MW00464190

Too
Mulch
to Handle

The English Cottage Garden Mysteries
Book Six

H.Y. Hanna

CONTENTS

CHAPTER ONE

Poppy Lancaster stared in angry dismay at the rose bush in front of her. The arching stems should have been covered with glossy leaves and clusters of buds, ready to open in a few weeks into gorgeous ruffled blooms. Instead, there were large gaps in the bush where the foliage had shrivelled and dropped off, leaving bare stems scarred a scaly brown and ending in clusters of blackened, deformed buds.

Poppy shook her head slowly in disbelief. What had happened here? She was sure the rose bush looked fine when she had glanced at it earlier in the week. How had it changed from that lush, healthy shrub to this sickly, deformed plant?

Gingerly, she lifted one of the clusters of deformed rosebuds and looked closely at the shrivelled flowers, then she stooped and peered into the bush, examining the undersides of leaves, inspecting the junctures of petioles. *Is it a fungal infection?* But the hours she'd spent poring over her grandmother's plant books meant that Poppy knew all the common fungal disease symptoms by heart. These weren't the ugly, dark blotches of black spot, or the powdery grey coating associated with mildew, and they definitely weren't the bright orange pustules of rust. *A pest then? Caterpillars? Aphids? A spider mite infestation? One of those big black beetles I've seen recently?*

But again, none of the classic symptoms from those well-known rose pests matched the damage she could see in front of her eyes. Besides, it was usually possible to spot pests—especially those of the chomping variety—if you examined a plant closely enough, but no matter how hard she looked, Poppy couldn't spot any malevolent visitor on the rose bush.

Frowning in confusion, she straightened and turned to scan the rest of the flowerbed. It was set alongside the path leading from the front gate, and although she had passed it several times, she had been too busy in the last few days to do more than give it a cursory glance. Now that she was looking properly, though, she was aghast to realise that the other rose bushes were beginning to show similar signs of disease. She had been waiting with delight and anticipation for the roses to open in the first glorious flush of blooms, but now she saw that many of the buds were blackened and deformed, and some had even shrivelled and looked as if they would drop off soon.

"No... no... no..." gasped Poppy, shaking her head in horrified denial.

This was the worst thing that could have happened, especially with the "Open Day" she was planning to host in a couple of weeks' time. The event was to be a belated "grand reopening"—a chance to put Hollyhock Cottage Gardens and Nursery back on the horticultural map at last—and she needed the gardens to be looking their best! They were the most powerful marketing tool for the nursery and she'd been working like a maniac in the last few weeks to prepare them for the event.

Besides, the cottage garden was also part of her late grandmother's legacy and Poppy was determined to live up to the horticultural reputation of the Lancaster name. True, no one had expected a city girl like her to even *keep* the unexpected inheritance she had received, never mind attempt to resurrect the failing family business. With no green fingers and zero gardening experience, no one would have blamed her if she'd decided to just sell up and take the money. But Poppy had embraced the challenge and, in fact, she had thought that the worst was behind her. She had managed to survive the long, barren winter and the killing spring frosts and had kept herself and the business afloat, despite not being able to grow or sell many plants. Now that summer was just around the corner, with months of warm, balmy weather ahead of her, she had been looking forward to a season of bustling business and booming plant growth. And what better way to relaunch the nursery and spread the news to new customers than with an Open Day where they could come and admire the gardens that had once made Hollyhock Cottage so famous?

But it'll be a total flop if the borders look like this, Poppy thought, dropping her gaze back to the rose bush beside her. People weren't going to be impressed if all they saw were beds of diseased rose bushes sporting naked, scarred stems and shrivelled flowers!

"My lordy Lord, Poppy—why the long face?"

Poppy looked up to see a middle-aged woman with a mop of grey curls coming down the path towards her. Nell Hopkins's normally rosy-cheeked smile was replaced by an expression of concern, and she made a tutting sound as she came to a stop beside Poppy. "Your breakfast is getting cold, dear. I thought you were just popping out for a minute to get the mail from the letterbox?"

"Oh, Nell, something is wrong with the roses!" said Poppy miserably.

"What do you mean?"

Poppy indicated the bush in front of them. "Look!"

Nell leaned forwards, then recoiled. "Ugh... they do look terrible, don't they? What's wrong with them?"

"That's just it: I don't know!" said Poppy in

frustration. "It doesn't look like any of the usual fungal diseases, and I can't seem to find any insect pests on the bush either."

"Maybe it's slugs?" Nell suggested. "I mean, people are always complaining about slugs in the garden, aren't they?"

Poppy shook her head. "I don't think slugs normally attack roses—they prefer tender leaves at ground level."

"Okay, what about rabbits then? Or deer?" said Nell. "Now, they nibble roses, don't they? I heard a couple of ladies in the village post office the other day complaining about rabbits damaging their gardens. And there are still deer roaming wild in the countryside in Oxfordshire, you know. Roe deer, I think—"

"How would a deer or rabbit have got in here?" asked Poppy, pointing to the high stone wall that formed the perimeter of the property, effectively turning the area inside into a walled garden.

"You know that wall is very old and several parts are crumbling," Nell said.

"Yes, but this doesn't look like rabbit or deer damage," Poppy argued. She indicated the misshapen stem nearest to them. "Look—it's not like leaves have been chewed off. It's more like there is some kind of disease affecting the plant, something that's making all the leaves grow contorted, and the stems brown and scaly, and making all the flower buds become deformed."

"Maybe you're looking in the wrong place," said Nell suddenly. She gave Poppy a meaningful look. "Maybe it's not a fungus or an insect or an animal at all."

"What else could it be? Aliens?"

Nell ignored her sarcastic tone. "Maybe someone sneaked into the garden in the night and deliberately sprayed the roses with a nasty chemical."

Poppy stared at her. "Why on earth would someone want to do that?"

"Well, it could have been a young man who wanted to give roses to the love of his life, but the poor lad can't afford to buy a bouquet and so he lost her to another man... and then he happened to be passing and looked over our wall to see our beautiful rose bushes, and it made him so angry and bitter that he felt compelled to destroy them—"

"Oh, Nell!" Poppy gave a laugh of mingled impatience and amusement. "That is the most ludicrous, far-fetched idea I've ever heard! This isn't one of those lurid novels you love to read. This is real life."

"Books are based on real life," said Nell with a sniff. "And don't you laugh at my novels, young lady. They contain far more wisdom than you realise."

Poppy suppressed the urge to roll her eyes. Still, she felt better now that she had shared the problem with Nell. Despite not really being "family", the older woman had slipped easily into the role of "substitute mother" after Poppy's own mother had passed away the previous year. In fact, Nell had probably eased into the role long before then—from when she'd first come into Poppy's life as the kindly cleaning lady who had agreed to sublet rooms in her London flat to the mother-and-daughter duo.

With her warm, soothing presence, Nell had provided the maternal nurturing that Poppy's own mother, Holly, had never been able to give her. Poppy had loved her beautiful, creative mother, but she had also realised that Holly Lancaster was essentially a "wild child" who had never grown up. Despite having a baby at eighteen, Holly had remained a carefree but also careless spirit, and Poppy had often felt more like the parent in their relationship. It had been a relief to find in Nell someone she could confide in and go to for advice and support.

Now she heaved a sigh and said, "Whatever it is, I need to get to the bottom of it quickly. I've spent a small fortune on organising and advertising the Open Day event, and the weather's getting warmer, which means more tourists in Bunnington. I think we're going to attract a lot of visitors. Everything *has* to look perfect for the Open Day!"

"Maybe you're worrying too much, dear," said Nell. "I mean, we're not a public park. We just want people to buy plants."

"But that's just it. The gardens are our best promotional tool. It's what makes us unique!" cried Poppy. "It's what makes people come here instead of going to the big, bland garden centres. And when they see the rose bushes in full bloom and how the traditional cottage-garden annuals and perennials all complement each other in the beds, it inspires them and makes them want to buy similar plants for their own gardens. I can't tell you how many times a customer has turned to me and pointed out a particular plant in the flowerbeds, asking if we sell it."

"All right, why don't you just get some pesticides and spray the bushes?" suggested Nell. "There's a huge garden centre in that business park nearby. I'm sure they stock all sorts of pest sprays. Go and buy yourself a couple of different bottles. It won't matter, then, if you're not sure what it is—I'm sure one of them will tackle the problem."

"I don't know..." said Poppy hesitantly. "I didn't find any insect sprays when I first moved in here. I don't know if my grandmother ever used them."

"Maybe someone removed them after she was taken to hospital. Anyway, even if she didn't use them, who says you have to follow exactly in her footsteps? There are lots of ways to garden, aren't there?"

Poppy straightened up. "You're right. And I do need to sort this out before our Open Day." She glanced at her watch. "Hmm... wonder if I've got time to pop out before I open the nursery for the day—"

"Oh, don't worry, dear; I can hold the fort for you. Go and take your time. I don't have a cleaning job until this afternoon, so I've got the morning off. It'll be nice, actually, to spend it talking plants and gardening with customers." Nell's eyes gleamed. "I'm hoping that Mrs Singh will return and tell me how her son got on with his blind date—you remember Mrs Singh, don't you? She came last week to buy some begonias."

"Um... yes," said Poppy vaguely, racking her memory and wondering how Nell seemed to remember all the customers' names.

"Actually, it wasn't really 'blind' as he'd already met the girl online," Nell continued. "Mrs Singh said her son had joined a dating app and that's how he got a girlfriend at last. Of course, I think she'd really prefer him to find a nice Indian girl, but she's getting so desperate for a grandchild now... and she sounds like a great catch—the girl, I mean, not Mrs Singh— young and pretty, with a great job in PR..."

Poppy chuckled to herself. Ever since Nell had left London to come and live with her in Bunnington, the older woman had embraced village life with a fervour, especially the part involving the local grapevine. Her gossip sessions with the various local residents who popped into the nursery were the highlight of her days and meant that Nell eagerly volunteered to help Poppy "man the shop front" whenever she wasn't out on a cleaning job.

"You know, Poppy, *you* should sign up for the app!" said Nell suddenly. "Mrs Singh says it has millions of users and you can sort people by their educational background, income, religion, body type—even star sign! You could meet all sorts of young men and—"

"I'm not joining a dating app," said Poppy firmly. "I'm not remotely interested in finding a boyfriend. I've got so much on my plate, I haven't got time for a relationship and besides—"

"You have to *make* time for a relationship!" said Nell. "It's not right, Poppy, for a pretty young girl like you to be spending so much time alone."

"I'm not alone," Poppy protested. "I have you... and customers coming daily... I never feel lonely. I'm always busy with the garden and new plants and—"

"Friends and work are not the same thing," said Nell, glowering at her. "I know the cottage garden and nursery are important to you, but you shouldn't be spending all your days just holed up here, digging in the dirt and talking to plants. You should be out dancing and having fun, meeting Prince Charming and being swept off your feet—"

"Nell!" Poppy gave an exasperated laugh. "We don't all want to live in the pages of a romance novel! Besides, you have to kiss a lot of frogs to find Prince Charming," she added wryly.

"So? That's part of the fun, dear," said Nell. "That's what being young is all about, isn't it? You're never going to be twenty-five again, you know. You should make the most of it, not hide away just because you're afraid."

"What do you mean? I'm not afraid," said Poppy indignantly.

"Then why do you always back out of any chance to meet someone? To go out on a date? Honestly, dear, when was the last time you went out for dinner—or even a coffee—with a young man?"

"I... I've been on dates!" Poppy protested. "Just not recently because I've been busy with the nursery. Besides, I don't want to be one of those girls who's always lurching from one love affair to another or thinks her life isn't complete unless she's with a man! I'm not going to waste my life chasing silly romantic dreams, just like Mum—" She broke off.

There was silence for a long moment, then Nell said gently, "You're not your mother, dear. Lord knows I loved Holly like a daughter, but she was wild and feckless. You're different. You have a strength and a resilience that your mother never had. Don't cut yourself off from life just because your mother didn't handle it well."

Poppy brushed some imaginary bits of soil off her hands, not meeting Nell's eyes. "Yes... well... anyway, I've got to go," she mumbled, turning to head back along the path.

"Not before you finish your breakfast, young lady," said Nell firmly.

Poppy obediently followed Nell back to the cottage, where she gobbled a couple of slices of buttered toast and washed them down with a cup of hot tea. Then—leaving Nell busily arranging plants for display on the trestle tables outside the cottage—she got into her little second-hand Fiat and headed out of the village.

CHAPTER TWO

It was a short drive to the large business park that sprawled alongside the motorway running past Bunnington. Like many industrial parks that had sprung up around the UK in recent years, this one pitched itself as more than just a collection of office blocks, laboratories, and warehouses, but also as a work campus and a "community". There were cafés and restaurants, a gym and yoga studio, a day nursery, landscaped gardens, post office, supermarket, and even a hairdresser on-site. And at one end was a large cluster of retail outlets, with the biggest store being the aptly named "Mega Garden Town", which dominated one corner of the business park and claimed to cater to every gardening need under the sun.

Poppy had heard a lot about this huge garden

centre but had yet to come and see it in person. Now, she paused in awe as she alighted from the car and stared at the sprawling complex in front of her. It looked as big as an airport! The whole of Hollyhock Cottage and Nursery could probably fit in the forecourt. And as she approached the sliding automatic doors which led into the main entrance of the place, she was staggered by the hordes of people coming out, pushing trolleys laden with plants, gardening supplies, and everything in between. There were elderly ladies clutching bags of bulbs, cooing couples admiring their new houseplants, fathers proudly regaling sons with the features of their new lawnmowers, and mothers juggling armfuls of potted annuals and hanging planters... not to mention the man wrestling with a mature banana tree!

Once inside, Poppy stood with her mouth slightly open, gazing down the enormous halls leading away in all directions, each filled with a mind-boggling array of products. The place was vast, more a city than a "town". She didn't realise that so much gardening equipment and paraphernalia existed! There were entire sections devoted to home decorating, from botanical-inspired cushions and lamps to beautiful wooden furniture imported from halfway across the world. There were walls hung with gleaming copper hand tools and exotic Japanese implements, racks of stylish gardening aprons and matching gloves, and even a small library filled with plant-related books.

Poppy squirmed as she thought of her own little nursery, with the ramshackle trestle tables set up alongside the single path, displaying a motley assortment of potted plants, and the small greenhouse at the back, nurturing a straggly collection of cuttings and seedlings. It all seemed like such a pathetic, amateur effort compared with this gleaming metropolis of horticultural excellence.

Then she gave herself a mental shake. *Remember, people don't come to Hollyhock Cottage for the same experience. Not everyone wants a big, slick garden centre. Sometimes people appreciate a more local, home-grown feel.*

Still... Poppy looked enviously at the products on display as she wandered past various shelves and units. She would have loved to have been able to expand her own range and offer things like pretty ceramic plant pots, bespoke gardening tools, or maybe even some mulches and fertilisers. After all, if someone was coming to her to buy a plant, it made sense that they should be able to satisfy their other gardening needs too. *Maybe if I have a really good couple of months over the summer and am able to save up some extra profits, then I'll be able to think about investing more in the business come autumn,* Poppy thought with a hopeful sigh.

Then she paused as she walked past a mini gallery exhibiting sculptures and figurines by local artists. All thoughts of "business investments" went out of the window as she stared at the gorgeous pieces on display. There were playful blue tits and jaunty red squirrels, somnolent barn owls and bashful hedgehogs, jewel-like ladybirds and acrobatic frogs, and a host of other wildlife found in British gardens... all brought to life through ceramic and clay, with beautiful patinas and burnished lustres.

"Oh!" Poppy's face broke into a delighted smile as she spied the quirky ceramic figure of a garden slug, its sinuous body draped lazily over a glossy green leaf, its tentacles alert and seeking. It had been created with such delicate vibrancy that you almost expected it to come to life.

She sighed wistfully. She would have loved to buy the slug—not for resale, not for display in the nursery—just for herself, to enjoy and treasure. But a glance at the price tag underneath the piece made her wince and hastily turn away. *Yikes. No way.*

Reluctantly, Poppy began making her way to the department dedicated to weed and pest control. She could have spent hours—days—wandering around the many halls, but she reminded herself sternly of the reason she had come in the first place. The pest control section was enormous and she stood for a moment in front of the shelves, eyeing the multitude of spray bottles and storage cans in bewilderment. Glancing around, she tried to see if she could find a member of staff to help her. The area was surprisingly empty, with no one else browsing nearby.

Then she spotted a young man standing behind a kiosk counter on the other side of the room. The sides of the counter were emblazoned with a large graphic showing various spray bottles against a background of lush green grass and colourful flowers, with a banner which read: "An exciting new range for the home gardener!" Next to the kiosk, a small pyramid of pesticide bottles, identical to the ones featured in the graphic, had been carefully stacked to form an impressive display—each bottle proudly displaying the same logo: a bell encircled by the name "Campana AgroChemicals". They were accompanied by a pile of glossy leaflets fanned out across the top of the kiosk counter.

A middle-aged woman was leaning across the counter, talking earnestly to the young man. At first, Poppy thought that the woman was a fellow customer looking for some advice, but as she got closer, she realised that this wasn't a friendly conversation. In fact, the woman had grabbed one of the leaflets off the counter and was waving it in an aggressive manner, thrusting it in the young man's face and jabbing him in the chest.

"...can't believe you have the gall to stand there and sell these poisons to innocent people! Do you tell them, eh? Do you tell them about the environmental pollutants, the harmful chemicals, the potential carcinogens in your pesticides?" the woman demanded.

"Aww, give it a rest!" said the young man with a

groan. "I'm sick of you coming in here every day, harassing me and my customers. People have a right to choose what to put in their own gardens and it's none of your busi—"

"No, people have a right to know the truth!" snapped the woman. "People need to be educated. If they knew what harm they were doing by spraying your pesticides, they would think twice!"

"Is this the thing about the bees again?" asked the young man with a weary sigh.

"It's not just the bees! Don't you realise everything is linked together in a great web? It travels all the way up the food chain and gets into our bodies and our children's bodies. Look at what happened with DDT: everyone thought it was a wonder-chemical— they thought it was the solution to every pest, big or small! And now, forty, fifty years after it was banned, we're *still* dealing with the effects. It's been linked to cancer, miscarriages, infertility, liver damage—even Alzheimer's! And that's not even mentioning what it does to wildlife and the environment."

"That was a totally different scenario," protested the young man. "The... the industry was less sophisticated then, and they didn't have the regulations we have today. Campana pesticides have been developed under strict safety protocols and—"

"Safety protocols?" scoffed the woman. "That's a joke! There isn't any proper regulation in the sector at all. Everyone knows that government environmental agencies are totally corrupt and in the pocket of pesticide companies. They just turn a blind eye and allow all sorts of dangerous substances to be licensed—"

"You don't have any proof of this," said the young man impatiently. "And if you did, then you should be taking it up with the government bodies, not hassling me. I'm just a salesman doing my job, okay?"

"You're part of the problem!" hissed the woman. "I've seen the way you operate, smiling and sucking up, and making people believe that you care about their gardens... when it's all fakery and lies! You work on commission, don't you? I know the Campana model. The more you sell, the more you make. So you just want to shift as many bottles as you can. You don't care how much damage you're doing to people's health or the environment, as long as you're filling your own pocket!"

"And you just want to scaremonger and fill people's heads with nonsense!" snapped the young man. "I've had enough. If you don't leave now, I'm going to call the centre security."

The woman glared at him, then she grabbed a handful of the leaflets and tossed them contemptuously, scattering them all over the floor around the counter. Turning, she stormed out of the department and disappeared into the next hall. The young man sighed and bent down to start collecting all the scattered leaflets. Poppy hurried forwards and crouched down next to him to help.

The young man looked up in surprise, his mouth

curving into a smile as his eyes fell on Poppy. "Cheers... really nice of you to help."

"Oh, it's nothing," said Poppy as they both straightened with their hands full of leaflets and replaced them on the counter.

The young man gave her a sheepish look. "Er... I suppose you saw what happened just now?"

Poppy nodded. "It did seem unfair of her to attack you like that. I mean, if you were just doing your job."

"You don't know the half of it," he groaned. "That crazy cow has been coming here and giving me a lecture practically every day. And I'm sure she's tried to vandalise some of my supplies. I was halfway through unpacking a load from my car this morning and, when I got back, there were several bottles missing." Then he gave a droll smile. "Ah well, you get all sorts of people coming to a big garden centre like this. I suppose it keeps the job interesting." He stuck a hand out. "I'm Thales, by the way."

"Tha-lis?" said Poppy, trying to copy his pronunciation.

He grinned self-consciously. "It's of Greek origin. Thales Georgiou."

"I'm Poppy Lancaster," said Poppy, putting her hand in his. "Which is just boringly English."

"Oh, I wouldn't say boring..." He held her hand just a fraction of a second longer than necessary. "And I'm beginning to think I should thank that crazy cow since it means that we got to meet, Poppy Lancaster."

Was he flirting with her? Poppy blushed, then was annoyed with herself. *For heaven's sake, anyone would think you're a teenager meeting a handsome guy for the first time*, she berated herself. Still, she had to concede that Thales Georgiou was incredibly charming—and good-looking too, with dark hair curling rakishly over his forehead, twinkling brown eyes, and a muscular physique that spoke of regular workouts at the gym. The fact that he was looking *her* over with equal admiration was immensely flattering and Poppy felt her cheeks warming again. She cleared her throat and mumbled:

"Um... actually, I was looking for something to deal with a pest on my roses."

"Ahh, then you've come to the right place," said Thales, his smile widening. He gestured to the pyramid of bottles next to them. "We've just launched a new range of pesticides especially for the home gardener. Each one is formulated to target and treat a specific variety of sucking and chewing insect, from greenflies and whiteflies to mealy bugs, weevils and spider mites..." He glanced sideways at her. "Do you know what you've got?"

Poppy shook her head. "I can't figure out what it is." She described the diseased rose bushes, adding as she finished: "I couldn't see anything on the leaves or stems, even though I looked all over. But I'm sure it's some kind of pest."

"Well, they can be sneaky little buggers," said Thales. "They hide under the leaves or inside the flowers. But don't worry—even if you're not sure what it is, I can help." He reached over and plucked a bottle off the top row of the pyramid. "This is our bestseller: a special broad-spectrum formula. It's designed *specifically* with the busy home gardener in mind. We know you haven't got the time to sit and figure out exactly what's attacking your plants, so we've done all the hard work for you. It doesn't matter what's attacking your roses—Campana's *Exit-Bug Supreme* will find it and take care of it for you, leaving your plant lush and healthy."

Poppy looked at the bottle askance. "It sounds almost too good to be true," she said with a wry laugh.

"Oh, it's true, believe me. I've tested the whole range in my own garden—I couldn't stand here and promote them to other home gardeners otherwise," said Thales smoothly. "It's because I know how fantastic the Campana products are, that's why I'm so keen for others to benefit from them too. I mean, I'll bet you're probably like me: you might only have a little suburban plot, but you're really proud of it and—"

"Er... actually, mine's not really a normal home garden. I mean, it's not huge but it's not a typical suburban plot either. It's actually part of a... well, you see, I run a small plant nursery," Poppy confessed, flushing slightly. She half expected him to laugh at her, but instead, he looked impressed.

"Really? Where is it? What's it called?"

"Hollyhock Cottage Gardens and Nursery. It's in Bunnington, a village not far from here—"

"Oh yeah, I know Bunnington," Thales cut in. "I've been popping in there a fair bit recently. Didn't realise there was a nursery there, though."

"It's a very small place. Nothing like this," said Poppy quickly, indicating the garden centre around them. "It belonged to my grandmother and I inherited it. It's really a cottage and surrounding gardens, with a small nursery attached."

"It sounds delightful. I love cottage gardens. All wild and rambling and full of flowers."

"It's not going to be full of flowers if I can't clear this mystery disease up," said Poppy worriedly. "And I've got a really important event coming up: an Open Day at the nursery in about two weeks' time. I really need the gardens to be looking their best."

"Well then, you haven't got any time to lose! Luckily, though, we've designed our formulas to be extremely fast acting. So if you go back and apply some today, I guarantee your pests will be gone in a week."

"Really?"

"Oh yeah. Just one spray and you can sit back and relax, knowing that all the visitors will be seeing your gardens in their full glory."

Poppy reached hesitantly for the bottle he was holding out to her.

"And... is it safe to use?" she asked, recalling the woman who had been harassing him earlier. "I mean,

I want to tackle the problem, but I don't really want to use dangerous chemicals or—"

"Oh, don't worry, it's *very* safe," Thales assured her. "All our pesticides are carefully formulated to the highest standards and extensively tested to make sure that they meet stringent regulations. We know our customers care deeply about the environment, and we do too. In fact, Campana pesticides have all been manufactured to ensure that they have a good profile for bees. This means you can use them with total confidence, knowing that you will not be harming any of the 'friendly insects' in the garden."

"Oh." Poppy looked down at the bottle she held in her hands. Thales was very persuasive and she couldn't help visualising the tantalising picture he'd conjured up: her troubles all solved and the cottage garden brimming with flowers and admiring visitors...

"I tell you what," said Thales, leaning closer and giving her a conspiratorial smile. "We had a promotion running last week where you could get twenty percent off your first purchase. It was part of the launch special. Officially, it ended last weekend... but what's a few extra days, eh? I'll pull a few strings and extend it so you can get the same discount. And take a bottle of concentrate instead of the ready-made spray," he added, swapping the bottle she was holding for another one from the pyramid. "You need to make it up in a spray bottle yourself but it's a lot more economical."

"Oh! Thank you. That's really nice of you," said Poppy with surprised pleasure.

"And what about a herbicide?" said Thales, lifting another bottle from the pyramid. "I'm sure weeds are a constant battle in a vigorous cottage garden."

"Oh God, you have no idea," said Poppy with a sigh. "But I've been managing all right without spraying so far. I've just been pulling them up by hand—"

"Aww, come on!" said Thales with an exaggerated expression of disbelief. "You're not telling me that you want to spend your life on your knees, digging and pulling up weeds, when there are so many other fun things you could be doing?"

"Like what?" asked Poppy with a laugh, responding to his teasing tone.

"Well... like going out for dinner and dancing." His brown eyes twinkled at her. "In fact, I'd like to personally volunteer to help you with that, if you'd let me?"

Whoa, he moved fast! Was he asking her out on a date? Poppy hesitated, unsure how to respond. In spite of what she had said to Nell, it was true that she hadn't been out on many dates and had little experience with casual flirtation. Now, she wasn't sure if Thales's remarks were serious or just a bit of rhetorical banter. It would be horribly awkward and embarrassing if she'd read more into it than he intended.

"Um... I... I like weeding," she stammered,

sidestepping his question. "I find it very meditative, you know... like... like you're totally in the moment and there's something wonderful about removing all the unnecessary, unwanted things from the garden beds, like cleaning out your life... and it's really satisfying afterwards when you see the pile of weeds you've yanked up..." She trailed off, embarrassed as she realised what she'd blurted out.

Thales raised his eyebrows, the teasing smile still in his eyes. "Wow, I didn't realise weeding could be so... er... spiritual."

Poppy flushed, then she cleared her throat and said, trying for a brisk, business-like tone: "Yes, um... anyway, I'll take a bottle of the *Exit-Bug Supreme*, please, but I won't need any herbicide."

"All right, I'll tell you what: I'll add in one of our special plant tonic sprays—how about that?" Thales said as he began ringing up her purchase.

As he was handing her the two bottles and the receipt, he gave her an inviting smile and said: "Hey, listen—I was planning to have a break soon: nip out for a quick vape and grab a cup of coffee. Fancy joining me? They do a mean Danish pastry in the café here."

"Oh... thanks... that sounds lovely but... um... I think I'd better head back and start spraying," said Poppy.

Thales raised his eyebrows again and she could see laughter in his eyes, but all he said was: "Well, some other time, then. I'll be here manning this kiosk for the next few weeks, so you know where to find me." He gave her a wink.

Poppy slowly retraced her steps to the main entrance, clutching the spray bottles in her arms. She felt slightly ashamed of her stammering replies and generally awkward response to Thales's overtures. She was twenty-five, not a gauche schoolgirl, and she should have been able to deal better with a bit of casual flirtation! *Maybe Nell's right. Maybe I need to get out and socialise more*, she thought as she stepped through the automatic sliding doors leading out into the car park. *Maybe I should have gone for a coffee with Thales. After all, what's the harm in—*

The next moment, all thoughts of dating were wiped from her mind as someone barged into her path and lunged in her face, yelling:

"You murderer!"

CHAPTER THREE

Poppy gasped and stumbled backwards. She recognised the middle-aged woman standing in her path: it was the same woman who had been haranguing Thales earlier. Now, she jabbed a finger at Poppy's chest and demanded:

"Do you know how many lives you're destroying with those poisons? Do you realise how much damage you are doing to the environment? And to yourself?"

"I—"

The woman looked down at the label on the bottle Poppy was clutching and her face screwed up in disgust. "*UGH!* The 'broad-spectrum formula'—that's the worst! I suppose he told you it would save time, didn't he? Said it would be the perfect solution to all the troubles in your garden, eh?"

"Well, yes, but—"

The woman thrust her face close to Poppy's. "And I suppose he didn't mention all the lethal chemicals that will leave toxic residues on the leaves and be absorbed into the plant, so that anything that comes into contact is killed? Not just the bees and butterflies but other insects too... like... like dragonflies! They're not just beautiful; they're insect-eating machines too, did you know? They get rid of your caterpillars and aphids and mosquitoes. And what about the earthworms and beetles and woodlice? You need them to break down all the leaf litter that feeds the soil; you'll be killing all of them too." She pointed at the bottle. "By spraying that, you'll be no better than a mass murderer!"

Poppy flinched. "I did ask Thales—the sales rep—whether it's safe," she said defensively. "He said that it had a 'good bee profile'—"

"'*Good bee profile*'?" the woman sneered. "What does that even mean? It's just a fancy marketing term, a way to greenwash the whole thing."

Poppy frowned. "Greenwash?"

"Yeah, greenwashing. It's when companies use false labels or vague claims to cover up the truth. They deliberately deceive consumers, just so you would think that their products are eco-friendly. It's all fake reassurance and lies." The woman shot Poppy a piercing look. "Did you read the label yourself before you bought the spray?"

"N-noo..." Poppy admitted. "I just... well, I thought

it would be fine. Thales said Campana AgroChemicals follows strict safety protocols and—"

The woman made a rude noise. "You stupid, gullible fool! Don't you know anything? There is no safe chemical pesticide! Even the ones that are 'approved' are dangerous at high concentrations and with consistent use. If you don't care about wildlife and the environment, at least think about yourself. You don't know how much you're inhaling and absorbing through your skin... and what about pets, eh?"

"What do you mean?" asked Poppy.

"Have you got a cat or a dog?"

"No, but my neighbours—"

"Well, you'd better tell them you're poisoning their precious fur babies. Oh yes, pets are really high risk: they chew on grass or brush up against plants and then lick their coats, and all the toxic chemicals are transferred into their systems..."

Poppy wanted to put her hands to her ears and block out all the horrible accusations and imagery that this woman was hurling at her. Backing away, she mumbled: "Um... thanks for letting me know..."—then turned and practically ran to her car, the woman's voice still ringing in her ears. It wasn't until she was pulling out of the car park that she breathed a sigh of relief.

The sight of a large crowd of people milling about the gardens was a pleasant surprise when Poppy arrived back at Hollyhock Cottage, and she forgot about the unpleasant encounter as she hurried to help Nell serve customers. Her friend was doing a brisk business in bedding plants, and Poppy was delighted to see that several customers were buying up large batches of osteospermums and petunias. At this rate, she would have to put in a new order of plug plants from the wholesale suppliers!

Feeling a renewed confidence, Poppy approached two women who were standing in the middle of the path, surveying the flower beds.

"Hello, ladies—is there anything I can help you with?" she asked pleasantly. "Any particular plant you're looking for?"

"What on earth happened to the roses?" one of the women demanded, pointing to the bush nearest to them. "They look like they've got some kind of disease!"

"Oh! Er... um... we've had a bit of a pest problem," stammered Poppy, taken by surprise.

"I brought Sara with me today because I wanted to show her your gardens. I've been telling her what a great place this is for inspiration." The woman looked at Poppy accusingly, as if holding her personally responsible for embarrassing her in front of her friend. "What's the 'problem' with the roses?"

Poppy saw the look of disdain on the woman's face and realised belatedly that, as a commercial nursery and member of the horticultural industry, she was supposed to be a professional expert and must never admit to having a "problem" in her own garden.

"Oh... it's just a small, temporary thing," she said hastily. "It'll be sorted soon. Er... I'm actually holding an Open Day on the last weekend this month and there will be all sorts of discounts and promotions, and a raffle with wonderful prizes, and tea and scones available..."

"That sounds lovely," the friend called Sara said. "Why don't we pop back then, Rachel? I haven't got anything on that weekend—have you?"

"Yeah, I suppose we could do that," said the first woman grudgingly. Then she brightened. "I know— we can bring my cousin, Em, as well. She's just bought a house and she's planning to redo the garden, so she'll be looking to buy lots of plants to add to her new borders." She glanced at Poppy. "You sure the roses and everything will be looking good by this Open Day?"

"Y-yes," said Poppy, crossing her fingers behind her back. "Yes, everything will be looking gorgeous by then."

She stood and watched with troubled eyes as the two women walked back up the path and let themselves out of the front gate. It had been stupid of her to make a rash promise like that, but what was she supposed to say? *It's vital to sound confident in business*, she reminded herself. *And besides, I am going to get on top of it—I've got the pest spray now, haven't I?*

Accordingly, as soon as the nursery was shut for the day, Poppy hurried to the greenhouse attached to the back of her cottage to find an empty spray bottle and make up a pesticide solution. The light breeze that had been wafting through the garden earlier in the day seemed to have strengthened, and the windows rattled in their frames, the wind whistling through the gaps and stirring Poppy's hair as she bent to read the instructions on the bottle. She paused and looked up, gazing out of the open greenhouse door. She could hear the rustling of the bushes and see the tree branches swaying outside.

Poppy frowned, looking back down at the instructions and noticing the line: "NOT RECOMMENDED FOR USE IN WINDY CONDITIONS."

"Maybe I should wait until tomorrow instead of trying it now?" she mused out loud.

"*N-oww!*" came a loud, bossy reply.

Poppy smiled as she glanced up again and saw an enormous orange tomcat standing in the open greenhouse doorway. "Hello, Oren. Come for your evening constitutional?"

"*N-ow!*" said the ginger tom as he strolled into the greenhouse and came over to join her.

"All right, I'll take your advice," said Poppy, grinning. "I'll give it a go now."

She began making up the solution, but she had barely finished diluting the mixture when she heard a thump, like the sound of something striking glass. She looked around. Oren, who had obviously got bored of watching her mix and measure liquids, had gone over to the other side of the greenhouse, where he was now sitting on a ledge above a large glass tank. The ginger tom was staring avidly into the tank, reaching down with a paw every so often to try and grope something inside.

"Oi! Oren, stop that!" cried Poppy, rushing over to the cat. "Stop it! Leave poor Solly alone!"

"*No-ww...*" said Oren petulantly, then turned to look back into the tank, his tail lashing from side to side.

"Shoo!" said Poppy, flapping her hands at the tomcat. When he ignored her, she picked him up and set him down on the ground, giving his bum a gentle shove away from the tank.

"*No-ww!*" Oren wailed mournfully. "*Noooooo-ow!*"

"Oh, stop being such a drama queen," said Poppy with a grin as she turned back to the tank.

Bending down, she peered through the glass into the tank, which was set up like a terrarium, its base covered with a mixture of soil, twigs, and fallen leaves. There were also a few pieces of stone and small rocks, plus a little pile of lettuce and cucumber, carrot slices, and tomato chunks in one corner. She was rewarded a moment later by a slimy brown shape squirming out from beneath a rock and crawling onto a twig. There it paused, elongating until two dainty tentacles appeared from its front end and waved around enquiringly.

"Hello, Solly," said Poppy with a wry smile, thinking—as she always did every time she saw him—that she must be the only garden nursery owner in the whole of England who was keeping a slug as a pampered pet! Still, a promise was a promise, and she felt that she had to honour her vow to Solly's owner to look after the beloved mollusc.

She reached into the tank and picked up one of the lettuce fronds, holding this out to the slug—and felt ridiculously delighted when the slimy creature began to nibble on the wilting leaf.

"*N-owww!*"

Poppy turned to see that Oren had slunk back and was now sitting a wary distance away from the tank, eyeing it sulkily. He saw her looking at him and quickly got up and came over.

"*N-ow?*" he said, butting her hand with his head. "*N-oww?*"

"I can't stroke you now—I'm feeding Solly," said Poppy, turning back to the tank.

"*N-OWW!*" said Oren, shoving his head hard against her hand.

"Hey!" cried Poppy as she lost her grip and the lettuce fell from her fingers, flopping onto Solly's head.

Oren gave a gleeful chirrup, then turned and looked up at her with big yellow eyes. "*N-ow,*" he said triumphantly.

Poppy gave an exasperated laugh. "Oh, Oren— don't tell me you're jealous of a slug!"

Shaking her head and still laughing, she picked up the tomcat again and put him out of the greenhouse. Then she retrieved her spray bottle and lugged it out to the rose bush by the path. After pumping the handle vigorously, she lifted the spraying wand and began directing a steady stream of pesticide at the leaves. A fine mist rose in the air and a strong chemical smell accosted her nostrils. Poppy stepped back, coughing slightly. *Ugh.* For all the promises of "all-natural ingredients" on the label of the pesticide bottle, it didn't smell very natural at all!

A movement near her feet made her glance down and she recoiled slightly as a cockroach crawled out suddenly from the leaf litter at the base of the rose bush. It was moving in an odd way, though—staggering drunkenly, its antennae limp and crooked. It didn't manage to get more than a few feet before it flipped suddenly onto its back, its legs jerking spasmodically. Then it froze and lay still. Poppy stared at it. She loathed cockroaches but there was still something awful in watching a living creature die, writhing and quivering like that.

It's just a cockroach, she told herself. *People kill them every day.* Trying to stifle the sense of guilt, Poppy lifted the spraying wand and stepped forwards again. She worked her way slowly around the bush and was just stepping behind it to tackle the other side when she noticed something—a small, frantic movement beneath one of the leaves. She bent for a closer look, then gasped as she saw what it was: a dainty baby praying mantis in the most beautiful translucent green. It was scurrying up the stem as fast as it could, tossing its head from side to side and fluttering its legs, for all the world like a dog trying to shake water off its coat.

"Oh! Sorry! Sorry!" cried Poppy, dropping the spray wand.

The baby praying mantis reached the top of the stem and paused, lifting one of its tiny, perfectly-formed front claws and wiping it over its face. Then it tilted its little head and fixed her with one of its compound eyes, as if looking at her with great indignation.

"I'm so sorry," whispered Poppy again. She knew it was crazy, talking to an insect, but that sense of guilt and remorse washed over her again as she looked at the tiny creature.

She watched it with nervous dread. She couldn't bear it if she had to watch it die an agonising death like the cockroach. The minutes stretched into each other but the baby mantis did nothing other than stand up, alert, its tiny claws raised in the traditional praying gesture that had given the insect its name.

Finally, Poppy breathed a hesitant sigh of relief. Maybe it had somehow escaped the spray. Maybe it would be okay. Carefully, she reached out a hand and laughed in surprised delight when the tiny creature climbed onto the tip of her finger. It perched there, balancing with dainty grace, and Poppy felt a rush of wonder and awe: having this wild creature climb onto her hand so trustingly... it felt like a rare gift, an honour... and her attack with the pesticide seemed even more like the ultimate betrayal.

Turning slowly, she moved carefully across the bed to a tall shrub several feet away and deposited the baby praying mantis on one of the leaves. Then she retreated to the rose bush. But as she looked at the spray wand she had dropped, she found herself unable to pick it up again. The voice of the woman she'd met at Mega Garden Town echoed in her head: *"By spraying that, you'll be no better than a mass murderer!"*

Poppy gulped and glanced over at the shrub where she had deposited the baby praying mantis. No, she couldn't do this. There had to be another way.

CHAPTER FOUR

Gathering up the spray bottle, Poppy returned to the cottage, her heart heavy. She couldn't bring herself to spray any more but... what was she going to do about the roses? In the cottage, she found Nell busily ladling split pea and ham soup into bowls for dinner. As they sat down to eat the hearty soup, accompanied by chunks of crusty bread, she recounted the whole episode to Nell.

"I don't know what to do," she said with a sigh as she finished. "I can't bear the thought of killing innocent insects but... I have to do something! Hollyhock Cottage has always been famous for its gardens—it'll ruin the nursery's reputation if people come and see ugly, deformed roses. And besides..." She paused in dismay as a new thought struck her. "Oh, Nell, what if whatever's on the rose bushes spreads throughout the garden and onto our sales stock? I can't offer diseased plants for sale! People will be totally disgusted and the business will never survive."

Nell looked at a loss as well. "Maybe you could try a different spray? I mean, maybe one that isn't so... er... toxic to other insects."

"Mmm... that woman at Mega Garden Town did say 'broad-spectrum sprays' are the worst because they kill everything indiscriminately," Poppy recalled. "Maybe if I can get a more specific formula... but that would require knowing what the pest is, and I have no idea..."

She sighed and subsided back into her chair. Morosely, she finished her soup and listened with half an ear as Nell recounted the gossip she'd heard from various customers and villagers who had visited the nursery that day.

"You know Mariam Hicks? Her niece has just gone into labour! It's her first baby, though, so the midwife says they should settle in for a long wait. And they don't know if it's a boy or a girl, but Mariam's hoping it's a girl so she can pass on the bracelet that's been in the family for generations. She showed it to me the other day: *gorgeous* piece! Vintage Victorian sterling silver with seed pearls. She was just on her way to Sanders Fine Jewellery—you know, that antique jewellery store on the village high street—to have it professionally cleaned, and I told her she should get it valued as well... Oh, and Mrs Singh's finally met her son's new girlfriend, but apparently, she was absolutely horrified: the girl has several tattoos!"

Poppy smiled to herself, wondering if the Indian lady would decide that her need for a grandchild outweighed her abhorrence of body art.

"It wouldn't be so bad if it was a *nice* tattoo, something small and dainty in a discreet place," Nell continued, pursing her lips. "But the girl's gone and got two enormous black pawprints tattooed onto her chest, right above her breasts! Can you imagine? Mrs Singh says it looks like she's been breastfeeding a grizzly bear!" She made a tutting noise. "Really, I just don't understand why young girls have to mutilate themselves like that. Anyway, I told Mrs Singh that you can get tattoos removed quite easily these days. One of my cleaning clients was telling me how she really regrets a tattoo she got on her shoulder in her teens, so she's having it zapped off with a laser—oh, speaking of shoulders, have you heard about poor Miss Finch?"

"Who?" Poppy looked up, struggling to keep up with Nell's stream of running commentary.

"The lovely old lady who comes in here regularly to buy potted colour for her containers. You know, the one with the nephew called Dennis—"

"Ohhhh... her," said Poppy, smiling as she recalled the little old lady with a tendency to overshare. "What happened to her?"

"She's wrenched her shoulder badly and her entire upper back is in a spasm. She gets terrible pain if she tries to do anything, like bending to pick something up." Nell shook her head in sympathy. "I went to see her this afternoon and the poor dear is beside herself. She's always been very independent, you know, and although she's in her late eighties, she still lives by herself in a house on the other side of the village. Her nephew Dennis usually looks in on her once a week, but he's away on a business trip at the moment and there are no other family close by. Anyway, I helped to make up her supper and make sure she was comfortable... but I'm worried about her. I wanted to pop in to see her tomorrow but I'll be leaving in the morning. I'm off to my sister's in Dorset, remember?" she said at Poppy's blank look. "I'm going to stay with her for a few days."

"Oh, yes, that's right. My God, has it come round already? I thought you weren't going for another week. Sorry, I've just been so busy in the gardens lately, I've totally lost track of time..." Poppy shook her head, as if to clear it. "Don't worry, Nell—I can look in on Miss Finch for you tomorrow."

"Would you, dear? That would be fantastic."

"It might not be until after the nursery closes, though," said Poppy.

"Oh, that should be fine. I know there are others in the village who will be checking on her during the day." Nell's face brightened as her eyes fell on the pot of leftover soup sitting on the stove. "In fact, I'll put some of this soup in a thermos before I leave in the morning and you can take it round to Miss Finch when you go. Then all she'll have to do is heat it up on the hob—where are you off to now, young lady?" she demanded as Poppy jumped up from the table and rushed to take her empty bowl to the sink.

"I thought I'd pop back into the greenhouse to finish a few things off," said Poppy. "There are some cuttings that I need to mist, and I might try to sow some of those leftover seed packets I found. Also, a couple of batches of the plug plants need to be 'potted on'—"

"Well, make sure that you put on gloves and those plastic safety goggles I got you the other day, to protect your eyes," said Nell. "And tie your hair back! You don't want to be pushing your hair out of your eyes and touching your face with your contaminated hands—"

Poppy heaved an impatient sigh. "Nell, you're talking as if I'm handling dangerous chemicals or something! It's only seeds and water and potting compost."

"Don't underestimate the dangers of gardening!" said Nell sternly. "I've read some horror stories in the papers. One poor man died in intensive care after he was infected by fungal spores while gardening. And there were all these cases in Scotland where people ended up in hospital with legionnaires' disease, all because they got infected by soil or water in their gardens. The RHS says that you should always wear gloves when handling soil or compost, or fertilisers and pesticides, and you should always open bags of compost at arm's length. They even suggest wearing a dust mask when you're turning the compost heap." Nell wagged a finger at Poppy. "If it's good enough for the Royal Horticultural Society, then it should be good enough for you."

"All right, all right..." said Poppy with a good-natured grin. "I'll make sure I suit up in full PPE before I go back into the greenhouse. Happy?"

CHAPTER FIVE

Poppy slept badly that night, with nightmares of giant insects rampaging through the cottage garden, chomping on everything in sight and reducing entire flowerbeds to stumps, whilst she kept stepping on baby insects and hopping about on one foot crying: "Sorry! Sorry!" She awoke tired and bleary-eyed, and her mood was not improved when she finally washed, dressed, and made her way outside to see that the rose bushes by the path looked worse than ever.

"How can anyone have a frown like that when they're standing in a garden as beautiful as this?"

Poppy whirled at the sound of the familiar voice and exclaimed: "Thales! What are you doing here?"

He came sauntering up the path from the front gate, his trademark boyish grin on his face. "Oh, I was on my way in to work—I live in that new residential estate between Bunnington and the business park—and I thought I'd make a little detour, see how you were getting on with the spraying." He turned to survey the flowerbed next to them and gave a low whistle. "Whoa—this looks pretty bad. But I'm sure *Exit-Bug Supreme* will sort it out in no time. Did you manage to spray the whole bed yesterday?"

"Oh... um..." Poppy stammered. She knew that she should just tell Thales the truth, but somehow she was too embarrassed to admit she'd decided not to use the pesticide because she couldn't bear to kill some insects. "Not yet... I mean, I was really busy yesterday..." She flushed and trailed off, recalling that she'd declined his invitation to coffee on the pretext that she needed to rush back immediately to get on with the spraying.

Thales raised his eyebrows slightly, as if he could read her thoughts, but all he said was: "Well, you really want to spray as soon as you can, so the pesticide formula can start working and get on top of things. If you delay, it could get even worse, especially with the weather turning warmer—that'll make the pest population really explode."

"Yes... yes, I'm sure you're right..." Poppy mumbled. Then, desperate to change the subject, she said hurriedly: "So... um... you live in that new residential estate? That's practically on the business park's doorstep, isn't it? Don't you mind living so close?"

"Oh no, I like it. Makes the commute a breeze. The Campana AgroChemicals head office and main warehouse is in the business park, you know. In fact, the residential estate is one of the side investments of the company and they were offering houses off-plan at a great discount for all Campana employees, so I snapped one up. It means I was able to get a place with a garden, when I probably would only have been able to afford a flat otherwise."

"Do you garden?" said Poppy in surprise, glancing down at his manicured hands.

He laughed at her look. "Oh yeah. Whenever I can. Don't write me off just because of my 'lily-white hands'—I use heavy-duty gardening gloves. And I moisturise. I'm the ultimate metrosexual, you know," he said, grinning unashamedly.

Poppy laughed as well, responding to his easy confidence. Thales really was very charming, and seeing him now in the bright morning light, she could appreciate his good looks even more—from the dark hair that flopped boyishly across his forehead and the designer stubble that accentuated the line of his jaw, to the beautifully thick lashes that lined his brown eyes. She realised that she was staring and hastily dropped her gaze, feeling a blush coming to her cheeks.

"So, what time do you close the nursery?" asked Thales casually.

"Oh... um... it depends on how busy it is, but usually around five," said Poppy, trying to match his casual tone.

"And have you got any plans for tonight? No? Well, how about dinner with me then?"

Poppy was surprised and flustered. Although Thales had laid on the charm when they met at Mega Garden Town, she hadn't really taken his attempts to invite her out seriously. She'd thought that it was just part of his casual flirtation routine. But here he was, already seeking her out again and losing no time in issuing a second invitation. It was clear that he really did want to take her on a romantic outing, and suddenly Poppy found herself unsure how to respond.

Perhaps it was because she'd never thought of herself as the kind of girl that men would instantly ask out on a date. Her mother, Holly Lancaster, had been that kind of girl, with her gorgeous honey-blonde hair and bohemian glamour. In comparison, Poppy felt that her own looks were very ordinary, from her dark brown hair and milky complexion, prone to freckling in the sun, to her not-particularly-curvy-nor-particularly-athletic figure. Her clear blue eyes were the only features she shared with her beautiful mother, but even then, she didn't know all the make-up tricks like Holly had to enhance her eyes and lashes. So now, to have a handsome charmer like Thales treating her like the kind of woman who could arouse an instant passion... it was flattering and thrilling, and yet slightly disturbing too.

"Um... that sounds lovely but I don't think it's a good idea," said Poppy at last.

"Why not?"

"I just think it's best to keep things... er... 'professional' between us," she said, trying not to sound prim.

"Who says we can't have an *enjoyable* professional relationship?" Thales said, chuckling. "Poppy, I'm not asking you to marry me or even be my girlfriend. It's just dinner and drinks." He leaned forwards, his eyes twinkling. "I'll be on my best behaviour, I promise."

Poppy flushed. Nell's words from the day before flashed through her mind: *"Why do you always back out of any chance to meet someone? To go out on a date?... When was the last time you went out for dinner—or even a coffee—with a young man?... You're never going to be twenty-five again, you know. You should make the most of it, not hide away just because you're afraid."*

Was Nell right—was she afraid? Was she just finding excuses to avoid a situation where she might lose her heart to a man... and thus her control over her life? A night out with Thales would undoubtedly be fun and—as he had said—it didn't have to mean anything. Not unless she wanted it to. What was the big deal in giving it a go?

And yet... for all his charm, there was something about Thales that made her vaguely uneasy. She couldn't quite put her finger on it, but it was there, like the feel of a cold draught at your back, even though you were facing away and unable to see the open window or door it was coming from.

She opened her mouth to answer but, before she could say anything, they were interrupted by the sound of a male voice, cursing angrily. They both turned to see a large ginger tomcat vault over the front gate of the cottage garden and come bounding up the path. It was Oren. A minute later, the gate crashed open and a tall dark-haired man burst through, chasing after the ginger tom. Oren dodged left and right, darting between Thales's legs and causing the sales rep to give a yelp of surprise.

"Come here, you mangy beast! I'm going to wring your neck if it's the last thing I do!" snarled the man as he lunged after Oren.

The ginger tom nimbly evaded his hands, then swarmed up a nearby drainpipe and was up on the roof of the cottage in the blink of an eye. He turned around and sat down, curling his tail around his paws and shooting them a triumphant look.

"*N-ow?*" he said cheekily.

"YOU SODDING FLEABAG!" roared the man, glaring up at the cat. "Don't think you're getting away with it! Just wait until I get my hands on you!"

Oren gave him another insolent stare and made a great show of licking his lips, then languidly began washing a paw.

The man made a noise of fury and, for a moment, Poppy thought he was going to climb up the drainpipe himself. Then he seemed to recall where he was and stepped back, glancing at them.

"Sorry," he said curtly. "Bloody cat ate my breakfast. Sausages, bacon, eggs, the whole lot! I put the plate down and turned my back for *one* minute, and he jumped up on the kitchen counter and polished off everything." He scowled as he saw Poppy's lips twitch. "Do you find that amusing?"

"Er... no, no, not at all," said Poppy, hastily wiping the grin off her face. Clearing her throat, she turned to Thales and said: "Thales, this is my neighbour Nick Forrest."

Thales stuck a hand out. "Good to meet you, Ni— wait a minute!" He broke off, a look of delighted recognition crossing his face. "Nick Forrest? Are you *the* Nick Forrest? The crime author?"

Nick gave him a wry smile. "For my sins," he said.

"Wow... it's an honour to meet you," said Thales, looking awestruck. "Your latest book was awesome! I read it in, like, one night."

"Thanks," said Nick, looking slightly embarrassed.

He shoved his hands into his pockets and hunched his shoulders slightly. But even with the self-effacing posture, he seemed to dominate the garden. Poppy was surprised and slightly annoyed to find that Thales suddenly seemed bland and insipid in the older man's presence, his superficial charm paling in comparison to Nick's more subtle and yet deeper charisma.

"You never told me you lived next door to a bestselling novelist," Thales teased Poppy, giving her shoulders a playful squeeze. "What a small world, eh?"

Poppy saw Nick's eyes linger on Thales's proprietary arm around her shoulders as he said coolly, "Yes, it's funny who your neighbours can be. So... are you here buying plants?"

Thales chuckled. "More like protecting plants, mate. I work for Campana AgroChemicals in their sales division. Poppy and I met at Mega Garden Town. I was there promoting our new pesticide range for home gardeners and she came in looking for help with pest control... I guess it was my lucky day!" he said, grinning. "Actually, I was just trying to convince her to have dinner with me when you and your cat showed up."

As if hearing himself being referred to, Oren called out: "*N-oww?*" Then he sprang down from the roof, landing on the ground next to Thales with a thump that made the sales rep jerk back in surprise.

"Bloody hell, he gave me a scare!" cried Thales.

"*N-ow?*" said Oren, giving Thales's leg a suspicious sniff. He flattened his ears suddenly and shot the sales rep a narrow look from his yellow eyes. "*N-ow? N-OW?*"

"Is it me or does the cat speak English? I swear, he sounds like he's talking,'" said Thales, eyeing Oren askance.

Poppy laughed. "No, you're not crazy. That's what

I thought, too, when I first met Oren. He always sounds like he's saying 'now?'"

Thales gave Nick a playful punch on the shoulder. "You should put that in a book, mate." Turning back to Poppy, he said, "Hey listen, I've just remembered— I have a bunch of brochures in my car. I was wondering: could I leave some here? Just for your customers to pick up, if they're interested in Campana products."

"Er... yes, all right," said Poppy reluctantly. She wasn't sure she wanted to promote Campana products in her nursery, but Thales had sprung it on her in such a way that she felt rude refusing.

"Great! Back in a moment..." Thales turned and hurried down the path, disappearing out the front gate a minute later.

Nick watched him go, then turned to Poppy and raised a sardonic eyebrow. "I didn't realise garden centres were the new dating mart."

"I'm not dating Thales," said Poppy quickly. "We just got chatting yesterday when he was telling me about his company's products."

"And... he somehow followed you home?"

"I told him about the nursery yesterday. He said he lived nearby and just popped in to see how I was getting on with the pesticide he sold me."

Nick snorted. "And you believed him? I didn't think you were the type to be that gullible and naïve."

Poppy bristled. "What's that supposed to mean?"

"It means that he probably uses that line on all

the pretty girls he sells products to," said Nick. "Be careful, Poppy. Thales is a 'player'."

"What? How can you possibly know that? You barely met him a few minutes ago," said Poppy indignantly.

Nick shrugged. "Call it a writer's intuition, if you like. We spend our time observing people and working out character motivations. Besides, I'm used to sizing people up quickly for my old job—it was one of the first skills we learned in the CID. And let me tell you, if Thales were a suspect in a case, he'd immediately be marked down as 'untrustworthy'."

"That's... that's total conjecture!" said Poppy hotly. "I think you're just making things up because you're jealous!"

"Jealous? Me?" Nick scowled. "Don't be ridiculous. I'm just trying to prevent you from getting hurt."

"I'm not an idiot," snapped Poppy. "I can take care of myself."

She was about to say more but, at that moment, Thales returned with a wad of brochures in his hands.

"Here you go," he said enthusiastically. "If you could leave them somewhere prominent, that would be great. Now..." He gave her a flirtatious smile. "You still haven't answered my question?"

Poppy hesitated. In spite of his cajoling, she *had* been thinking of refusing Thales's invitation, but now, as she saw Nick eyeing the younger man askance, she felt a surge of annoyance.

Giving Thales a dazzling smile, she said: "You know what, Thales? Dinner tonight sounds really nice. Thanks for the invitation—I'd like to accept."

"Really? That's fantastic!" said Thales, his face lighting up. "What time would you like me to pick you up?"

"Any time after five—oh no, wait, I've just remembered... I need to pop across to the other side of the village after work today, to check on an elderly lady." Poppy gave him an apologetic look. "I'm not sure what time I'll be finished there, though. Sorry, maybe tonight's not such a good idea after all—"

"No, no, I'm not letting you wriggle out of it now," said Thales teasingly. "Listen, the Campana head office is right on the edge of the business park, on the side near Bunnington—in fact, there's a public pathway that connects the two. I'll just wait for you at my desk. Don't worry, I've got loads of paperwork and admin to catch up on, so I'll happily keep myself busy until you're done. Give me a ring when you've finished and tell me the address of this old lady's place—"

"Why don't I just walk over to you myself?" Poppy offered. "If there's a public path and it isn't too far..."

"Yeah, it shouldn't take more than fifteen, twenty minutes. I've done it myself several times. Okay, well, if you're happy to walk, I'll just wait for you at HQ."

"It seems a shame for you to have to hang around, waiting in the office, though," said Poppy hesitantly.

"Are you sure you want to—"

"Absolutely!" Thales gave her a suggestive look. "You know what they say about anticipation increasing the pleasure."

Poppy blushed, then—aware of Nick watching them—she lifted her chin and said, "I'll see you tonight then."

CHAPTER SIX

Poppy had expected Miss Finch to live in one of the quaint old stone cottages that made Bunnington such a picturesque village, but to her surprise, the address that Nell had given her led to a newly built residential estate on the outskirts of the village. It was an extensive development, and if Poppy had realised the size of the place, she would have driven over in her car. Instead, she had opted to walk, and now she found herself wandering around the grid-like streets, past modern townhouses and bungalows, trying to get her bearings and figure out which was Miss Finch's house.

She found it at last: a neat little house right at the edge of the estate, next to open land which sloped away towards a shallow valley occupied by a large industrial park. *The business park*, Poppy realised, pausing to take in the view. Yes, she could see the huge sprawling complex of Mega Garden Town in the far distance, surrounded by rows of office blocks and warehouses, interspersed with car parks and landscaped gardens. Closer in, she could see an enormous warehouse attached to a building which had a familiar logo painted on its side: a bell encircled by the name "Campana AgroChemicals". *That must be where Thales's office is*, thought Poppy, and she was pleased to see the start of a paved pathway a bit further beyond Miss Finch's house. It led straight down over the hill to a side entrance of the business park and was bordered by globe lights which would mean safe walking, even in the dark.

Turning back to Miss Finch's house, she went to the front door and rang the bell. "Just a minute!" came a frail voice, and there was a long wait before Poppy heard the slow shuffle of footsteps on the other side of the door.

"Don't worry—take your time," she called out. "It's Poppy from Hollyhock Cottage, Miss Finch."

The door opened at last to reveal a little old lady dressed in a flannel housecoat, with one hand gripping the opposite shoulder in a gingerly fashion.

"Hello, Poppy dear," she said, smiling warmly. "How nice of you to drop by! I'm sorry it's taken me so long to answer the door—I've hurt my shoulder, you see, and I can't move about very quickly."

"Yes, Nell told me what happened and I came to see how you are. Nell would have come herself but she had a visit to her sister planned, and she had to leave Bunnington this morning."

"She was so good to come over and help me yesterday," said Miss Finch, stepping back to let Poppy into the house. "Do come in, dear. I wish I could offer you a cup of tea, but I'm finding it difficult to lift anything with this arm at the moment—"

"Oh heavens, don't worry about me! In fact, can I make *you* a cup of tea? That was the reason I came: to see if there was anything I could help you with around the house."

"Ooh, a cuppa would be lovely," said Miss Finch with a sigh. "The doctor said I should try to rest the shoulder and not do too much, especially with my upper back, but I'm not used to sitting around doing nothing." She made a rueful face. "Actually, even sitting down and getting up can be painful. I never realised how one uses the muscles in one's back to do so many things! But I've managed all right and Maggie from next door popped in earlier to help me make some lunch and tidy up a bit around the house..."

"Oh, speaking of meals, I've brought this for your dinner," said Poppy, lifting up the thermos she was holding. "It's some of Nell's split pea and ham soup."

"Ah, bless her," said Miss Finch. "That Mrs Hopkins is a real treasure!"

Poppy settled the elderly lady in the sitting room, then hurried into the kitchen to make the tea. As she stood filling the kettle at the sink, she looked out of the kitchen windows and noticed a pretty garden outside with a small patio area bordered by large terracotta pots. One of them was brimming with marigolds and petunias, but the rest seemed to be only half filled with soil. There was more soil scattered in piles on the ground next to the pots, and at the edge of the patio sat a half-opened bag of potting compost, together with several plastic trays holding more petunias, nasturtiums, and a variety of other flowering annuals. It looked like someone had been planting up the containers but had been interrupted and never finished the job.

"Were you doing some gardening, Miss Finch?" Poppy asked when she took a tray with teapot, teacups, and a plate of biscuits back into the sitting room. "I saw the half-filled pots out on the patio."

The old lady sighed. "Yes, I was in the middle of replacing the spring annuals with some lovely new flowers. I think that might be partly how I hurt my shoulder, actually. I tried to shift one of the terracotta pots to a different position and it was very heavy, so I had to give it a big shove. I didn't feel anything then, but when I came in to fetch my glasses, I bent over to pick them up from the table and felt the most dreadful pain in my shoulder and upper back..." She winced at the memory, then she looked out sadly through the glass patio doors at the pots outside. "I hate leaving the pots half-finished like that and I'm worried about the flowers drying out in their punnets, but the doctor gave strict orders for me to avoid gardening for a week."

"I could finish the pots for you, if you like," Poppy offered. "It won't take me long. You just need to tell me exactly which ones you want to go in which pots."

"Would you, dear?" Miss Finch cried, her entire face lighting up. "That would be wonderful! Thank you so much." Then she paused and looked embarrassed, fidgeting with the buttons on her housecoat. "Oh, but... I don't get my pension until the end of the month, so I wouldn't be able to pay you until—"

"Oh no, I wouldn't think of accepting payment," protested Poppy. "Honestly, Miss Finch, I'd be delighted to help. It's no big deal. Think of it as an extended service for buying the plants from the nursery."

"You're such a good girl," said Miss Finch, reaching out to pat her hand. "Just like my nephew, Dennis. He's always coming here and checking on me, to see if I need a hand with anything. He's my sister's boy and he came very late in life, you know. She'd almost given up hope of having any children, and then Dennis arrived. We were so delighted— although when we saw him, we were very worried, too, because he was born with his little winky all crooked! Yes, completely bent to one side. Can you imagine?"

Oh no, here we go again... thought Poppy, bracing herself for another account of Dennis's wonky appendage. It seemed to be Miss Finch's favourite topic of conversation.

"The doctor did assure us that it's quite common in baby boys. Apparently, it's even got a name... now, what was it called? Chorizo? Cholera? Ah... 'chordee'—yes, that's right, 'chordee'. What an odd name, don't you think? But then it seems a very odd thing to happen, really. The doctor said they don't know what causes it—something goes wrong when the baby is developing in the womb, I suppose..." Miss Finch mused. "Dennis is very tall, you know. Perhaps all the cells and whatnot went into growing his legs and so there weren't enough left for his manhood?"

"Uh..." Poppy stared at the old lady, wondering how on earth to reply. She hoped she would never have to meet Dennis in person—she'd never be able to look the poor man in the eye!

"Still, it doesn't seem to have caused Dennis any trouble in the bedroom, I can tell you," continued Miss Finch, smiling proudly. "My sister says girls were always hanging all over him. Perhaps they found it a novelty... although I don't suppose he would have shown them his willy, do you?"

"Er... I... I don't know," stammered Poppy.

"Well, it's just that young people seem so relaxed about everything these days. And boys are always very proud of their members, aren't they? Not that Dennis is a boy anymore, of course. He's well into his fifties now. But I always tell him: I can still remember the first time I saw you in hospital, with your wonky willy!" said Miss Finch with a reminiscent smile.

"I... I think I'd better get started on those pots," said Poppy, rising hastily from the sofa. Then she caught sight of the clock on the mantelpiece and paused as she remembered her date with Thales. It wouldn't be fair to keep him any longer than necessary. "Actually, Miss Finch, if you don't mind, can I come back to do them tomorrow? I've... er... sort of got a date tonight."

"Oh goodness me, yes, of course," said Miss Finch, making a flapping motion with her hands. "Go on, dear. I wouldn't want to keep you from your date."

"No, no, it's all right—there's no rush. I tell you what, I'll pop outside now and water the plants, then they should be fine until tomorrow afternoon when I can come back."

"That would be wonderful. Thank you, dear," said Miss Finch gratefully. "There's a watering can by the pots and an outside tap just around the side of the house."

It was still fairly light when Poppy stepped out onto the patio, despite it being nearly seven o'clock, and she was glad that the clocks had changed to British Summer Time. It meant that she would still have ample time to walk over to the Campana head office before twilight fell. Quickly, she gathered the watering can, then made her way around the side of the house. There was a narrow alley which connected the back garden to the front of the property, and it was divided from the house next door by a tall hedge.

Poppy could see a dense tangle of tree branches, shrubs, and bushes poking over the hedge from the other side. Whoever lived there was obviously a keen gardener, who had filled every inch of their outdoor space with plants.

She bent by the tap and placed the watering can beneath the spout. As she waited for it to be filled, she heard the faint sound of a doorbell chiming. She was about to call out to Miss Finch that she would get it, when she realised that it was actually coming from the neighbour's place. The next moment, she heard the front door of the adjoining house open and a woman's voice say sharply:

"Whatever you're selling, I'm not interested!"

"Oh, I'm not selling anything," came a smooth male voice. "I'm with Top Notch Estate Agents and I wanted to let you know that we've recently sold several similar houses to yours at *very* attractive prices. We have many buyers still interested, so if you've been thinking of moving—"

"I told you: I'm not interested!"

"Well, I'll just leave these leaflets with you, shall I? This one tells you a bit more about our agency and these are some of the recent properties that we—"

"I don't want your bloody leaflets—and you should be ashamed of yourself! Look at all the paper you've wasted printing these. All people will do is shove them in the bin, d'you know that? Do you realise how many trees are cut down and killed, just to provide paper for poxy little businesses like yours to make junk advertising that nobody wants?"

"I—"

"One tree produces enough oxygen for three people to breathe, you know! And it's not just the lost trees—paper production is the third largest industrial polluter. They use chlorine-based bleaches and all of that releases toxic waste into the air and the waterways and even leaches into the soil. You might think that paper is biodegradable anyway, so it doesn't matter, but when paper rots, it emits methane gas which is *twenty-five times* more toxic than carbon-dioxide..."

Bloody hell, what a diatribe! Bet he's wishing he never rang that doorbell, thought Poppy with amusement as she listened. Still, she had to admit that the woman's words did make her feel uneasy and she felt a stab of guilt at the number of times she had thoughtlessly crumpled a piece of barely used paper and thrown it into the bin.

She turned off the tap and started to lift the watering can, then, on an impulse, put it down again and made her way over to the hedge. There had been something familiar about the woman's voice... Standing on tiptoes, she peered over the top, trying to see through a gap in the dense foliage. She was just able to make out the front corner of the house. She moved further along and craned her neck until she was able to see around the corner and get a partial view of the front porch. A young man stood uncertainly on the lower step, clutching a sheaf of leaflets and cringing slightly as a wiry, middle-aged woman yelled at him while jabbing a finger in his chest.

Poppy's eyes widened. She had been right. It was her—the anti-pesticide woman at Mega Garden Town! Poppy almost ducked as a reflex, before she reminded herself that the woman couldn't see her. Still, she hurriedly backed away from the hedge, grabbed the watering can, and returned to the patio, not wanting to risk attracting the woman's attention.

Miss Finch looked up anxiously when Poppy finally rejoined her in the sitting room. "Was everything all right, dear? I thought I heard raised voices."

"Oh, that was your next-door neighbour —"

"You didn't run into trouble with Maggie, did you?" said Miss Finch with consternation.

"No, no, she wasn't talking to me. She was talking to an estate agent who came to her door, looking for business."

"Ah... no doubt she sent him off with a flea in his ear," said Miss Finch, chuckling. "She can be quite blunt, Maggie, but her bark is worse than her bite."

Poppy couldn't help an incredulous snort and Miss Finch said, "Oh, it's true, dear. I know Maggie can seem terribly stroppy, but she means well. She's a good person at heart."

"Yes, I suppose she's right about the environment," Poppy admitted. "I *am* pretty careless when it comes to wasting things and not making sustainable choices. I really ought to try harder."

"It's not very palatable to hear, but everything Maggie says is true. She just isn't very... er... tactful sometimes," said Miss Finch with a rueful smile. "She's had a very hard time of it, you know. Her husband left her when her daughter was just a baby, and she's had to bring the girl up on her own. Plus, she's had to look after her own mum, too, so Maggie has her hands full, really, and yet she still always finds time for others. She's always checking on me and offering to pick things up for me from the shops or help out around the house."

"Oh. That's really nice of her," said Poppy, her feelings softening towards the woman.

Perhaps Maggie's belligerent manner was a sort of defence mechanism, a way to cope with a harsh world that had never been easy to her. Poppy resolved to try and think of the woman more charitably... although she still hoped that she would never have to speak to her face to face again!

CHAPTER SEVEN

Twilight was falling by the time Poppy arrived at the head offices of Campana AgroChemicals. It had been a windy walk, and she was glad that she had opted for a practical blouse-and-capri-pants combo, paired with her favourite cardigan. However, as she stepped into the gleaming foyer, she caught sight of herself in the reflection of the glass door and paused in dismay. She had a large smudge of dirt on her nose, her hair was wind tossed and standing up in wild tendrils around her face, and there were bits of soil clinging to her capri pants, probably from when she'd knelt down to water the flowering annuals on Miss Finch's patio.

She decided that, before she sent Thales a text telling him that she'd arrived, she would take the chance to clean herself up first. It was quiet in the building—the quiet of a workplace where most of the staff had left for the day. She approached the empty reception desk, the receptionist no doubt having gone home already, and leaned over the counter to peer down the corridor beyond. She was pleased to spot a door with a sign displaying the universal stick figure for "Ladies". Quickly, she darted around the reception desk and hurried down the corridor.

Several minutes later, she stepped back from the sink in the bathroom and checked her reflection in the mirror. She felt much better with her face clean, her hair smoothed down again and anchored with hairpins, and the soil stains brushed off her clothes. Poppy leaned forwards, looking into the mirror, and adjusted the collar of her blouse to show off the gold locket she wore around her neck. Although not valuable in the monetary sense—the locket had belonged to her mother and its value was more sentimental than anything else—it looked very pretty as part of the ensemble. And she was pleased now that she had chosen to eschew the usual choice of a dress for a "date". She hadn't wanted Thales to think that she'd made too much effort to impress him, but she hadn't wanted to look too slovenly either, and the pretty blouse paired with capri pants seemed to strike the perfect balance.

Her confidence restored, Poppy pushed the swinging door and stepped out, nearly colliding with a man who was just walking past in the corridor.

"Oops, sorry!"

"Excuse me—" The man paused and looked at her curiously. "Can I help you? Our offices are closed for the day. You don't look like you work here..."

"Er... I'm here to see Thales. Thales Georgiou."

The man raised his eyebrows, his gaze roving over her frilly blouse and tight-fitting capri pants. "You have a meeting with him?"

"No... I mean, sort of. We're supposed to meet up for dinner," said Poppy awkwardly.

The man's eyes filled with sudden contempt. "Oh. You're one of Thales's girls," he said, curling his lips back in distaste.

Poppy stared. What was that supposed to mean?

"Well, I'm heading back to my desk anyway—I'll take you to him, if you like," said the man, jerking his head down the corridor. "His desk is next to mine."

"Oh... I thought I'd just wait in the foyer. I didn't want to disturb him if he's in the middle of work—"

The man gave a sarcastic laugh. "I doubt it. Pretty Boy is probably just dolling himself up and dousing himself with more of his noxious aftershave. Come on."

He turned and began walking down the corridor. Poppy hurried to keep up with him.

"So... do you work with Thales?" she asked, glancing surreptitiously at the man beside her. He looked to be in his fifties, with salt-and-pepper hair combed into a neat side-parting and cold blue eyes in a narrow face. He was wearing a navy suit with a conservative tie and carried a bulging manila folder under one arm—the image of a stuffy banker or accountant, and the complete opposite of Thales's trendy, urban style.

The man gave a curt nod. "We both work in Sales. I'm the senior sales rep—Thales only joined the company six months ago," he added.

And has probably smashed your sales targets in that time, despite his lack of experience... which really gets up your nose, thought Poppy dryly.

They turned a corner and walked into a large open-plan office. Thales was standing by a desk in the far corner and it seemed that his colleague's acerbic comments were accurate, after all, because he was pouring liquid from a cologne bottle into one palm and splashing it liberally around his neck. His face lit up as he saw them and he tossed the aftershave into a desk drawer before hurrying over to greet them.

"Poppy! You look gorgeous," he said, grasping both her hands and enveloping her in a musky fragrance as he leaned close to kiss her on one cheek.

Poppy stepped back in surprise at the unexpected familiarity and felt her cheeks burning under the colleague's caustic gaze. Hastily, she pulled her hands out of Thales's grasp.

"Did old Sidney find you and bring you in? Hope he didn't bore you with his standard spiel. He's always spouting slogans at anyone who will listen; thinks they're really funny and clever," Thales chortled. "Like this one: *'The bug killer that bugs would use.'* He gave Poppy a wink. "Sidney thinks he's a real poet, you know."

The older man flushed. "I... I never said that! Everyone knows that slogans play a key role in marketing. They encapsulate your brand and make it memorable."

"Oh yeah? So how does *'the bug killer that bugs would use'* encapsulate the Campana brand? Like, are we the pesticide that suicidal aphids would use?" Thales threw his head back and laughed uproariously.

"You... you..." Sidney spluttered, his face going beetroot in colour. A vein stood out at his temple and his jaw was clamped so tight, Poppy thought she could hear his teeth cracking.

"Hey... I'm just joshing you, mate," Thales said, grinning and giving his colleague a playful dig in the ribs.

Sidney did not look remotely amused. Turning, he stalked over to the desk beside Thales's and placed the folder carefully next to the keyboard. Then—with a curt "Good night" to Poppy—he walked stiffly out of the room.

"Whoa... think I might have offended old Sidney there," said Thales, chuckling. "Don't worry. I'll apologise to the old fart in the morning." He turned towards his monitor. "Lemme just shut down my computer..."

"If you're still in the middle of something, I can

wait," Poppy offered.

"Nah, I was finishing up when you came in. I was just wondering whether to bother contacting the police."

"The police? Why?" said Poppy, startled.

"To report that bloody cow at the garden centre."

"Oh... is that really necessary?"

"Well, I'm sick of having to put up with her stupid lectures all the time. If I report her for assault and vandalism, maybe the police will pick her up and clap her in a cell for a couple of days. That'll teach her a lesson," said Thales with relish.

Poppy felt a stab of compassion for Maggie. "That's a bit harsh, don't you think?"

"Harsh? I think it's too good for her! These bloody tree huggers need to know that they can't go around imposing their own stupid beliefs on others."

"The thing is, she's sort of right, you know," said Poppy uncomfortably. "I mean, pesticides *can* be very harmful to wildlife and the environment, and there are even health risks to humans—"

Thales groaned. "Oh God, don't tell me she's brainwashed you too? Yes, there are some bad pesticides out there, but I can tell you, Campana products are not one of them. Anyway, let's not ruin the evening by talking about that crazy cow." He grabbed his jacket from the back of his chair, then snapped his fingers and turned back to her excitedly. "Actually, before we leave, I want to show you something. So far, Campana has focused mostly on fertilisers and pesticides, but we're just starting to develop a range of mulches and composts and we've come up with a new mulch product that's going to revolutionise the industry! We've used a special chemical to coat the bark chip and other materials, so that they'll be more resistant to rain and UV light. You'll love it; you might even like to stock it at your nursery. I could give you a great stockists' discount," he added with a persuasive smile.

Poppy gave a helpless laugh. Thales really was the consummate salesman. Even when he was going on a date, he couldn't resist the opportunity to gain a new customer. "I'm not really selling any non-plant products at the moment," she said.

"Well, then, I'll be your first stockist partner," Thales replied, not missing a beat. He grabbed her hand. "Come on, I'll give you a quick tour."

They left the office and went down the corridor, heading deeper into the building. After a while, they came to a set of double doors with glass vision panels. The doors were also covered with various warning symbols and signs saying: "DANGER", "CHEMICAL HAZARDS", and "NO UNAUTHORISED PERSON ALLOWED BEYOND THIS POINT". Thales peeked through one of the glass panels, then, throwing Poppy a mischievous look, he pushed a door open and dragged her into the laboratory with him.

"Thales!" cried Poppy, pulling back. "Should we be in here?"

"Well, I won't tell if you don't," said Thales with a wink. "Come on, where's your sense of adventure? This is our R & D laboratory, you know, where all our top-secret pesticide formulas are developed. Don't you want to have a peek?"

Poppy glanced uneasily around. To be honest, the place didn't look that interesting or exciting, despite Thales's words. It reminded her of laboratories she'd been in at school—albeit a much larger version—with the usual layout of long white workbenches running the length of the room and a couple of sinks by the walls. The only thing that seemed radically different was a large cabinet in one corner, with a glass-fronted chamber filled with bottles and jars, and a thick duct pipe leading up into the ceiling.

Thales saw her looking at it and said with a smirk: "That's the fume cupboard. It's where all the hard stuff is—you know, the chemicals that can kill you with one whiff."

Poppy thought of all the warning signs outside and turned hastily for the door. "We really shouldn't be in here."

She stepped back outside without waiting for Thales, forcing him to join her. As they turned away from the laboratory door, they saw a couple coming down the corridor towards them: a distinguished-looking older man in a grey three-piece suit accompanied by a slim young woman.

"Ah, Thales—still here?" said the man with a genial smile as he spotted them. "I can see why you've been our 'Top Salesman of the Month' several times running. You never seem to stop working."

"I'm just giving a potential stockist a tour of our facility, sir," said Thales smoothly. He led Poppy forwards to meet the couple. "This is Poppy Lancaster. She runs a nursery in Bunnington."

"Lancaster?" The man looked at Poppy curiously. "You're not related to Mary Lancaster, by any chance?"

"Yes, she was my grandmother," said Poppy.

The man smiled. "Ahh! Hollyhock Cottage Garden and Nursery, isn't it? Your grandmother was well known and respected in the garden trade, Miss Lancaster." He held a hand out. "I'm Bill Campana."

"Mr Campana is the CEO of the company... and my awesome boss," said Thales. Then he glanced at the girl standing behind the older man and added in an offhand voice: "And that's Nina. She's Mr Campana's PA."

Poppy glanced at Thales, then at the girl, wondering if she was imagining the current of hostility that seemed to pulse between them. Nina was dressed like the epitome of an executive PA stereotype, in a tailored shirt and trousers, with her hair pulled back in a sleek bun and a pair of glasses perched on her nose... and yet something about her made Poppy feel that she wasn't the type who appreciated taking orders from anyone.

Now, she stepped forwards and said in a light, cool voice: "Actually, Mr Campana, this is a good chance for Thales to sign those papers you wanted."

"Ah, yes, of course," said Bill Campana. He gave the girl a fond smile. "Thank goodness I have you, Nina. You always think of everything."

Nina pulled a sheaf of papers out of the leather portfolio she was carrying and handed them to Thales.

"What—no pen?" said Thales insolently. "And you call yourself a PA?" He said it jokingly but there was an undertone of malice in his voice.

Nina compressed her lips, but before she could reply, Mr Campana reached into his inner jacket pocket and pulled out a fountain pen.

"Here, use this," he said, passing the pen to Nina.

She handed it to Thales, who twirled it and tossed it up in the air before catching it with a flourish and finally scribbling his name in the places she indicated. It was a bit of cocky showing-off and Poppy saw Mr Campana smile indulgently, but Nina stiffened and narrowed her eyes. As she reached out to take the pen back, she fumbled slightly and, the next moment, ink squirted from the end of the fountain pen to splash all over the front of Thales's pristine white shirt, leaving huge black splotches.

"Hey!" cried Thales angrily, jumping back and staring down at his shirt in dismay.

"Oh, I'm sorry," said Nina smoothly. "I guess your reflexes weren't fast enough that time. Would you like me to look up some local dry-cleaners for you?"

"Never mind," snapped Thales. He looked as if he

wanted to say something else but then he glanced at his boss and bit back his words. Instead, he took a deep breath and plastered a breezy smile on his face. "Don't worry about it. I never liked this shirt anyway, so you've just done me a favour and given me an excuse to get rid of it."

"Oh dear..." said Mr Campana. "What an unfortunate accident. That has never happened with that pen before."

"Don't worry about it, sir," said Thales, adding with a cheeky grin: "In fact, I would say getting squirted by one of your pens is an honour!"

The older man laughed and patted Thales on the shoulder. "You're a good lad, Thales. And thank you, by the way, for dropping the things off at my place. I hope it didn't take you out of your way too much."

"Not at all, sir. Anywhere in Oxfordshire is an easy drive, really."

Campana laughed again. "Maybe at your age, Thales. At mine, I like to follow the speed limit." He turned to Poppy. "I'm delighted to know that Mary's granddaughter is following in her footsteps and continuing the family business. I think an interest in gardening is a wonderful legacy—I got mine from *my* grandmother." A reminiscent smile spread over his face. "I remember as a young boy spending hours in her garden, watching her sow seeds and plant flowers. I just love getting my hands in the soil, you know—I still do all my own gardening."

Poppy looked at him in surprise. Somehow, she'd

expected someone like Bill Campana to have a full-time gardener.

The CEO saw her expression and gave a sheepish laugh. "It drives my wife crazy. She keeps telling me to hire someone, but I refuse. Oh, we have someone who mows the lawns and trims the hedges, but for the 'real' gardening..." He smiled. "It's actually really relaxing after a long day at work to muck around in the flower beds. And besides, I think it keeps me in touch with our customers—you know, it helps me appreciate their priorities and concerns." He glanced at his watch. "Goodness, is that the time? We'd best get going, Nina, or I'm going to be late." He nodded to Thales and gave Poppy a warm look. "Well, it was lovely to meet you, Miss Lancaster. I hope to see you again soon."

CHAPTER EIGHT

Thales hung back until his boss and Nina had exited the door at the end of the corridor, then led the way back to the foyer. As they stepped out into the car park, he turned to Poppy and said: "Hey—do you mind if we stop off at my place so I can change my shirt?" He indicated his front ruefully. "Can't really go to dinner looking like this. My place is just five minutes' drive away."

Thales pointed up the slope that Poppy had walked down earlier and she was surprised to realise that he lived in the same residential estate as Miss Finch.

"Oh, of course," she said, following him to his car.

It was a sporty model, with two doors and very low-slung seats. Poppy bent to get in the front passenger seat, then paused as she saw that there was a half-open box of gourmet chocolates lying on the seat.

"Oops, sorry..." said Thales, leaning across from the driver's side to pick up the box. He waited until she had settled in and fastened her seat belt, then held the box out to her. "Chocolate?"

Poppy glanced down, noticing that there was a handwritten card tucked into the side of the chocolate tray. Without meaning to, her eyes scanned the writing, then she stiffened as she read the words:

Can't wait to see you again, Thales.
You know I'm yours. Always.
Jules xxx

Poppy stared at the card. Nick Forrest's warning about Thales being a "player" echoed in her mind. Something of her thoughts must have shown on her face because Thales said quickly:

"These are from my ex-girlfriend—she turned up at Mega Garden Town lunchtime today and took me by surprise. She hasn't taken our break-up very well. I tried to explain to her that it wasn't her, it was me, you know? But she keeps asking me to give us another chance. Anyway, she's been going through a rough patch lately so..." He gave a helpless shrug. "I felt like I had to spend a bit of time with her, you know? But we just went to the centre café. It was only a quick—"

"It's okay," said Poppy, shifting uncomfortably. "You don't have to explain—"

"But I *want* to," said Thales. "I don't want you to think that I'm two-timing you or anything."

"Well, since we're not really dating, you wouldn't be able to," Poppy retorted.

Thales didn't answer. Instead, he held the box out to her again. "Fancy a chocolate?"

"No, thank you," said Poppy, slightly taken aback at his insensitivity. The last thing his ex-girlfriend would have wanted was for him to be offering her heartfelt gift to his new date!

"Sure? They look pretty good, actually. I have to say, Jules always did have an eye for gourmet goodies," said Thales, selecting a large truffle and popping it into his mouth.

He tossed the box onto the back seat, then turned back to the steering wheel. But as he was about to start the engine, he made a noise of annoyance and said: "Ah... bugger! I was going to show you our new mulch. Meeting Mr Campana completely sidetracked me."

Poppy wondered if it was the encounter with Thales's boss that had thrown him or the unpleasant little interlude with his boss's PA.

"Never mind," continued Thales, brightening. "I've just remembered—I've got a bag of the stuff in my boot. I can show it to you when we get to my place."

The drive to Thales's house was as short as he'd promised and Poppy soon found herself back in the grid-like streets of the residential estate. They turned into a road which looked vaguely familiar—she realised that she'd walked through it when she was searching for Miss Finch's house—and pulled up in front of a row of terraced housing. Thales's was the one on the end, and Poppy waited as he opened the boot to reveal a plastic sack emblazoned with the Campana company logo and the words: "Moisture-Shield Mulch". It was a big, bulging sack and Thales grunted as he lifted it out.

"Are you all right? Can you manage?" asked Poppy, putting out a hand to help as she watched him stagger while trying to heft the sack up into a fireman's carry over one shoulder.

"Oh... fine... fine... no... no problem..." panted Thales.

Poppy wanted to roll her eyes. No doubt, showing that he could handle the heavy sack was a sign of his supreme virility and, like a typical male, Thales would rather collapse than admit that he was struggling. She gave up and instead followed him as he tottered up to the front door.

"Let me at least get the door," she said, taking the keys from his clenched fingers and unlocking the front door.

"Wait... wait until you see... this... stuff... in action... You're... going to be... amazed," said Thales, puffing. He paused and sagged against the door frame, leaning the sack against the wall for a moment to take the weight off his shoulders. "Whew! I've got to admit, this thing is pretty heavy," he said with a rueful laugh. "Gotta do more workouts at the gym."

Poppy glanced into the house. "Can't you leave the bag out here?"

"Nah, I need it out the back. I've got this little courtyard garden and I've just finished planting up the borders and mulching most of the beds. Just got a bit left to do—I ran out of mulch last time. Luckily, though, I work near a ready source of the stuff," he said with a wink.

"Do employees get a discount on all products?"

"Yeah. Fifteen percent, which is not bad but I... er... sort of got this one for free," said Thales, grinning. "Hey, they're hardly going to miss a bag here and there, and I reckon it's one of the perks of working for a gardening supplies company, you know?"

Poppy made a non-committal noise of reply. She was beginning to feel uncomfortable with the glimpses she was getting of Thales's character: the vindictive satisfaction from getting Maggie into trouble, the arrogant malice in his interaction with Nina, and now the sly delight at "stealing" company products. It was all a far cry from the charming, attentive persona she'd first met at the garden centre. And she couldn't help thinking again of Nick's comments. It annoyed her to think that the crime writer might have been right in his snap assessment of Thales's personality.

No one's perfect, she reminded herself. *Everyone's*

*got some quirks or flaws. It doesn't mean that they're
bad people or that you shouldn't socialise with them.*

Thales took a deep breath, then hefted the sack of
mulch up again. They walked into the house, which
was very obviously a bachelor pad, and out to the
shaded courtyard at the rear. This had been cleverly
landscaped to give a sense of space, despite the small
size. The stone path leading down to the compact
shed at the bottom of the garden was bordered on
either side by asymmetrical beds arranged in a zigzag
fashion, which lent it a feeling of depth. The beds
themselves were planted with a variety of grasses,
ferns, and foliage plants, each with different heights
and leaf textures, so that the overall effect was one of
green harmony. Poppy had to admit that Thales had
done a very good job. He might have been a bit of a
rogue but he knew how to garden.

He dropped the mulch down by the path and
heaved a sigh of relief. Then he turned to her and
gestured proudly around the courtyard. "What d'you
think?"

"It's gorgeous," said Poppy with honest
admiration. She pulled out her phone. "Can I get a
couple of pictures? I'm still fairly new at gardening,
you know, and I'm always collecting images for
inspiration. You've done an amazing job, especially
in such a narrow space."

Thales smiled with satisfaction at her words and
watched as she snapped several shots from different
angles. "Yeah, I'm pretty chuffed with it—I've just got

to finish up this corner."

He indicated the bed closest to them, where Poppy could see that most of the surface had been covered by a fine bark chip mixture, except for a triangle of exposed soil on the side next to the path.

Glancing down at his stained shirtfront, he said, "Listen, are you really hungry? 'Cos if you don't mind waiting an extra few minutes, I can finish this corner and quickly show you what this new mulch is like. It's a really fantastic product! Honestly, you'll be amazed."

Poppy laughed at his enthusiasm. Thales really was a supreme salesman—he never stopped promoting his products at any opportunity! Still, she was keen to pick his brains about how he had landscaped his courtyard, so she was more than happy to delay their meal.

"Yes, of course," she said. "But do you mind if I just pop to the loo first?"

"Sure, take your time." He gestured back towards the house. "The toilet's the second on the left as you come in the front. Don't shut the door fully, though. It's been playing up and the handle keeps jamming in the latch."

Poppy returned to the house and wandered back down the hall until she found the downstairs lavatory. Like the rest of the house, it was very much a masculine domain, with minimal toiletries and the seat left up on the toilet. Still, she was relieved to see that there was ample toilet paper and soap for hand washing. She completed her business, gave her appearance a quick check in the mirror, then turned to go. To her annoyance, however, when she tried to turn the door handle, it stuck fast. She tried again, twisting and jiggling it from side to side, but it refused to turn.

Oh no... Suddenly, Poppy recalled Thales reminding her to leave the toilet door slightly ajar. She'd completely forgotten, pulling it shut behind her by reflex. Now she realised that the latch in the door had jammed, exactly as Thales had predicted. Cursing under her breath, she crouched down to look more closely at the handle. It looked completely normal, but when she tried again, heaving and pulling with more force, it remained unresponsive.

"Bugger!" Poppy muttered. She hesitated, then— swallowing her embarrassment—called through the door: "Thales? Sorry, but I'm stuck in the toilet!"

There was no answer. Poppy took a deep breath and tried again, raising her voice: "Thales? Can you hear me? The toilet door's jammed! I can't get out!"

Again, there was no answer. She tried a few more times, raising her voice louder until she was almost shouting herself hoarse, but each time, she was greeted with silence. He probably couldn't hear her, out in the courtyard at the rear, Poppy realised, especially with the toilet being at the front of the house. And she also realised that she had left her phone out in the courtyard with him, so she couldn't even use it to call and alert him to her predicament.

"Bugger, bugger, bugger!" she muttered in frustration.

It looked like she had no choice but to sit there and wait; surely Thales would wonder where she was eventually and come looking for her? Poppy flipped the lid down on the toilet and sat gingerly on the cold plastic surface. Minutes passed and she fidgeted on her makeshift seat. She didn't know if it was just because she was stuck there without a phone or watch but it seemed like a long time had gone by. Where *was* Thales?

Finally, she heaved an impatient sigh and stood up again. She'd had enough of just sitting there, waiting to be rescued—she had to try and get out herself. Once again, she attempted to force the handle to turn, throwing her weight against it and yanking it as hard as she could. But it was difficult to manoeuvre in the cramped space of the toilet and, in any case, no matter how much force she applied, it didn't seem to make a difference. Finally, she stopped, panting and sweating. No, this couldn't be done by brute force. There had to be another way.

She crouched down to look at the handle again, squinting at the gap between the door and the jamb. Then, on an impulse, she reached up and pulled out one of her hairpins. Carefully, she straightened the wire, then inserted it into the gap. She jiggled it experimentally in one direction, then the other, all while trying to turn the handle. Suddenly, there was a loud *click!* and the handle depressed smoothly. The door swung outwards, throwing her off balance, and she had to grab the towel rail to stop herself sprawling forwards.

Whew! Poppy breathed a sigh of relief as she rose and stepped out of the toilet. How long had she been stuck in there? Surely it couldn't have been more than a few minutes, otherwise Thales would have come looking for her, but it felt like an age! Smoothing her clothes down, she hurried back through the house and stepped out into the courtyard.

"My God, Thales, you were right about the toilet door!" she gasped. "I got completely stuck! You know, you should get a locksmith to come and look at that—"

She broke off with a gasp as she caught sight of the figure sprawled face down beside the nearest bed.

"Thales!" she cried, rushing forwards and dropping to her knees next to him.

There was a bloody gash on his forehead and his legs were twisted underneath his body. The bag of mulch was open next to him, its contents spilling out onto the path. What had happened? Had he been lifting the heavy mulch to pour it into the bed and then lost his balance and fallen, hitting his head on the stone walkway?

"Thales?" she said, putting a hesitant hand on his shoulder.

Then she jerked back, her heart pounding. He was so still. So unnaturally still.

"Thales?" she said again, in a whisper. Slowly, she reached out to touch his neck. The skin felt slightly warm, and yet...

She whirled, searching for her phone. She saw it lying on the low wall bordering one of the zigzag beds and snatched it up. Her fingers felt numb as she groped for the keypad, struggling to press "999".

"Emergency. Which service?" came a disembodied voice.

"I... I don't know... he might be... I don't know..." gasped Poppy, her voice breaking. "Ambulance, I think... or the police... But you need to come quickly!" She broke off suddenly as she realised that she had no idea what address to give. She hadn't been paying any attention when she arrived and couldn't remember what the name of the street was, never mind the house number. Panic filled her.

"It's all right, luv. Help is on the way," said the voice soothingly. "Can you tell me—is the patient conscious?"

"No, I found him on the ground. He's... he's not moving."

"Is he breathing?"

"I... I don't know! Oh God, I don't think so..." Poppy glanced over her shoulder at Thales's still body, then swallowed painfully. "I... I think he might be dead."

CHAPTER NINE

Poppy tried not to fidget as she sat in the waiting area of the police station. It was still hard to believe that she was here, about to go into a police interview, instead of standing by the trestle tables in her cottage garden, chatting to customers about growing hollyhocks and delphiniums. In fact, the events of the night before seemed like a surreal dream now. *Or more like a nightmare*, she thought with a grimace. She could still vividly see, in her mind's eye, Thales's still form as he lay slumped on the ground, and she could still vividly remember the clammy feel of his skin...

The paramedics had looked grim when they arrived and Poppy had stood watching, hugging her arms around herself, as they'd strapped Thales to a stretcher and loaded him into the waiting ambulance. It had driven away, its sirens screaming, but from the expression on the paramedics' faces, Poppy didn't think there was much reason for hope. She had spent a restless night wondering what had happened and had tried to call the hospital first thing that morning, but had been fobbed off by a harassed ward sister who had refused to give out information to anyone who wasn't officially "family". So when she'd got the call asking her to go down to the police station for further questions, it had almost been a relief.

And now, Poppy's relief increased as she heard her name being called and looked up to see a dark-haired woman in her late thirties approaching. Detective Inspector Suzanne Whitaker was not what you'd normally expect for an officer in the CID. With her sleek bob and elegant suits, she looked more like a high-flying publishing executive or maybe even someone who worked for a fashion houses in Paris or Milan. But her glamorous looks belied a calm efficiency and shrewd mind which made her a brilliant lead investigator on criminal cases.

"Poppy!" Suzanne greeted her with a warm smile. "How nice to see you—although it's a shame it's for this reason."

Poppy sprang up from her seat. "They said it's about Thales Georgiou—do you know how he is? I haven't been able to get any news from the hospital."

Suzanne gave her a look of compassion. "I'm sorry, Poppy. He was pronounced dead on arrival.

They tried but they couldn't save him."

"Oh." Poppy stopped, stunned. Somehow, even though she had been expecting the news, it still hit her with a sort of horrified shock. It didn't seem possible that Thales, with his insolent grins and easy, boyish charm, Thales, who had been laughing and teasing her only a day ago, could be dead and gone.

"Was he a good friend?" asked Suzanne gently.

"Um... no, not really. I was... we were on a date."

"Ah, I see." Suzanne gave her a thoughtful look. "I think you'd better tell me all about it. Come on through to my office." She turned and began leading the way back down the hallway to the inner CID offices. "You know, I've been meaning to give you a ring to see if we could catch up over coffee sometime, but I just never seem to get a free moment," she said with a rueful smile. "My weekends have been completely shot the past few weeks, what with the workload from the extra cases we've had..."

"Oh, I would love to meet up sometime," said Poppy. She had first met Suzanne when she'd become embroiled in a murder case straight after moving to Hollyhock Cottage. The detective inspector was like the big sister she'd never had: cool, confident, and poised at all times, and Poppy had developed a slight case of hero worship for the older woman. So she was flattered and delighted that Suzanne seemed to be seeing her as a friend. "Just let me know whenever you're free."

"Mm... yes, well, in the meantime, I suppose we'll have to make do with chatting about murder," said Suzanne wryly.

Poppy stopped in her tracks. "*Murder?*"

Suzanne paused as well. "Yes, that's why you've been asked to come in for further questioning. This is now officially a murder investigation."

"But... I don't understand... I thought Thales hit his head when he fell? He was trying to carry this really heavy bag of mulch and I think he lost his balance."

Suzanne shook her head. "I haven't got the full autopsy results yet, but based on the preliminary examination, there's strong evidence that Thales was fatally—and deliberately—poisoned."

"He was *what?*" Poppy stared at her in disbelief.

"I'm waiting for the toxicology report to confirm, but the forensic pathologist thinks it was probably cyanide. It's a very fast-acting poison. It can kill in a few minutes if inhaled, although it can be slower if ingested in the stomach."

Poppy shook her head, unable to believe what she was hearing. It all seemed too melodramatic and surreal. "Why would anyone want to poison Thales?"

"That's what I'd like to find out," said Suzanne grimly.

A minute later, they arrived at the CID unit at the rear of the building. Poppy had been here once before and, like last time, she was surprised at how "ordinary" the place looked. Somehow, after watching all the crime dramas on TV, she'd expected to see a hive of crime-fighting activity, with detectives clustered tensely around a whiteboard showing a web of suspects or bent over their desks, examining photographs of gruesome weapons. Instead, the reality was disappointingly mundane. From what she could see, all the officers were simply tapping away on their keyboards or talking on their phones in a desultory fashion.

Suzanne led the way into her private office and Poppy settled into a chair facing the desk as the other woman opened a folder and leafed through the papers inside.

"I've got the preliminary statement you gave Uniform last night," she said, drawing out a sheet of paper. "But in view of the nature of the case now, I'll need to go over everything again."

Poppy nodded. "Ask me anything you like."

"How long had you been going out with Thales?"

"Oh, we weren't going out. I mean, he wasn't my boyfriend or anything," said Poppy hurriedly. "In fact, I only really met him a couple of days ago." She recounted the story of how she'd met the sales rep at Mega Garden Town and his persistence in asking her out on a date.

"You liked him," said Suzanne. It was a statement, not a question.

Poppy blushed slightly. "Yes... Thales was very charming and he made me laugh and... I mean, I wasn't looking for a relationship or anything. I just thought... well, Nell had been telling me I should go out more and I thought dinner with Thales would be fun."

She didn't add that she had actually been planning to refuse Thales's invitation but had been annoyed by Nick's obvious disapproval of the younger man and had been goaded into accepting the date. Somehow, she didn't like to admit that Nick Forrest had "got" to her. Although, of all people, Suzanne would probably have been the most sympathetic, Poppy reflected. After all, the detective inspector had worked alongside Nick when they had both been sergeants in the CID, and she was also Nick's ex-girlfriend. They'd remained good friends, even after splitting up, but Suzanne was more familiar than most with the crime writer's infuriating manner and unpredictable moods.

"Thales invited you to dinner in his home?" asked Suzanne.

"No, no, we were going to a restaurant but there was a sort of accident with a fountain pen—I met Thales at his work, you see—and he got ink stains all over his shirt, so he wanted to stop off to change before we went to eat."

"So you were with him at the Campana head office before going to his house," said Suzanne, making a note in a pad. "Did you meet anyone there? See anyone interacting with him?"

"There was his colleague, Sidney—I don't know his last name, sorry. He was actually the one who took me into Thales's office."

"A colleague, you say?"

"Yeah, they both worked in Sales, although Sidney was more senior, I think. He..." Poppy hesitated. "I got the impression that he didn't like Thales much."

Suzanne raised her eyebrows. "What gave you that idea?"

"Oh, just the way he was talking about Thales and some of the things he said. Like, when I told him that I was there to meet Thales, he said: 'Oh. You're one of Thales's girls'—in a really sarcastic tone of voice."

"So Thales was in the habit of meeting girls at his place of work?"

Poppy shifted uncomfortably, recalling once again Nick's warning about Thales being a "player". She didn't like the thought that she could have been one of his easy conquests.

"Maybe Sidney was just being nasty," she said quickly. "I mean, he was the complete opposite of Thales, you know. Like, stuffy and conservative, and totally humourless. I'll bet he resented Thales being so much more junior and yet being much more popular and doing so much better at work. Apparently, Thales was 'Top Salesman of the Month' multiple times running."

"Professional jealousy is quite a far-fetched motive for murder," said Suzanne sceptically.

"But resentment can fester, can't it?" Poppy said. "I mean, people can get really bitter about things and then it becomes a sort of obsession, and one day, they just lose it?"

"Mmm... I *have* worked on cases where the victim was killed because they'd inadvertently offended someone who then brooded on it for ages. And you're right, if you let something eat you up inside, then one day, with the right trigger, you can just snap. But, in all those cases, the victims were killed in an act of sudden violent assault: a blow to the head or an impromptu stabbing with a sharp object. That doesn't fit in with this case, which is a poisoning. That's a very premeditated type of murder."

"Sidney would have had the perfect opportunity, though," Poppy persisted. "His desk is right next to Thales's. He could easily have put something in Thales's coffee, for example, without anyone noticing."

"*Was* there a cup of coffee on Thales's desk?"

Poppy screwed her face up in an effort to remember. "Y-yes, I think so... I think there was a half-drunk mug on his desk, with some dark liquid in it. I don't know if it was tea or coffee. I didn't see Thales drink from it though..." She sat up excitedly as a thought struck her. "You know, Thales gave me a little tour of the facility and he showed me their R & D laboratory. There were all sorts of chemicals in there, which means that Sidney would have had an easy source of cyanide!"

"That depends on whether they used cyanide in the laboratory," said Suzanne cautiously. "And don't forget, that would also apply to any other employee in the company. Anyone else could have got hold of the chemical from the lab and tampered with Thales's drink."

"Yes, but the office was already closed for the day and most of the staff had left by then. And you said that cyanide is really fast acting, so if someone had put something in his coffee earlier, wouldn't he have been showing symptoms already?" Poppy pointed out. "Thales was fine until after we got to his house, so he had to have been poisoned in the hour or so before that, at the most?"

"Was there no one else in the Campana offices?"

"The only other people I saw were Thales's boss, Mr Campana, and his PA."

"Bill Campana, the CEO?"

"Yes. He and his PA were just leaving. We bumped into them during our tour of the place." Poppy paused, then added, "Actually, I think you should question Nina the PA as well."

"We're intending to question all the staff but it'll take some time," said Suzanne with a sigh. "Why do you mention Nina specifically?"

"It was just... I don't know, I thought there was something odd about the way she was with Thales. And the way he was with her."

"Odd?"

"Yeah, like... there was a nasty little exchange between them. Oh, they weren't outright hostile to each other or anything, but there was a sort of undercurrent... I'm almost sure that Nina did something on purpose to get the ink on Thales's shirt... and he also seemed to be taunting her—" Poppy broke off with an embarrassed laugh. "Maybe I was just imagining things."

"No, no, go on," said Suzanne with an encouraging smile. "I know from past cases you were involved in that you have a good instinct for these things. You are far more astute than you give yourself credit for, Poppy."

"Thanks." Poppy flushed with pleasure at the compliment. "Well, there's not much more, really. I just felt that there was some sort of 'history' between them."

"Well, I'll certainly remember that when I question her," said Suzanne, making another note in her pad.

Poppy hesitated, then asked in a low voice: "Do you think if I'd done CPR or something, I might have saved him?"

"I think nothing could have saved him," said Suzanne gently. "The toxin was in his system already. The only way to save someone with cyanide poisoning is to administer the antidote. So you did the right thing by calling an ambulance. In fact, if you had attempted any first aid, you might have made things worse or even exposed yourself to the poison."

Poppy drew back. "Really?"

"Yes, for example, if you'd attempted mouth-to-mouth. Ingestion is the most common method of poisoning, so if Thales had swallowed the cyanide, traces of it might still have been in his mouth and on his lips... Speaking of which, did you see Thales eat or drink anything at his house?"

"Not at his house, but now that you mention it, he did have some chocolates," said Poppy. She explained about the box of chocolates from Thales's ex-girlfriend that had been in the front passenger seat of his car. "Apparently, she'd come to Mega Garden Town at lunchtime that day and Thales said he'd felt obliged to go to the café with her."

"Ex-girlfriend?" said Suzanne, looking up with interest. "I wonder why they split up and who was the one who broke it off?"

"I think it was Thales. He mentioned that she'd taken their break-up very badly and kept trying to convince him to get back together."

"Hmm... that's very interesting. Did you happen to get her name?"

"I think it was Jules," said Poppy, searching her memory. "Thales made some comment about how she always knew her gourmet food. The chocolates looked like something from a luxury boutique, not the kind of box you'd buy at the supermarket."

"And you definitely saw him eat some?"

"I know he had at least one. I saw him put a truffle into his mouth, then he tossed the box onto the back seat. In fact, I'm sure it's still in his car."

"I'll make sure Forensics tests the chocolates."

"The only thing is... if Thales *had* eaten something poisoned with cyanide, wouldn't I have smelled it on him when I found him?" asked Poppy. "The only smells I remember were from the garden—you know, like earthy smells: soil, mulch, wet leaves, that kind of thing. But don't they say that you can smell almonds on someone's breath when they've been poisoned with cyanide?"

"Don't let Nick hear you say that," said Suzanne with an expression of mock horror. "It's one of his pet peeves: that mystery novels—especially the older ones—always use that plot device. Someone would sniff a body and announce that they could smell bitter almonds and then deduce that the cause of death was cyanide poisoning. Or conversely, they would sniff the body, say that there *wasn't* any almond smell, and therefore they could rule out cyanide poisoning." Suzanne shook her head and laughed. "Nick thinks it's the laziest, most awful gimmick."

"But... isn't it true?" asked Poppy, confused. "I've always heard that cyanide has the smell of almonds."

"It's actually a bit of an urban myth. Oh, it's not completely untrue: there can sometimes be a bitter almond smell associated with cyanide poisoning, but it's not always there and not everyone can detect it. In fact, I think up to fifty percent of the population can't smell the odour. That's why Occupational Safety and Hazard rules always state that odour alone isn't enough to warn of hazardous exposure to cyanide."

"So... you mean, there could have been cyanide

there but I couldn't smell it?"

"Possibly, but it would have been trace amounts. Even if you couldn't smell it, if there had been enough in the air to inhale and cause damage, you would still have shown the other symptoms like dizziness and nausea, or respiratory distress, like struggling to breathe." Suzanne paused, then said gently, "Poppy... you did everything right last night. Don't feel bad. You couldn't have helped Thales any more than you did. His death isn't your fault."

CHAPTER TEN

Poppy stepped out of the police station and took a sharp breath as a gust of cold wind hit her in the face. *So much for "early summer weather"*, she thought, shivering. It felt more like winter was just around the corner! She rubbed her bare arms, regretting that she hadn't thought to grab her favourite cardigan before leaving the cottage that morning. Then she paused, frowning. *Wait a minute...*

One reason she hadn't grabbed the cardigan was because it hadn't been in its usual place, slung across the back of the chair next to her bed. At the time, she had been impatient to leave and had abandoned her search after only a cursory look around the cottage. But now it hit her that the reason she hadn't been able to find it was because she hadn't brought it home in the first place. Yes, now that she thought about it, she couldn't remember having it with her when the police finally dropped her back at Hollyhock Cottage late the previous night.

Did I leave it at Thales's house? she wondered. She turned and dashed back into the police station, finding her way back to Suzanne's office. Luckily, the detective inspector was still at her desk, reading through some papers. She looked up, startled, to see Poppy again.

"A cardigan? No, I don't remember seeing that in the reports, but I can check with Forensics, if you like?"

"Please," said Poppy gratefully. "It's a cropped cardi in a vintage style, raspberry pink, with hand-beading on the front. It was my mother's—I'd be really gutted if I lost it."

Suzanne put down her phone a few minutes later. "No, sorry. The SOCO team didn't find any woman's cardigan at Thales's place. Perhaps you left it at the Campana head office?"

Poppy thought for a moment, then she brightened. "You know, I think you're right! I popped into the toilet there before I saw Thales, just to fix my hair and clean up a bit, and I remember now that I took off my cardi because I didn't want to get it wet at the sink. I must have left it hanging over the towel rail."

"Well, someone's probably handed it in to the company's Lost Property then," said Suzanne reassuringly.

"I hope so. I'll stop off at Campana AgroChemicals on my way back to Bunnington and ask. Thanks!"

Twenty minutes later, Poppy pulled into a space in front of the Campana head office and killed the engine. She sat for a moment, staring at the building in front of her and trying to overcome the sense of disbelief that she had been happily strolling in there, less than twenty-four hours earlier, looking forward to a date with Thales... and now he was dead. *Murdered.*

She got out of the car, trying to shake off her morbid thoughts, and hurried into the foyer. There was a young woman behind the reception desk this time, who looked up expectantly as Poppy approached.

"Can I help you?"

"Yes, I was here yesterday and I think I left my cardi in one of the toilets. Would you know if anyone found it?" Poppy described her cardigan again.

"If it was found, it would have been handed in to Bev, our office manager. Hang on a tick—I'll give her a ring and see if she's got anything like what you described..." The receptionist pressed a number on the switchboard and spoke briefly, then turned back to Poppy with a smile. "Yes, she's got it. If you'd like to go down to her office—it's down the corridor, first left, and then take the right turn at the end and it's the third door on your left." She turned and pointed at the corridor beyond the reception desk.

Poppy thanked her and hurried to follow the girl's directions while she could still remember them! Eventually, she found a door marked "Office Manager" which was slightly ajar. Knocking softly, she pushed it open and stepped inside. She found a plump middle-aged woman sitting behind a desk, chatting to a bearded man in a neon-yellow safety vest, who was leaning against a filing cabinet.

"...cannae believe 'at he's dead! Ainlie saw him yesterday—came tae pick up 'at mulch fo' the gaffer—an' we had a blether about th' footy. Disnae seem real 'at he's dead," the man was saying.

"Yes, I was so shocked when I arrived and heard the news this mornin—" the woman broke off as she saw Poppy and gave her a friendly smile. "Hello! I'm Bev, the office manager. You must be the girl who's lost her cardi."

She reached into a drawer in her desk and pulled out the cardigan, neatly folded. "Here you go." She handed it over. "One of the cleaners found it in the front toilet. Here for a late meetin' yesterday, were you?" she asked, her eyes curious.

"Um... sort of... I came to meet Thales Georgiou after work," said Poppy, caught unawares by the woman's nosiness.

The bearded man straightened and looked at her with new interest.

Bev's eyes gleamed. "Ooh—you're not the girl who found him, are you?"

"Yes, I am," admitted Poppy.

"Och! Must have bin awfie," said the bearded man, giving Poppy a look of sympathy.

"This is Cam, our warehouse manager," said Bev, gesturing to him. "We were just talking about Thales and saying how shocked we were to hear the news. Everyone in the building's been talking about nothing else all morning, you know. Is it true that Thales was *poisoned*?"

Poppy hesitated, unsure what Suzanne had revealed in the official press release. "It's possible... The police are still investigating."

Bev gave a delicious shiver. "Poison! S'like something on the telly. I couldn't believe it when I arrived this morning and heard the news. Here I was expecting Thales to come swaggering in as usual, full of stories 'bout his date the night before, and instead, there's police removing everything from his desk as evidence in a murder inquiry!"

"Aye, speakin' of which, a' better get on," said Cam, turning towards the door. "Polis all over th' warehouse this mornin' an' nae work getting done."

With a nod to both women, the warehouse manager left. Poppy turned to leave as well, but Bev quickly began talking about Thales again, asking for more details of what his body had looked like. It was obvious the office manager loved to gossip and, on an impulse, Poppy decided to use this to her advantage. Leaning forwards, she adopted a conspiratorial manner and said in a low voice:

"I keep wondering how anyone could have done

anything like that—I mean, Thales was such a nice guy. Everyone loved him, didn't they? Who could possibly have wanted to poison him?"

"Oh, you'd be surprised!" said Bev with a knowing look. "There're a few who wouldn't hesitate. That Sidney Maynard, for one. Sour as a rancid lemon, he's been, ever since Thales joined the company. Wouldn't surprise me at all if he'd tried to bump Thales off..."

Poppy blinked in surprise at the woman's bluntness, but before she could comment, Bev continued with relish:

"...and then there's the girls. Thales was a bit of a lad, you know, and he had a bit of a 'love 'em and leave 'em' habit—oh, not that he meant any real harm," she said, with an indulgent smile. "Just sowing some wild oats, like all the lads. And why not? He was young and good-looking and he always gave the girls a good time. But some of them didn't take it so well." She clucked her tongue. "I lost count of the number of times I had one of the female staff in here, crying their eyes out over Thales dumping them."

"Like Nina? Mr Campana's PA?" asked Poppy quickly.

Bev snorted. "Her? You wouldn't catch Miss Hoity-Toity shedding tears over any man—"

She broke off as her phone rang and Poppy was chagrined to hear that the office manager was needed to sort out a problem on the other side of the building. Another half an hour with Bev and she would probably have known everything about everyone at Campana AgroChemicals!

Thanking the woman once again for her cardigan, Poppy left and started to make her way back to the foyer. As she tried to retrace her steps through the warren of corridors, she passed a familiar-looking set of double doors with glass viewing panels and warning labels stuck all over its surface. It was the door to the R & D laboratory that Thales had shown her the day before, on their mini tour of the place. Before she realised what she was doing, Poppy had darted over and pressed her nose against one of the glass panels.

She looked in. There was no one in the lab, although the lights were all on and there were signs of activity and equipment laid out on the workbenches. Perhaps the researchers had popped out to the toilet or for a cup of tea? She craned her neck, peering around the sides of the viewing panel and straining to see the labels on some of the bottles lined up on the shelves. Did they have cyanide in here? She had no idea what cyanide might look like— was it a liquid? A powder? She was just wondering if she dared to sneak in and get a closer look at some of the labels when she heard someone clearing their throat loudly behind her.

Poppy whirled around and flushed as she found herself facing Sidney Maynard. Recognition dawned simultaneously on his face.

"Can I help you?" he asked frostily.

"I... um... I came to pick up my cardigan from the office manager's office... I left it here last night," stammered Poppy.

The unspoken reference to Thales hung in the air between them. Sidney looked a bit awkward and he cleared his throat again.

"I... er... heard that you were with Thales when it happened... I'm sorry. It must have been a terrible experience for you."

"Yes, it was." Poppy paused, then—deciding that if Bev knew, it was hardly a secret anymore—she added: "The police believe that he was poisoned."

"Er... yes, I'd heard," he said, shifting uncomfortably.

"They think it could have been cyanide," she continued, watching him. "Like maybe someone had put it in Thales's coffee or something when he wasn't looking. Someone here in his office... isn't that creepy?"

"It certainly isn't a pleasant thought," said Sidney without expression.

"I was wondering where someone could have got the cyanide from. Do they use it in the lab here?" asked Poppy, indicating the door behind her.

Sidney nodded. "Cyanide compounds are quite commonly used in chemical synthesis. But they are very carefully regulated," he added quickly. "It wouldn't be easy for any employee to just walk into the lab and help themselves. Cyanide salts are always kept in a locked cabinet to prevent unauthorised access."

"But if someone managed to get the key, they could remove a bit of cyanide, couldn't they?"

"It isn't like cutting a slice of cake," said Sidney, giving her a patronising look. "Cyanide is normally stored in the form of crystalline solids like potassium cyanide or cyanogen bromide. However, these still require training and knowledge to handle safely. If someone didn't know what they were doing, they could easily poison themselves. The dry salts are hygroscopic—they absorb moisture from the air very easily," he explained, seeing Poppy's blank expression. "And when they do, they react to form hydrogen cyanide, which is a gas that's flammable and highly toxic if inhaled. It's why anyone producing a reaction with cyanide compounds normally uses a fume cupboard and wears proper protection."

"Wow... you seem to know a lot about working with chemicals," said Poppy, giving him a look of exaggerated admiration.

Sidney coughed modestly. "I'm a chemist by trade. I used to work in the research lab here, actually, before I transferred to Sales."

They were interrupted by a young man wearing a white lab coat coming around the corner of the corridor. He joined them and said cheerfully:

"Hey, Sid—you coming down to the pub this weekend? There's a company quiz on. R & D versus Marketing. Come on, you can't let your old teammates down."

"I'll try my best," said Sidney.

"Great!" The young researcher gave Poppy a polite nod, then he shouldered the door of the laboratory open and went in.

Sidney turned back to Poppy and said, "Can I see you out?"

She had been hoping to snoop around the place a bit more, perhaps try to find Bev again, but faced with his pointed offer, she couldn't think of a way to refuse. As they stepped back into the front foyer, however, Poppy gave the man next to her a sidelong glance and said casually:

"I suppose the police will be wanting to interview you in particular."

Sidney stiffened and stopped. "What do you mean?"

"Oh... just with you being Thales's colleague and having your desk next to his. You must have a better idea than most about his comings and goings in the office?"

Sidney compressed his lips. "Thales and I worked in the same department but we were not friendly." Then, realising how that could sound, he added hastily, "Not that I would have wished him harm, of course."

"I was chatting to Bev, the office manager," said Poppy. "She thought that there were quite a few people in the company who *could* easily have wished him harm... in fact, she mentioned *you* as one of them."

"Me?"

"Well, it was obvious that you didn't like Thales. You made that clear even to me, just in the short time we spent talking last night. You had a lot of good reason to resent him, didn't you? He was a lot more junior than you and yet he was beating you at sales targets—"

"You think I hated Thales because he was a better salesman than me?" said Sidney scornfully. "Don't be ridiculous! I knew that with Thales being a lot younger, he had the greater advantage in terms of energy and stamina... plus, he had good looks and charm. I accepted that I was never going to compete with that." He gritted his teeth. "What really got to me was Mr Campana treating Thales like some 'golden boy' and holding him up as a shining example for the rest of us to follow, when he had no idea just how much Thales was shafting his company!"

"What do you mean?"

Sidney glanced over at the receptionist, but she was busy on a call and not paying them any attention. Still, he shifted so that his back was to her and lowered his voice. "Thales was a petty thief," he said bluntly. "He was always nicking things and helping himself to stuff on the sly: office supplies, stationery, food and drink from the communal kitchen, products from the warehouse... Now, you might think this is small fry, but it's still taking advantage and stealing things that don't belong to you. Did you know that petty employee theft costs businesses in the UK nearly two hundred million pounds per year?"

Poppy was silent. She was uncomfortably reminded of her own uneasy feelings about Thales's loose morals. "If it bothered you so much, why didn't you report it?" she asked at last.

"Report it?" Sidney gave a snort. "I would have been laughed out of the building. It's not like Thales was embezzling from the company accounts. People would have just accused me of petty jealousy."

Which would have been true, thought Poppy.

He must have read her mind because he scowled and said, "Look... okay, I admit it: maybe I *was* a bit jealous. But just because I thought Thales was a cocky git who was always shooting his mouth off— either about how many girls he'd had or the sales he'd made—that doesn't mean that I wanted to kill him!

"And besides," he continued, "I'd seen what happened when someone made an enemy of Thales and what he'd do in retaliation. I need this job: I've got a mortgage, and a wife and kids to support. If I can just keep my nose to the grindstone for a few more years, I've got a good retirement coming up with the company pension. I don't want to risk any of that."

"What d'you mean by retaliation?" asked Poppy.

"Nina—Mr Campana's PA. She's known around the company as a bit of an 'ice queen', which was like waving a red rag at a bull, as far as Thales was concerned. He saw every female rejection as a challenge to his ego: the more a girl refused, the more it made him want to 'win' her over. It was all just a game to him, really. But Nina wouldn't play. No matter how many times Thales tried to get her to go out with him, she always turned him down. Any normal chap would have accepted it and moved on, but oh no, not Thales. He couldn't bear the thought that he'd finally met a woman he couldn't charm."

"So what happened?" said Poppy, trying not to think of her own inadvertent part in Thales's "game".

"Well, I happened to be in the same office one day and I overheard Nina threatening to report Thales to HR for sexual harassment if he didn't leave her alone. Thales was bloody furious. He saw me watching them and he came up to me afterwards and tried to turn the whole story around: called Nina a slag and said that *she* was the one who'd been harassing *him* and begging him to take her to bed. It was just a face-saving exercise, because he couldn't bear for anyone to know that his charms had failed him for once. But I wouldn't have put it past him to begin spreading smear stories about Nina around the office."

"People would believe him?" said Poppy.

"People always latch on to what they really want to believe, whether or not it's the truth," said Sidney cynically. "Thales already had most of the females in the company eating out of his hand, and Nina hadn't done much to make herself likeable, so it wouldn't have been that hard to convince everyone that he was the wronged party all along. He could have made life absolute hell for her, you know." He gave Poppy a meaningful look. "So if you really want to find someone who had reason to wish Thales dead, you should be speaking to Nina."

CHAPTER ELEVEN

Poppy found it hard to concentrate on work the rest of the day, as her mind kept returning to the mystery of Thales's murder. Sidney Maynard had given a convincing account of why he couldn't be a suspect, but it didn't change the fact that he was one of those at the Campana head office who'd had the best opportunity of poisoning Thales.

And the means too, thought Poppy, recalling the man's background as a chemist and his familiarity with the workings of the R & D lab. From his exchange with the young researcher about the company pub quiz, it was obvious that Sidney had remained on friendly terms with the research staff at Campana AgroChemicals. It would have been easy for him to find an excuse to go into the lab and steal some cyanide mixture to use as a murder weapon, and he would have known the safest way to handle the toxic compounds too. In fact, in spite of what he'd said, killing Thales would have benefited Sidney in many ways: not only would it have got rid of a thorn in his side, it would also have removed the threat to his career and eventual retirement.

And Nina? Where did she fit in all this? From what Sidney had said, it sounded like the PA had good reason to hate Thales. She could have wanted to get rid of him too—if not for revenge, then for self-protection. Poppy could still vividly recall the malicious glee in Nina's eyes when she'd managed to manipulate the fountain pen to misfire on Thales's shirt. True, it was a big jump from ink stains to murder, but it showed that the girl wasn't afraid to grab an opportunity to attack Thales if she could. And she would have had access to the cyanide in the R & D lab too. Maybe not as easily as Sidney, but surely, as a clever and capable young woman who was PA to the boss, she could have thought of some ploy?

But what about Thales's ex-girlfriend, Jules? Wasn't she also a possible suspect? After all, her chocolates were the last thing that Thales had eaten before he'd collapsed. But how would she have got hold of cyanide? Surely she didn't have access to some convenient laboratory filled with lethal chemicals too?

By the time five o'clock rolled around, Poppy was exhausted from all these wayward thoughts running through her head while she was trying to tend to plants and deal with customers, and she was relieved when she could officially shut the nursery. She remembered that she was supposed to return to Miss Finch's place to finish planting the old lady's annuals, and so she hurried to lock up the cottage and make her way across the village.

As she drove past the village green, however, she saw the figure of an old man dressed in mismatched tweeds and a purple-spotted bow tie standing next to a taxi. It was her neighbour, Dr Bertram Noble—"Bertie"—who lived in the property adjoining Hollyhock Cottage, on the other side to Nick Forrest. Bertie was a retired Oxford professor who personified the stereotype of the "mad scientist". He combined a brilliant mind with a tendency to create outrageous inventions—most of which never seemed to work as planned. Since moving to Hollyhock Cottage, Poppy had had more than her fair share of trouble with Bertie's wacky machines and unpredictable concoctions. Still, there was an adorably childlike quality about the old inventor that made you somehow forgive all his foibles, and Poppy had grown incredibly fond of her eccentric neighbour.

Now, she frowned as she saw that he seemed to be in some distress: he was arguing with the taxi driver while struggling to balance an enormous box in his arms, and his little terrier Einstein was circling excitedly around him, tangling his leash between Bertie's legs. Poppy slowed her car and pulled up alongside, just in time to see the driver point at Einstein and say:

"I'm not havin' that mongrel in my car and that's that. They never said when they booked the job that you were bringin' a dog with you. I don't carry animals, mate."

"Oh dear," said Bertie, looking distraught. "But if I take Einstein back home first, it'll delay me even further and I shall miss the train to Oxford. It is imperative that I get to the station on time."

"Not my problem, mate," said the taxi driver unsympathetically. "If you want to get the train, hop in, but I ain't takin' that mutt."

"But I cannot just turn Einstein loose here in the village green—"

"Bertie, is there a problem?" called Poppy, leaning out of her car window.

Bertie turned to her with relief. "Oh, Poppy, my dear—I *am* in a quandary! I have a very important meeting in Oxford that I simply must attend, but this gentleman is refusing to take Einstein in his car."

Poppy hesitated, then said: "Don't worry, Bertie. *I'll* take you to the nearest train station. And you can leave Einstein with me; I'll look after him until you get back from Oxford."

Bertie's eyes lit up. "Oh, would you? That would be simply marvellous!"

The taxi driver shot Poppy a dirty look, muttered a curse, then swung his car around and took off in a cloud of dust.

"What a horrible man," said Poppy, gazing after him with dislike. "Good riddance!" She hurried to alight from her car and help the old inventor, who was still struggling with the enormous box. "Here, Bertie—let me help you with that—my goodness, it's heavy! What *is* this thing?"

"It is my latest invention," said Bertie proudly. "It's a prototype for a new kind of portable laser polarimeter, which can identify organic matter simply by the unique spread of its scattering matrices in aqueous suspensions. I believe it will revolutionise laser phase microscopy! Of course, I still need peer assessment by others in the field, which is what my trip to Oxford is for. I have a special meeting set up with the top chemists and biophysicists from the University to show them my new invention."

A few minutes later, they were all settled in the car, with the enormous box safely stowed on the back seat and Bertie in the front next to Poppy. Einstein sat on his master's lap, panting excitedly as he gazed out of the window, his ears pricked and his little tail wagging happily.

"Bertie, you wouldn't happen to know where someone could get cyanide, would you?" asked Poppy as they drove out of the village.

"Oh, I have some in my fridge, my dear, next to the Branston pickle and the mayonnaise," said Bertie.

Poppy gave him a startled look. "Er... is that a

good idea?"

"Branston pickle and mayonnaise? Well, it depends on who you ask, I suppose. There are purists who believe that Branston pickle should only ever be served as part of a 'ploughman's lunch', but I have known individuals who have theirs with Welsh rarebits, devilled eggs, even stirring it into pasta—"

"No, no, not the pickle—the cyanide!" said Poppy. "Isn't it dangerous to have it sitting around in your fridge? I mean, isn't cyanide, like, one of the most toxic chemicals ever?"

"Well now, it depends on your definition of 'dangerous'," said Bertie, adjusting his spectacles. "Thallium is probably worse because, aside from being highly toxic, it is also radioactive and carcinogenic; I probably would not keep that in the fridge... and then there's arsenic trioxide, of course, which is particularly risky because one could easily mistake it for sugar or salt... ah, and benzene, which catches fire really easily—although, of course, cyanide compounds can be very volatile too." Bertie paused thoughtfully. "Hmm... perhaps I shouldn't have it next to the Branston pickle since that contains vinegar and you should really keep cyanide salts away from acids—it reacts to form hydrogen cyanide gas, you see, which can kill in seconds."

"Oh. Great. That's good to know," said Poppy, reminding herself never, ever to open Bertie's fridge!

"Yes, well, if you ever inhale hydrogen cyanide, you'll be pleased to know that at least you won't have to suffer for long," said Bertie cheerfully. "It works much faster than if you'd ingested cyanide, because the toxin wouldn't have to be absorbed through the stomach lining. Cyanide gas enters the bloodstream directly and the cyanide molecules immediately bind to the mitochondria in your cells, preventing them from using oxygen and causing systemic death. It would be over before you knew it."

"Thanks. That's really comforting," said Poppy dryly.

She wondered if whoever had poisoned Thales had known all this too. Had they chosen cyanide because they knew that once exposed to it, there was little chance of recovery? It would make them a particularly cold-blooded killer. She could certainly imagine Sidney Maynard and Nina planning such a murder, but the ex-girlfriend? Could someone who had loved Thales so much really be able to kill him in such a horrible way? Still, didn't they say there was a thin line between love and hate?

"To return to your original question, my dear, cyanide exists naturally in all sorts of places," said Bertie, cutting into her thoughts. "In fact, many fruits, vegetables, and nuts that are consumed every day contain cyanide."

Poppy looked at him in surprise. "Really? But how come people aren't just dropping dead everywhere?"

"Well, it's only trace amounts usually, and your body can detoxify small doses of cyanide. So ingesting modest quantities of these foods as part of your daily diet would not normally do you any harm. Plus, things like apple pips have a hard coating which can't be digested, so even if they *are* swallowed, they would pass right through your digestive system," Bertie explained.

"Okay, so what about other sources?" asked Poppy. "Is cyanide hard to find?"

"Oh no, cyanide is widely used in manufacturing. You can obtain cyanide in the form of cyanide salts, such as sodium and potassium cyanide, which are widely used in laboratories. And it is also used in industrial processes like steel manufacturing and electroplating and fumigation. Jewellers use it, too, to clean gold and silver."

Poppy started to ask where Bertie had got *his* cyanide, then decided that she didn't really want to know. The old inventor probably had an industrial supplier who got him "hard chemicals" from the underground scientific community!

She dropped Bertie off at the station just in time for him to catch his train and, after watching him safely on board, she got back into the car and headed for the residential estate. Einstein pressed his black nose to the rear window and whined as they drove away from the train station, obviously looking for his master. Poppy glanced at the terrier anxiously, wondering if she had been a bit hasty in offering to dog-sit. Still, she'd looked after Einstein before and, as long as she kept him on his leash, she hopefully wouldn't have any trouble. Besides, she was sure that Miss Finch liked dogs and would welcome a visit from the little terrier.

By the time they arrived at the old lady's house, Poppy was relieved to see that Einstein seemed to have perked up and temporarily forgotten about Bertie. He jumped out of the car, looking curiously around, and pulled eagerly on his leash, practically dragging Poppy up the path towards Miss Finch's front door. They hadn't gone a few steps, though, when they were assailed by the most revolting stench.

"Ugh, what's that smell?" muttered Poppy to herself, wrinkling her nose. It was exactly how she imagined a rotting corpse would smell.

Far from being disgusted, though, Einstein seemed to be delighted by the horrible odour. His nose began to twitch like crazy and he whined excitedly, straining on the end of his leash.

"Hey! Einstein... stop that!" admonished Poppy.

The little terrier ignored her. Instead, he lunged on the end of his leash, trying to pull Poppy off the path and towards the hedge separating Miss Finch's place from the house next door.

"Einstein! Stop... What are you—stop it!" gasped Poppy, struggling to hold on to him.

The next moment, the leash was yanked out of her hands. With a yelp of elation, the little terrier dived into the hedge and disappeared.

"Einstein!" shouted Poppy. "Come back here!"

She hurried around the hedge and entered the

neighbour's garden from the path at the front. She was just in time to see a scruffy black terrier wriggle out of the bottom of the hedge and turn into the narrow alleyway that ran down the side of the house, joining the front garden with the back. It was similar to the one on Miss Finch's side, although this was more heavily planted with tall shrubs and perennials. Poppy remembered standing on tiptoes, peering over that hedge the day before, trying to see through the dense foliage.

"Einstein!" she called as the terrier trotted away down the alleyway, trailing his leash behind him.

The little dog ignored her calls. She saw his tail wagging madly as he followed the narrow path between the plants and disappeared into the back garden. Poppy hesitated a moment, then approached the front door. This was Maggie's house—the woman who had accosted her at Mega Garden Town. She could still vividly remember the scene she had witnessed over the hedge the previous day and she didn't relish receiving the same treatment as that hapless estate agent. Nervously, she pressed the doorbell, bracing herself and rehearsing what she was going to say. The long silence that followed seemed almost like an anticlimax. She tried again. Still, no one answered the door. Had Maggie gone out?

Poppy left the front door and made her way around to the side of the house again. She peered down the alley leading to the rear of the property, trying to see through the plants crowding in on either side. There was no sign of Einstein and she fretted over what the mischievous terrier could be doing in the back garden. From the amount of plants and the general state of the front garden, Maggie seemed like a keen gardener; she certainly wasn't going to be happy if Einstein started digging up her prize roses or vegetable beds or something!

If I just pop quickly down to the back and grab him, I can be back here in a few minutes and no one will ever know, Poppy thought.

Making up her mind, she hurried down the path and, a minute later, emerged in the garden behind the house. It was filled almost to bursting with plants. There were climbers like honeysuckle and clematis festooning the walls, enormous shrubs with sprawling canes crammed next to bushy perennials, and ornamental grasses shooting up like random fountains between beds of flowering annuals and burgeoning vegetables. From what she had seen peeking over the hedge, Poppy had guessed that Maggie's place was heavily planted, but she'd had no idea it was such a rich, lush, secret garden filled with so many varieties! The only thing that spoiled the ambience was the awful, putrid smell, which seemed even stronger now. Poppy pinched the bridge of her nose and breathed through her mouth, trying not to gag.

There was a path of stepping stones snaking between the beds, almost obscured by the overflowing foliage, and Poppy followed this deeper into the garden, her eyes wide with admiration and wonder as she took in all the plants around her. She'd almost forgotten about Einstein until she saw the little terrier up ahead. He had climbed into one of the vegetable beds and had his nose shoved deep in the soil, snuffling around excitedly. The smell of rotting here was particularly strong. The next moment, he began digging with great fervour, tossing clumps of soil into the air around him.

"Einstein! No!" gasped Poppy in horror as she saw a plant being raked up and thrown aside. "Stop!"

The little terrier paid her no heed. He kept digging, pausing only to thrust his muzzle into the hole every now and again in olfactory ecstasy before resuming his excavation.

"Einstein! Stop that!" hissed Poppy, running over to grab him.

She caught the end of his leash, but her elation was short-lived as the terrier jerked sideways, throwing his weight against the leash, and she heard a *SNAP!* The next moment, she was left holding the dangling leash whilst the terrier jumped out of the bed and bounded away to the bottom of the garden.

"Einstein!" cried Poppy, infuriated.

The terrier paused next to an ancient-looking wooden shed and sniffed the door curiously. Poppy rushed after him but, before she could reach him, Einstein shoved his nose into the gap where the shed door had been left ajar and wriggled through, disappearing inside.

"Arggh!" groaned Poppy. She grabbed the shed door and flung it open, then stopped in surprise.

A woman stood inside, bent over a wooden bench on which there were various piles of dried leaves, nuts, seeds, and bark, as well as what looked like a giant mortar and pestle, and several jars of coloured liquids and oils. The pungent, spicy aromas of rosemary and lavender wafted out of the room, mingled with a sweetish smell that reminded Poppy of alcohol.

The woman looked up, scowling, and Poppy stifled a gasp. It was Maggie. The other woman straightened and came quickly out of the shed, jerking the door shut behind her. Yanking earphones out of her ears, she glared at Poppy and snarled:

"This is a private garden! You're trespassing! What are you doing in here?"

CHAPTER TWELVE

"Oh... I... um..." Poppy stammered, all her carefully rehearsed explanations forgotten. "Sorry... I was chasing my dog. I mean, he's not my dog—he belongs to my neighbour—but I'm looking after him..."

Maggie glanced impatiently down, then her face softened as she saw Einstein. The terrier came forwards and sniffed her gumboots for a moment, then cocked one of his back legs against them. Poppy gasped in horror and made to grab Einstein, but to her surprise, Maggie burst out laughing.

"Cheeky little bugger," she said with a smile, using one foot to nudge the dog away.

She bent to pat Einstein and Poppy relaxed slightly. Obviously, Maggie loved animals and found the terrier's impudence endearing rather than annoying.

"That's Einstein," she said quickly. "He ran into your garden. I think it's something in your vegetable bed. The smell—it was really attracting him."

Maggie chuckled. "I reckon it's the blood and bone."

"The what?" Poppy stared at her, wondering if she'd heard wrong.

"It's a type of organic fertiliser. Haven't you heard of it?"

"And it's really made of blood and bone?" asked Poppy disbelievingly.

"Yes, it's bloodmeal and bonemeal, usually made from by-products of the meat-processing industry. After the carcass is processed and the meat taken for human consumption, the bones and blood and other remnants are cleaned, boiled, dried, and ground up into a fine powder." Maggie gave an emphatic nod. "You won't get a better natural fertiliser than this. The bonemeal's a great source of phosphorus—gives you great flowers and strong roots. You want beautiful roses? You want to grow good carrots and parsnips? Use this. And lush green foliage too—that comes from the nitrogen in the bloodmeal. Plus, it feeds the soil: breaks down naturally, great for all the microorganisms, great for soil structure."

She lifted her chin defiantly as she saw Poppy's still sceptical expression. "This is what our grandparents and great-grandparents used in their gardens. Back when everyone hadn't been brainwashed into using synthetic chemical fertilisers," she added with a dark look. "It doesn't leach into the groundwater and contaminate all the rivers and seas—" She broke off and looked closer at Poppy, frowning slightly. "Sorry, have we met before? You look very familiar."

Poppy gave a dry smile. "Yeah. At Mega Garden Town. I was just coming out with some pesticides—"

"Oh, you're *that* girl!" Recognition dawned in the woman's eyes and she looked suddenly embarrassed. "Sorry... I might have been a bit overzealous that morning. It was just that I couldn't bear for you to be sucked in by all that false advertising." She cleared her throat and added gruffly, "Hope I didn't frighten you."

"No, no... it's fine..." said Poppy, feeling embarrassed in her turn. It was silly—she had been so irked at the time, but now seeing Maggie so contrite, she felt an almost-overwhelming urge to apologise for her own annoyance! She gave the woman a sheepish smile. "Actually, I took your words to heart. I mean, I decided not to use the pesticide I bought."

Maggie's eyes lit up. "That's fantastic! I'm so glad to hear that. There are so many alternatives to spraying chemicals, you know. People are told that pesticides are necessary to keep their gardens looking nice and free of pests and disease, but it's all absolute bollocks!" She waved a hand at the area around them. "I don't use chemical sprays at all and look at my garden."

"Really?" said Poppy, suitably impressed as she turned to gaze at the beds and borders around her. She had to admit that Maggie's garden looked incredible. There was the odd chewed-up leaf, and some yellowing and spots here and there, but overall, the plants were all lush and healthy, with strong stems, vigorous growth, and big, colourful blooms on the flowering varieties. "You don't use any pest control at all?"

"Well, I do use some natural organic pesticides and fungicides," Maggie admitted. "But only if it's really necessary and only as a last resort! I don't just reach for a spray at the first sign of trouble. I use a more holistic approach: I boost the plant's own defences through feeding the soil, and I encourage natural predators, like ladybirds and hoverflies and lacewings. They feed on the aphids and caterpillars and mealybugs and other pests, you know." She looked at Poppy earnestly, her cheeks flushed and her eyes almost feverishly bright. "You might think that a chemical spray is a good solution, but actually, all you're doing is killing the 'good guys' helping to keep things in check... which means then the pest population *really* explodes and the pests start to develop resistance too... so then you have to use even *more* toxic pesticides... and it just becomes a never-ending, vicious cycle, see?"

"But if I do nothing, won't pests and disease just destroy the whole garden?" Poppy protested.

"It's not about 'doing nothing'," said Maggie impatiently. "There are ways to manage your garden without harming the beneficial insects and other wildlife, and without poisoning the environment. Nature is all about balance, you see. Every living thing has a job, a role in the ecosystem. They all keep each other in check. So when there's an insect infestation, you need to look for the real cause. Like maybe there are nutrient deficiencies or a lack of good bacteria and fungi in the soil—so the plants are weakened and stressed. Or maybe you haven't attracted enough beneficial insects to your garden or allowed them the chance to grow and multiply." She wagged a finger in Poppy's face. "Of course, this all takes time. It's not a quick fix. You need to invest in the soil, to nourish it and build it up; you need to plan your garden to include companion plants that attract insect predators—"

"But what if you *do* need a quick fix?" asked Poppy desperately. She told the woman about the upcoming Open Day at her nursery and her dilemma with the deformed roses. "I'm a plant nursery. The cottage gardens represent the business—it's our professional image. I can't have them looking pest-ridden and awful. I need to do something about it."

"Sounds like you might have thrips on the roses," said Maggie knowledgeably. "They're tiny sap-sucking insects; they especially like feeding on the sugars in new shoots and they cause deformities in the flowers and stems, and lesions on the leaves.

Hmm... a bit unusual to have them this early in the season, though—they usually thrive in warmer weather—but I suppose you might have a micro-climate around your roses, since it's effectively a walled garden, isn't it?"

"Yes, that's right." Poppy furrowed her brow. "But I've looked over the roses really carefully and I couldn't see anything."

"Oh, thrips are really tiny. In fact, the eggs are laid *within* the plant tissues and the larvae that hatch feed on the tissues from inside the plant, so you can't see them with the naked eye. Even the adults can be really difficult to see. They often hide deep inside a flower—particularly if you've got roses with lots of petals—or they hide in the crevices between leaf joints and under the leaves themselves." Maggie gave her a pat on the arm. "But don't worry, your Open Day isn't lost. You can treat your roses with neem oil."

"Neem oil?"

Maggie nodded. "It's an organic pesticide, made from the extract of the *Azadirachta indica* tree. It's got fantastic insecticidal properties but it only targets chewing and sucking insects, so it leaves all the beneficial insects that eat the pests well alone. It works on mites as well. But the best thing is that it's non-toxic to bees, butterflies, fish, and other wildlife—although, of course, you shouldn't treat the roses when bees are actively foraging. Wait until late in the afternoon, when they've headed back to the hive."

"Oh. Okay... I suppose I could give that a try."

"Mind you, don't expect it to work overnight," Maggie said, giving her an admonitory look. "That's the big difference with organic treatments. You don't kill the pests instantly; takes a while for things to work. Also, because neem oil degrades when exposed to UV light, it won't remain on the plant for long. So depending on how bad the infestation is, you might need to repeat the treatment a few times.

"And if it rains, you'll need to respray as well, because it's easily washed off by the rain—yes, I know, it's a bit more hassle," she said, seeing Poppy's expression. "I know everyone wants instant gratification and convenience nowadays. They just want the silver bullet, the lazy quick fix—and the pesticide companies exploit that!"

Poppy sighed impatiently. "I'm not afraid of the hassle, if it's the 'right' thing to do. I mean, I make the effort to always buy free-range eggs, 'cos I don't want to support battery hen farms. But I was hoping my garden could look good in time for the Open Day in two weeks' time."

"Well, you've got a couple of weeks; the neem oil should have started to make a difference by then. And remember the perfect pest-free garden doesn't exist. It's a modern obsession, wanting everything to be pristine and perfect. Look at all those Photoshopped photos of people in magazines! It's completely unnatural." Maggie leaned forwards and looked Poppy in the eye. "It's actually good if your nursery garden is more realistic—it'll help to educate your customers and adjust their expectations."

"I suppose you're right," said Poppy doubtfully.

"I am, trust me," said Maggie. "It's only because you've been brainwashed by all the smooth-talking salesmen like that smarmy git at Mega Garden Town. Can you believe it? Spouting all those lies, and then he had the bloody cheek to accuse *me* of scaremongering. Wait till I see him next time—I'm going to give him a piece of my mind!"

Poppy stared at her.

"What's the matter?" asked Maggie, noticing Poppy's expression.

"Um... Thales—that salesman you're talking about—actually, he's dead."

"Dead? What do you mean? I saw him only yesterday. How can he be dead?"

"That's what the police are trying to figure out."

The other woman was silent for a moment, then she asked casually, "Do they have any idea who murdered him?"

Poppy glanced sharply at her. "I never said that he was murdered."

Maggie looked flustered. "Oh, well, I just assumed that... when you said the police were involved... I mean, if he had just dropped dead of a heart attack or something... Are you saying he *wasn't* murdered?"

"No, the police do think his death is suspicious," Poppy admitted.

Maggie straightened and said briskly, "Listen, why don't you come in for a cup of tea? It's the least I can do after jumping down your throat at the garden centre."

Poppy hesitated. She'd only been intending to grab Einstein and head straight back next door to Miss Finch. On the other hand, she did want to talk to Maggie about Thales some more...

"Thanks. That would be lovely," she said at last. Then she glanced at Einstein, who had found a large twig and was chewing the end of it with gusto. "Is there somewhere I can tie Einstein up?"

"Oh, bring the little monkey in," said Maggie with a smile. "Four-legged creatures are always welcome in my home." She turned towards the house. "Follow me!"

CHAPTER THIRTEEN

Poppy followed Maggie through patio doors similar to the ones in Miss Finch's house and into a small sitting room. It had a cluttered but comfortable feel, with mismatched cushions thrown haphazardly across the sofa, a random collection of houseplants and ornaments decorating various shelves, and a rambling bookcase that took up an entire wall, filled to bursting with books all shoved in anyhow, vertically and horizontally. Tucked into the corner next to the bookcase was an old-fashioned rocking chair and Poppy was surprised to see that there was an old lady sitting there. She looked to be in her early seventies, with silky white hair, carefully pinned back in a bun, and beautifully delicate, almost translucent skin. There was a pair of knitting needles, tangled around a ball of wool, on her knees, although her hands rested idly on her lap. She smiled vaguely as they came in but Poppy got the impression that she didn't quite register their presence.

"That's my mother, Valerie," said Maggie, indicating the old lady. "And I just realised: we haven't been properly introduced! I'm Margaret—Margaret Simmons—but everyone calls me Maggie."

Poppy smiled and introduced herself as well. "I actually came over to look in on Miss Finch, next door."

"Ah yes, the poor dear," said Maggie, grimacing slightly. "She's really wrenched that shoulder something awful. I've been popping over to check on her as well—"

The sound of a laugh startled them and they turned to see Valerie sitting upright in the rocking chair, looking at Einstein, who had trotted over to her and jumped up to put his front paws on her lap. His tail wagging excitedly, he sniffed the ball of wool on Valerie's lap, then snatched it in his jaws and began shaking it furiously from side to side, as if trying to kill a small animal.

"Einstein!" gasped Poppy, rushing forwards. "I'm so sorry; I don't know why he's being so naughty today—"

"Oh no, don't worry about it," said Maggie, smiling as she watched Einstein begin to dance around on his hind legs, the ball of wool still clutched in his mouth. Valerie gave another delighted gurgle of laughter.

"That's the most animated I've seen Mum in ages," said Maggie, watching with pleasure as her mother reached out a frail hand and patted Einstein on the head.

"Your mother likes dogs?" said Poppy.

"She used to love them. But after—" Maggie broke off. She gave Poppy a sad smile. "Mum's not really been herself the last twenty years. She can't remember things anymore and gets confused easily. She doesn't talk much anymore either."

"Oh. I'm... I'm sorry," said Poppy, unsure how to respond.

Maggie turned back to look at her mother, who had started to rock the chair back and forth, then she sighed and laid a gentle hand on the older woman's head, stroking back the silvery white hair. Poppy felt a sudden lump come to her throat as she watched the tender, protective gesture. She thought of her own mother: Holly Lancaster had died of cancer over a year earlier and Poppy would never share such a moment with her.

Not that Mum would have been seen dead sitting in a rocking chair with a blanket on her knee and knitting needles in her hands, thought Poppy with an inward smile. No, her mother would probably have been the leading member of a 'granny groupie' band, wearing miniskirts and big bohemian hairstyles to her grave!

"Would you like tea or coffee?"

Poppy came out of her thoughts to see that Maggie was standing paused in the doorway of the sitting room, obviously on her way to the kitchen.

"Oh, tea would be great, thanks."

"Come and have it in the kitchen with me if you like," offered Maggie, throwing a look over her shoulder at her mother. Valerie had settled back into the rocking chair once more and was smiling down at Einstein, who had lain down at her feet. "Mum looks happy with her new friend."

Poppy followed the older woman into a small but cheerful kitchen, brightly lit by large windows above the sink, and watched as Maggie filled the kettle and set it to boil.

"So... um... do you go down to Mega Garden Town often?" she asked, keen to bring the conversation back to Thales.

Maggie shrugged. "Whenever I've got some free time. I like to walk around and see what the big companies are peddling." She shot Poppy an ironic look. "As the Chinese general Sun Tzu said in *The Art of War*, 'If you know the enemy and know yourself, you need not fear the result of a hundred battles'... Wise chap, that Sun Tzu."

"So I suppose you saw a lot of Thales?"

"Only in the last month or so. I suppose he'd been posted somewhere else before that. Campana launched that new 'home-gardener' range earlier last month so he's been there almost every day promoting that." Maggie curled her lips back in disgust. "Look,

I'm sorry he's dead but I still think that young man had rotten morals. It was all a game to him, really—smarming up to people, getting them to like him, manipulating them into doing what he wanted, which was to buy what he was selling, of course. He would probably have sold his own grandmother if he could have put a tidy sum in his pocket!"

Poppy was struck by how much Maggie seemed to dislike Thales. She wondered what the woman had been doing the day before and whether anyone could vouch for her whereabouts the whole afternoon, but she couldn't think of a way to ask that wouldn't have come across as confrontational. Somehow, it seemed too rude to be drinking the woman's tea and asking her for an alibi! So instead, she said:

"Did you ever see anyone with Thales at the garden centre who seemed a bit odd? Did he have any enemies that you knew of?"

Maggie shrugged again. "Dunno. I wasn't following him all the time, you know. We just had run-ins now and then, usually when I went into the pest control section. I did see him a couple of times outside the centre, lugging things back and forth from his car... oh yes, there was that girl—young woman, I mean—who was with him at lunchtime yesterday. Think she might have been a girlfriend or something."

"How could you tell?"

"I overheard a couple of things they said—I went into the café myself to grab a takeaway coffee and I passed them sitting at a table by the cashier—and it sounded like they were having a lovers' tiff. The girl looked like she'd been crying and she kept grabbing Thales's hand and he kept shaking her off. They were still arguing when I left the café."

Was this Jules, the ex-girlfriend who had given Thales the chocolates? wondered Poppy. It would fit the timing; she recalled Thales saying: "*She turned up at Mega Garden Town yesterday lunchtime and took me by surprise...*"

She opened her mouth to ask more but, before she could say anything, they were interrupted by the sound of the front door opening and closing, and quick footsteps in the hallway outside. The next moment, an attractive young woman carrying a cardboard box walked into the kitchen.

"Hi, Mum, I got off early today. Do you need me to run down to the shops? I was thinking of checking to see if they've got those biscuits that Gran really likes—" The young woman broke off. "Oh. I didn't realise you had visitors."

"This is Poppy." Maggie looked from one girl to the other. "This is my daughter, Nina."

Poppy stared at Bill Campana's PA. "Er... hello."

The girl gave her a cool nod, then turned to her mother and held up the cardboard box, saying: "Mr Campana's really kindly given me some of their new fertiliser. They're factory rejects, 'cos the packaging's too damaged for retail display, but the stuff inside's perfectly fine—"

"I don't want them."

"Mum, there's nothing wrong with them, and you need fertiliser for the garden. This will save us money and—"

"I told you, I'm not taking anything from Campana!" spat Maggie. "I don't know how you can bear to work for them! Especially for that greedy bastard who doesn't care if he destroys the whole planet, as long as he can fill his pockets—"

"That's not true!" protested Nina. "Mr Campana *does* care, and he's been changing the company's practices to become more sustainable. Like these factory rejects from the warehouse—he's always encouraging staff to buy these at a great discount, so that they're not wasted, and he's always taking them home himself to use in his own garden."

"Pah! That's just window dressing. Why doesn't he fix the real problem? Why doesn't he do something about his filthy chemicals polluting the environment and killing all the wildlife?" her mother snarled. Then she glanced at Poppy, who was shifting uncomfortably as she watched the tense exchange between mother and daughter. "You see? They've even brainwashed my own daughter."

"I'm sure Poppy doesn't want to be dragged into our sordid arguments," said Nina. "Besides, as the owner of a garden nursery, she's hardly unbiased herself."

"You know each other?" said Maggie in surprise.

"Yes, I met your daughter when I was at the

Campana head office yesterday evening," Poppy explained.

Maggie looked at her sharply. "The Campana head office?"

"Apparently, Poppy was the one who discovered Thales's body," said Nina coolly. "That's what I heard in the office." She turned to Poppy and added with false sympathy: "I hope his death wasn't too much of a shock to you. Not exactly how you expected your date to end, was it?"

"You were Thales's girlfriend?" asked Maggie, with a look of mingled accusation and betrayal.

Poppy squirmed. "No, nothing like that! I just... um... accepted his invitation for dinner. But it wasn't anything serious—I mean, I wasn't 'dating' him. I'd only met him the day before, actually..." She trailed off, flushing as she realised that made it sound even worse.

"Why didn't you tell me? Why did you act like you didn't know him?" demanded Maggie, her eyes suspicious. "You came here, pretending to be interested in organic gardening, and all the time, you were really trying to quiz me about Thales... Are you a spy for Campana, eh?"

"No!" cried Poppy. "No, it's not like that at all. I wasn't trying to deceive you about Thales. It just didn't come up in conversation... I mean—"

Maggie compressed her lips, her eyes hard. "I don't think you should stay for tea, after all. In fact, I think you should leave now."

Poppy started to protest, then stopped herself as she saw the look in Maggie's eyes. It was no use. The woman had completely turned against her now.

Nina stepped forwards, saying in a neutral voice: "I'll see you out."

They walked silently through the house, but as they got to the front door, Poppy gave a little gasp and said: "Oh—Einstein! Sorry, my dog's still in the sitting room."

"Wait here. I'll get him," said Nina.

Poppy hovered by the front door, glancing idly at the framed photographs on the small hall table. They were mostly of Valerie and Nina, showing the grandmother and granddaughter in a variety of shots from when the girl was a toddler to her early twenties. In the earlier pictures, Valerie was an active, smiling middle-aged woman, holding her granddaughter's hand on a country hike, laughing as they baked cookies together, grinning as they floated in large inflatable rings next to each other in a turquoise swimming pool. But Poppy felt a stab of sadness to see that the later photos were mostly of Nina standing with one arm protectively around her grandmother's shoulders as Valerie smiled vacantly into the distance.

She picked up the frame nearest to her: a picture of Valerie, Maggie, and Nina, standing together in front of a Christmas tree. It looked like it had been taken in recent years. Nina had both arms around her grandmother in a fierce hug and Maggie stood next to them, gazing down at her mother with the same tender, protective expression that she'd had when smoothing back Valerie's hair earlier. Poppy stared at the photo, filled with a sense of wistfulness. Her own mother and grandmother had been completely estranged—in fact, she had barely even known her grandmother's name or where she lived, until the day that letter had arrived, telling her that she'd inherited Hollyhock Gardens and Nursery. Poppy wished that she could have known what it was like to grow up with a grandmother, to feel that special bond of wisdom and love.

"He didn't have a leash so I had to use some of Gran's yarn."

Poppy jumped and hurriedly replaced the framed photo on the hall table as Nina returned with Einstein in tow, leading the terrier by a long piece of wool tied to his collar.

"Thanks," she said, taking the end of the yarn. She turned towards the front door, then paused and swung back to face Nina. She just couldn't leave without at least trying to defend herself.

"Nina, I hope you'll believe me: I genuinely wasn't trying to deceive your mother or anything like that," she said, looking earnestly at the other girl. "Einstein had run into your garden and I came over to fetch him, and then your mum and I got chatting about gardening. I'm struggling with pest control over at my nursery and your mother gave me some very helpful tips. It just so happened that the conversation turned to Thales, but I wasn't deliberately trying to hide the fact that I'd agreed to go out to dinner with him or that I had been at the Campana head office."

Nina shrugged. "I wouldn't worry about it. Mum's completely irrational when it comes to Campana AgroChemicals. She hates anything to do with them. She even thinks I'm a traitor to work for them." She heaved a frustrated sigh. "It's a good job and it pays well, and the money really helps with Gran's special care. It's not even as if I'm doing what Thales did— promoting the company's products to the public. But Mum just can't understand."

"That must make it hard for you," said Poppy sympathetically.

"Yeah, I've lost count of the number of rows we've had about my job. It's a great position working directly for the CEO, which could lead to all sorts of opportunities..." Nina paused, her eyes distant. "It's a means to an end. That's all."

"Are you hoping to move into one of the other departments in the company eventually?" Poppy asked, eyeing the other girl speculatively. She was remembering what Sidney Maynard had told her about Thales's vindictive smear campaign against the girl. Had that damaged her prospects at the company?

Nina met her gaze, her face bland. "I'm sort of playing things by ear."

Something about the girl's cool, offhand manner was really beginning to annoy Poppy, and she was seized by an impulse to break through that icy exterior, to provoke some kind of reaction.

"I hope you haven't been hassled by the police?" she asked with false solicitude. "The murder investigation must be especially tough on you, given your history with Thales."

"What do you mean?"

"Oh, you know... just with what happened between the two of you..." Poppy trailed off suggestively.

"Have you been listening to office gossip?" said Nina with a contemptuous smile. "That's it, isn't it? You think I might have a motive to murder Thales because he didn't like it when I refused to go out with him? Do me a favour! Any girl who's worked in an office has had to learn to deal with misogynists and perverts. Thales was just like all those other cocky bastards who think they're God's gift to women." She gave a scornful laugh. "Do you think I'd put my whole life and career at risk for a pathetic git like that? He wasn't worth it."

Poppy couldn't help agreeing as she finally walked away from Maggie's house, with Einstein trailing behind her. The whole idea seemed too far-fetched and ludicrous. Even if Nina *had* been furious at Thales for bad-mouthing her within the company, surely she wouldn't resort to committing *murder* in retaliation?

CHAPTER FOURTEEN

Poppy held the watering can under the tap, watching as water gushed into the opening and mixed with the fertiliser she had already added to form a foamy solution. When the can was full, she switched off the water and gave the contents a quick stir with an old chopstick, before lifting it in both hands and carrying it carefully over to the large wooden bench in the centre of the greenhouse. Here were arranged row upon row of seedlings and plug plants, each being nurtured until ready for sale to the public.

Poppy bent over a group of pots, each holding a miniature rosette of lush green leaves: *Digitalis purpurea*—foxglove. She picked up one of the pots and tipped it upside down, squeezing the sides gently until the plant slid out. The roots were neatly embedded in a compact plug of potting compost, and Poppy examined them closely: they were thick and healthy, with so much branching that you almost couldn't see the compost through them. She smiled with satisfaction. The foxgloves were growing well and could be put out for sale soon. Hopefully they would be snatched up by customers and taken to their new homes where they would shoot up as wonderful spires of gorgeous bell-shaped flowers.

She gazed down the bench at the rows of different plants arranged in groups according to size and variety, all of them healthy and growing strongly, and felt a flash of pride at what she had achieved. She'd never thought that she would get here, but somehow, she had managed to survive her first winter at the nursery, and now the agonising months of painstakingly raising and nurturing batches of flowering annuals and popular summer perennials seemed to be paying off. She hoped this latest feed with fertiliser and seaweed tonic would have them looking their best for display during the nursery's Open Day.

It'll be a small sop if the flower beds are looking awful, though, she thought with a sigh. She had been so distracted by Thales's murder that she had forgotten about her own problems for a while. In fact, she had spent most of the time since coming back from the residential estate earlier that evening thinking about her encounter with Maggie and Nina. But now, Poppy reminded herself that she was still dealing with ugly, deformed roses and had no idea how to fix them. She couldn't bring herself to try the Campana pesticide again but she also couldn't bear the thought of just leaving the roses to remain looking deformed and diseased either. Besides, aside from aesthetics and the threat of infection to her sales stock, what if the infestation became so bad that it killed one of the roses? This cottage garden was a legacy from her grandmother, with many of the rose bushes having been here for decades—she couldn't stomach the idea of losing any of them.

Maybe I should try that neem oil spray that Maggie suggested, she mused. The woman might have been a bit of a nutter, but she did seem to know her gardening. Her own plant collection was certainly impressive, especially if she'd achieved all that only with organic sprays and without using chemical pesticides!

A clatter on the other side of the greenhouse made Poppy glance up. It sounded like a terracotta pot or something had been knocked over. The sound brought back a memory: her first night here at Hollyhock Cottage, after she'd left her life in London and moved to Bunnington to take on this unexpected inheritance. She had been standing in this very spot in the greenhouse and had heard the same sound of terracotta shattering, only to discover that the culprit had been a big orange tomcat wandering around like he owned the place. Poppy smiled again at the memory. It had been her first meeting with Oren and she had been almost immediately smitten by the big ginger tom—although she certainly hadn't wanted to admit it at the time!

She turned now and peered at the other side of the greenhouse, wondering if Oren was up to his old tricks again. She could see several groups of unused terracotta pots neatly stacked along the far wall, but none of them had been knocked over and she could see no sign of the tomcat. Puzzled, Poppy walked over to the other side of the greenhouse and looked around. The stacks of pots, the tools leaning against the wall, the bags of potting compost, the boxes filled with balls of twine, bunches of labels, gardening gloves, seed packets... everything looked neat and untouched.

Then her gaze fell on the corner where Solly's tank should have been resting on the makeshift stand she had erected from an old wooden stool. She was dismayed to see that the rickety stool had been knocked over and the tank now lay on its side, on the floor. Luckily it had fallen onto a couple of folded burlap sacks, which had cushioned the impact, and so the glass sides had not shattered, but most of the contents had been tipped out. Soil had spilled everywhere, along with the twigs, stones, and leaves she had gathered as environmental enrichment for Solly. The lettuce leaves and vegetable and fruit pieces she had placed in the tank earlier were also scattered all around, making a big mess. Worst of all, though, there was no sign of a slimy brown slug.

"No, no, no..." Poppy muttered under her breath as she crouched down next to the fallen tank. Where was Solly? Had he escaped?

"*N-oww?*"

A big ginger tomcat stepped out suddenly from behind a pile of wooden crates and strolled over to rub his chin against the side of the overturned tank.

"Oren! You did this, didn't you?" said Poppy, glaring at the tomcat accusingly. She recalled his constant attempts to stick a paw into the tank the last time they had been in the greenhouse together. If he had been trying that again, he could easily have shoved the tank sideways and the weight would have caused the stool to tip over.

"*No-o-ow!*" said Oren, giving her an innocent look from his big yellow eyes, as if to say: "I don't know what you're talking about!"

Sighing, Poppy began to scoop as much of the mess back into the tank as she could. She checked to see that Solly wasn't clinging, out of sight, to the underside of anything, but the slug was not to be seen. Turning, she gazed around the floor of the greenhouse. How was she going to find one missing slug in here? Then she noticed a moist shimmer on the ground. Tilting her head, she looked closer. It was a slime trail, she realised—the wet mucus catching the light from the overhead bulb. If she cocked her head at a certain angle, she could see the reflected light glistening along a wavy line which led across the stone floor and out of the open greenhouse door. It looked like Solly had made a bid for freedom and had slimed his way out to the garden as fast as he could!

Keeping her head tilted at an angle so she could see the moist glistening from the slime, Poppy followed the slug's track out of the greenhouse, but as soon as the ground changed to earth outside the door, she lost the trail.

"Great," Poppy muttered, crouching down and looking around.

It was late now and, even with the longer days, the sun had already gone and twilight had set in. She peered into the gathering darkness. She was barely able to make out the details of the plants in the borders around her—everything had been reduced to dark shapes and shadows moving in the murmuring breeze. How was she supposed to find a runaway slug in these conditions?

I could go back in the house and get a torch, I suppose, she thought, without much enthusiasm. But even with that, could she really hope to find Solly in the jumble of foliage and vegetation of the garden? *I'm just as likely to step on him and squash him by mistake!* she thought, wincing.

As she was standing there, debating what to do, Poppy heard another sound: a metallic rattle and clanging, this time. It was faint and seemed to come from the front of the property. She was puzzled for a moment, then she realised what it was: the sound of something being put in the letterbox. With her cottage being situated deep in the centre of the gardens, she had recently decided to mount a small letterbox on the wall next to the front gate, so that the postman didn't have to actually enter the gardens and walk the long path to the front door to drop off the daily mail.

Now, she realised that someone must have shoved something into the letterbox. Odd... who could it be at this time? Certainly not the postman, and it seemed unlikely to be a villager or even a neighbour, given the late hour. Curious, she followed the path around the side of the house, past the various beds and borders, and the trestle tables set up in front of the cottage to display plants for sale, and finally made her way to the front gate. Leaning over, she reached for the flap at the back of the letterbox and flipped it up to see what was inside.

There was a folded piece of paper. Poppy drew it out and held it up to the faint glow of light from the cottage windows. The black scrawled words jumped out at her:

> *STOP DIGGING IN GARDENS THAT*
> *ARE NOT YOUR CONCERN.*
> *CATS AREN'T THE ONLY THINGS*
> *KILLED BY CURIOSITY.*

Underneath was a crude drawing showing a spade next to a rectangular mound of earth, with a headstone at one end and a bunch of flowers growing at the other. Poppy caught her breath. It was a threat, a warning—there was no doubt about it. Someone was warning her that if she continued to dig for information, she could be digging her own grave as well.

She looked up quickly and leaned over the front gate, peering up and down the lane outside. It was empty. Whoever had dropped off this note was long gone. She hesitated for a moment, then turned and began walking back up the path, towards the cottage—still staring down at the paper she held in her hand. Her mind raced as she wondered who could have put it in her letterbox. It was obviously someone who didn't want her asking questions about Thales's murder—yes, although it hadn't been specifically mentioned, she was sure she was being warned off the murder investigation into his death.

She had just rounded the corner of the cottage and was heading towards the rear door, which led back into the attached greenhouse, when she heard a sound behind her. She stiffened and paused, listening. Had it been a creak? Like the sound of a gate opening?

Poppy whirled around and peered back up the path, her heart suddenly thumping. She was around the side of the house now and so the view of the front gate was obscured by the corner of the building. Had someone come in through the front gate? Maybe whoever had put the note in the letterbox hadn't left after all? Maybe they were here in the gardens with her now—hiding behind the bushes, lurking in the shadows, watching her, waiting to catch her unawares...

She swallowed, trying to ignore the prickle of unease that was rapidly turning into a surge of fear. Nell was away, Bertie was in Oxford, and from what she could see of Nick's house beyond the wall at the edge of the garden, it seemed empty, the windows dark and shuttered. The crime writer seemed to be out as well. So she was all alone here at the cottage, which was at the edge of the village, down a lonely cul-de-sac...

Don't be silly, she admonished herself. *Loads of women live alone and it's not like you're in the middle of an inner-city slum. You're in a sleepy little village in the English countryside—what could happen to you here?*

Still, she wished suddenly that she hadn't taken Einstein back to Bertie's house when she had returned from Miss Finch's place earlier. She would have felt a lot safer having the feisty little terrier with her. Glancing down, she caught sight of a galvanised-metal watering can sitting by the edge of the path, where she had left it earlier. Bending slightly, she groped with one hand until she could feel the handle. The can was still half filled with water, which sloshed gently as she lifted it up. The weight of it felt comforting and she gripped the handle more tightly.

Slowly, she began walking backwards up the path, so that she could keep her eyes fixed on the direction of the front gate and make sure that no one could come up the path and surprise her from behind. She was almost at the greenhouse; if she could just get inside and then lock herself in the cottage...

There was a sudden rustle in the bushes behind her, the sound of twigs snapping underfoot, and then something touched her shoulder. A hand.

Poppy screamed and whirled around, raising the watering can and swinging it, as hard as she could, at the dark shape that loomed up behind her.

CHAPTER FIFTEEN

"What the—? BLOODY HELL!"

A male voice cursed loudly as liquid from the watering can sloshed everywhere. Poppy stumbled back and stared in disbelief at the tall man standing in the faint glow of light from the greenhouse windows. It was Nick Forrest, with a black scowl on his face and the contents of the watering can sprayed all over him.

"Nick! What are you doing here?" gasped Poppy, her fear turning to anger. "Why are you creeping up on me?"

"I wasn't creeping up on you," he growled, "I was in the garden and saw you walking oddly, backwards on the path. So I came over to see what was going on. You're the one who turned on me like some murdering banshee!"

Poppy felt a sudden, crazy urge to laugh. Now that she had calmed down, she was beginning to see the funny side of things. Nick looked a sorry sight, with smelly brown water running down his face and dripping off the end of his nose, and the front of his shirt and trousers soaked through.

"I'm glad you find it so amusing," he said through gritted teeth, pulling at the neck of his damp shirt.

"Sorry," said Poppy, sobering. "I heard the gate creak—I *think* it was the front gate, I'm not sure now—and then I heard rustling and I thought someone was creeping up behind me—" She broke off and gave Nick a slightly shamefaced look. "I'm probably a bit paranoid and jumpy, what with the murder and then—"

"Murder?" said Nick, his brows drawing together. "What murder?"

"Thales Georgiou; you know, the guy you met yesterday—"

"Yes, I remember," said Nick, his mouth hardening. "Your date for the evening."

Poppy gave a humourless laugh. "Yeah, well, it was probably the shortest date in history. We didn't even make it to dinner. We stopped at Thales's place for him to change his shirt and I went to use the loo, and when I came out..." She swallowed, the memory of Thales's body slumped on the ground still fresh in her mind. "He was lying face down in the courtyard out the back. I... I don't think he was dead yet, but he looked... I thought..." She took a breath, then said in a rush, "But Suzanne said I couldn't have saved him, no matter what I did. She said the poison worked too quickly."

Nick gave her a searching look. "Are you all right? It must have been a pretty nasty experience." He paused, then added in a neutral tone: "I know you liked him."

"Oh, I didn't—I mean, it wasn't as if he was my boyfriend or anything," said Poppy awkwardly. "I hardly knew Thales, really. We'd only met the day before. But yeah, I did like him. He was... he was charming... and nice company..." She took a shuddering breath. "It's just that you don't really expect someone you meet like that to be *murdered*, you know? And I can't shake the feeling that maybe... maybe I could have done something to save him."

Nick put out a hand and touched her gently on the arm. "You look like you could do with a stiff drink. Listen, why don't you come back to my place and I'll make you a hot toddy or something? And have you eaten? I haven't had dinner yet myself and I can rustle up some food for us, then you can tell me all about it while we're eating. It might help you feel better."

Poppy looked at him, surprised at the gentleness in his voice and manner. This was a side of Nick she rarely saw. Since becoming his neighbour nearly a year earlier, she had got used to the crime author's mercurial moods—he could blow hot and cold in the space of a few minutes—and she had learnt not to mind Nick's usually brusque tone and grumpy manner. She knew that, more often than not, it was related to how well his writing was going, and that underneath the prickly exterior, he was empathetic and kind, with a quiet compassion that often expressed itself in actions rather than words.

"Why don't you come into the cottage and *I'll* make dinner instead?" she offered on an impulse. "You cooked for me last time; you know, when I brought you back from the police station and you made that amazing omelette—"

"Yes, I remember," said Nick, looking amused. "But there's no need for you to feel obliged to return the gesture."

"No, no, that's not—I didn't feel obliged, I just thought it would be nice..." Poppy trailed off, feeling suddenly shy. She cleared her throat and added hurriedly, "Not that I'd really be making dinner—I wouldn't dare subject you to my cooking skills!—but Nell's left one of her delicious beef casseroles and there's plenty for two."

Nick chuckled. "With such a gracious offer, how can I refuse? Lead the way."

They went into the cottage together, and after Nick had dried himself off as well as he could, he joined Poppy in the kitchen. He set about making a classic hot toddy—whisky and honey thoroughly mixed and then topped with boiling water and finished off with a splash of lemon juice and a stick of cinnamon— whilst she warmed the casserole on the stove. The kitchen was a cosy room and there was a companionable silence as they worked together. Poppy couldn't help feeling the strong sense of domestic harmony in the scene. Growing up, she'd never known what it was like to have "a man in the house". Although her mother had never lacked for male friends, she had always remained a free spirit, preferring to keep her lovers at arm's length and preserving the home domain as a private world for Poppy and herself. Now, Poppy wondered if this was what it would be like to have a father in the home. *Or a husband*. The thought jumped unbidden into her head and she felt her cheeks warm. She was glad she was facing away from Nick, so that he couldn't see her face.

They piled the cutlery and crockery onto two trays, doled out portions of the casserole, together with a piece of crusty bread each, and then carried everything through to the sitting room. There, they found Oren already ensconced in his favourite seat: the saggy old armchair by the fireplace. The tomcat was lying on his back, with his four legs splayed out in opposite directions, his furry belly exposed, and an expectant expression on his whiskered face.

"*N-oww? N-ow?*" he said, eyeing the trays they were carrying, sounding like an aristocrat complaining that the servants were late with his dinner. He raised his nose in the air and sniffed in an exaggerated manner, obviously scenting the wonderful aroma of tender stewed beef and braised vegetables.

"Not for you, mate," said Nick, giving Oren a stern look. "You've got your own dinner waiting for you at home. Proper cat food, as recommended by the vet, so you don't end up overweight again."

"*Noooo-ow!*" said Oren, rolling back upright and giving them a feline scowl. Then he sprang off the armchair and trotted over to Poppy to rub himself against her legs. Looking up at her with big yellow eyes, he meowed softly: "*N-ow? N-owww?*"

"Don't even *think* about giving him anything," said Nick as Poppy's fingers twitched.

"I wasn't doing anything of the sort," she said indignantly.

Nick shot her a leery look. "Oren's coming to you because he knows you're the soft touch."

"Rubbish!" scoffed Poppy, although she remembered guiltily that she *was* one of the reasons for Oren's recent weight gain, because she simply couldn't resist giving him extra treats on top of his normal daily rations.

Pretending not to hear the cat's insistent demands, she marched across the room and plonked her tray down on the coffee table in front of the sofa. Nick joined her and they were silent for a few moments as they both tucked into the casserole. Oren sat and watched them petulantly, the tip of his tail flicking from side to side. Finally, he stalked over to where Poppy was sitting and jumped up onto the sofa next to her.

"*N-ow?*" he said, staring intently into her face.

Poppy shifted uncomfortably, keeping her eyes on her plate, but she could feel Oren's unblinking gaze practically boring a hole through the skin on her cheek. *Bloody hell, there's nothing like the passive-aggressive intensity of a cat who wants something!* She speared a morsel of beef with her fork and hesitated. Surely it couldn't hurt to give Oren a little piece like this? Maybe if she just pushed it to the edge of her plate...

She glanced up to see Nick watching her blandly. Hurriedly, Poppy lifted the morsel and put it into her own mouth, trying to act as if that was what she had been intending to do all along.

Nick's lips twitched but instead of commenting, he said: "So... is Suzanne in charge of the case?"

"Yes," said Poppy, glad to have something to distract her from Oren's basilisk stare. "She called me in for an interview this morning at the police station—I didn't know until then that they were treating it as a suspicious death. I mean, I really thought Thales had just lost his balance and fallen and hit his head or something."

"And the police think that it was poison?"

Poppy nodded. "Cyanide. Although Suzanne hadn't had the full autopsy report so she wasn't sure how it had been administered. She did say the most common way was by eating or drinking something laced with cyanide."

"Mmm... it wouldn't be the fastest way to kill

someone though," mused Nick. "You said that you didn't even make it to dinner, but did you see Thales eat or drink anything while you were with him?"

"Suzanne asked me that, and the only thing I remember is the chocolates from his ex-girlfriend." At Nick's blank look, she tried to explain: "They were in Thales's car. I saw them when he was driving us over to his place. I didn't have my car, you see, 'cos I walked over from the residential estate to meet Thales at the Campana head office—" She broke off as she saw that Nick was looking more confused than ever. Sighing, she said:

"I'd better tell you everything from the beginning. It started with my visit to Miss Finch..."

CHAPTER SIXTEEN

Poppy tried to make sure she didn't leave out any details, and she was surprised to find that, as she told the whole story, the tightness in her neck and shoulders began to ease. Perhaps Nick was right and just recounting what had happened had a cathartic effect. Or perhaps it was because he was a good listener. At any rate, Poppy found that she felt a lot better when she'd finished the whole account. She clasped the hot toddy between her hands and sipped the warm, spicy drink appreciatively. The soothing sweetness of the honey, the slight burn from the whisky, and the fragrant aroma of the lemon and cinnamon all combined into a wonderful, heady brew. The warmth seemed to seep from the mug into her veins, down her limbs, and through her whole body, and she leaned back into the sofa with a sigh.

"So... who are the suspects?" asked Nick.

"Hmm...?" Poppy blinked and came out of her brief stupor.

She found Nick regarding her with an intent expression that made her feel as if she were back in a police interview room! She knew that Nick had given up a successful job in the police force to pursue a career in writing, and although he had become one of the top-selling crime novelists in the United Kingdom, she often wondered if he missed the life of a CID detective. He certainly seemed to remain in regular touch with Suzanne—she didn't think she'd ever seen such friendly "exes" in her life—and he kept up keenly with news about local investigations.

She realised suddenly that Nick was still waiting for her to reply and hurriedly pulled her thoughts back to the current case. "Um... well, there's the ex-girlfriend. You know, the one who gave Thales the chocolates. Apparently, she was devastated by their break-up and had been trying to convince him to give them another chance."

"Forget the girlfriend. It's not her," said Nick.

"How do you know?" said Poppy, annoyed that her suggestion had been dismissed so quickly. "Don't they say: 'hell hath no fury like a woman scorned'? Maybe she got angry and frustrated when Thales refused to take her back and decided that if she couldn't have him, nobody should."

"Maybe. But if she had really wanted to murder him, the last thing she would have done was to be seen in a public place, having coffee with him, just a few hours before his death. Also, why would she put the poison in a box of chocolates with a card attached that had her name on it?" asked Nick scathingly. "Nobody would be that stupid. Even if she had wanted to use chocolates, surely she would have just left them anonymously?"

"I suppose so," Poppy conceded. "Although… maybe she just didn't think things through. I mean, sometimes people do things on the spur of the moment, don't they? Not everyone spends all their time meticulously planning how to commit the perfect murder," she added tartly.

"Like me, you mean?" said Nick, grinning. "Fair point. But think of the practicalities as well: how would she have got hold of cyanide in the first place? It's not exactly something you can buy easily over the counter these days. I'm telling you it's not the girlfriend." He paused, then said, "I'm more interested in the colleague."

"Sidney Maynard? But surely he's just as 'obvious'?" Poppy protested.

"Not necessarily. In fact, he was perfectly placed to do something *without* it seeming obvious. You said his desk was next to Thales's, wasn't it? And they both worked in Sales. So it would have been perfectly natural for him to go over to Thales's desk when the latter wasn't around. He could have pretended to search for something—a report, a brochure, even a spare pen—and no one would have paid any attention since it was expected for a colleague from the same department to hover around the area. It would have been very easy for him to doctor something with poison."

"But... don't you think he'd still be an obvious suspect if he tried anything? I mean, the fact that he's sitting so close means that he'd also be the most likely person to drop something into Thales's coffee or—"

"No, not poison in the coffee. That would have been too easily traceable and Maynard strikes me as the kind of man who'd be meticulous in his planning. No, he'd go for something more subtle." Nick paused, thinking. "Cyanide can also be absorbed through the skin."

"Through the skin? You mean like via a cream?" Poppy looked at him doubtfully. "Well, it's true that Thales seemed really into personal grooming, but I don't think even *he* kept a moisturiser at work—"

"I wasn't thinking of moisturiser. You mentioned just now that when you first met Maynard, he made a snide remark about Thales putting on aftershave for his dates?"

"Yes, that's right," said Poppy, surprised that Nick had recalled such a small detail she'd mentioned in passing. "He said: '*Pretty Boy is probably dousing himself in aftershave*'—or something like that."

"And that's exactly what Thales was doing when you went into his office, wasn't it? Well, that would have been one perfect way to poison him. Maynard wouldn't even have had to worry about manoeuvring himself into place at the right time to doctor Thales's coffee. All he had to do was get hold of the same brand of cologne, dissolve some potassium or sodium cyanide in the bottle, and then switch it for the one in Thales's desk drawer."

Poppy frowned. "But doesn't that mean anyone in the head office site could have done it?"

"They could," Nick agreed. "But Maynard is one of the most likely. He worked with Thales. He was familiar with his habits. In fact, his comment showed that he knew Thales used cologne liberally—he used the word 'dousing', didn't he?—so he knew that it would probably be a lethal dose. What's more, Maynard was friendly with the R & D lab staff and had access to a ready supply of cyanide compounds."

Poppy had to admit that she herself had had the same thought during that conversation with Sidney Maynard when she'd bumped into him outside the laboratory door.

"Do you really think that being jealous and resentful of Thales is enough of a reason to murder him, though?" she asked, recalling Suzanne's scepticism of that motive.

Nick shrugged. "People have murdered for a lot less. In fact, I can remember a couple of cases during my time in the CID which arose from workplace competition getting very nasty."

Nick's words made Poppy think of Nina. "What about the PA?" she asked. "By the same reasoning, she could have had motive too. Although... she probably wouldn't be as familiar with Thales's habits, though," she added as an afterthought. "Nina works for the CEO and isn't in the same office as Thales was, so it would probably have been a lot harder for her to tamper with anything of his."

"Plus, you're basing your suspicions of her on what Maynard told you," Nick reminded her. "The man may have his own reasons for badmouthing her. Such as being rejected by her himself."

"Oh. I hadn't even thought of that."

"Hurt male pride can lead to a lot of malice," said Nick cynically.

"But Nina didn't deny it when I spoke to her earlier today," Poppy said. "I saw her at Maggie Simmons' house—you know, the woman who'd been harassing Thales at the garden centre. Nina happens to be her daughter, can you believe it?" Poppy shook her head wryly. "Talk about a division in the family! Maggie thinks her daughter is a traitor for working for a company that makes 'evil' products, while Nina obviously thinks it's a great job and really likes her boss. Anyway, she didn't deny that Thales had been harassing her."

"Did she seem angry or distressed about it?"

"No," Poppy admitted. "She seemed very cool and offhand when talking about Thales. Totally different to Sidney Maynard, who seemed really bitter and resentful. Still, I suppose being badgered for a date is not quite in the same league as being humiliated and upstaged by a cocky younger colleague. You should have seen Sidney's face when Thales was making fun of his slogans. He looked absolutely mortified!"

"As I said, hurt male pride can lead to a lot of things, including violence. Although I have to say..." Nick looked thoughtful. "This doesn't feel like a 'violent' murder. Oh, the intent to kill is there, don't get me wrong, and cyanide is a particularly nasty poison, but the whole set-up, the method—"

"I know what you mean," said Poppy quickly. "It feels less like a sudden, violent impulse and more like a cold, deadly fury, a thirst for revenge..."

Nick gave her an amused look. "Are you sure you're not a writer? That's a very eloquent description. Maybe you can help me write this book. God knows, I need all the help I can get," he said with a groan. "I've hit a snag in the plot and it's been driving me crazy all day. I thought I had everything worked out, but now that I'm actually writing the scene, it all feels too contrived somehow. I know something's wrong but I can't figure out how to fix it. I've been redoing the book using different plotting techniques: the snowflake method, screenwriting beat sheets, plot diagrams, hero's journey... but nothing's working!"

Watching him, Poppy wondered again why anyone would want to be a writer. Nick seemed to spend most of his life in mental torture, and the rest of the time in a bad mood because all that mental torture had still got him nowhere!

"Maybe you should give it a rest," she suggested. "Don't they say it's good to take a break and sometimes your brain will come up with the answer when you're not forcing it?"

"That's why I came over. I thought maybe a walk in your gardens, sitting on that bench in the alcove for a bit... the fresh air and setting might trigger an idea... Something about Hollyhock Cottage always seems to help the creative process. I can't seem to get the same effect in my own garden." He paused, then added: "Sorry again about frightening you earlier. I suppose next time I should call out, rather than just come up behind you."

"Oh... it's okay. I think I was just extra jumpy, actually, because of the note. I thought maybe whoever had left it had come back—"

"What note?"

"Oh? Didn't I tell you?" Hurriedly, Poppy dug into her pocket and pulled out the crumpled piece of paper whilst she told Nick about the anonymous visitor who had left it in her letter box.

"You should report this to Suzanne in the morning. Threatening notes shouldn't be ignored," said Nick, frowning down at the crumpled piece of paper in his hands.

Poppy sat up straighter as a thought struck her. "Hey—I wonder if it would be possible to get a sample of Sidney Maynard's handwriting so I can compare it to the one on the note?"

"That won't do you much good," said Nick, holding the paper up to the light and looking at it more closely. "These words haven't been handwritten; they've been printed."

"Printed? But they look like handwriting..." Poppy protested, snatching the note from Nick's hands. As she held it up to the light, however, she realised that he was right. The words looked like a handwritten scrawl, but when she examined them closely, she could see that they were actually printed using some kind of font that resembled handwriting.

"Whoever it was, was very careful," commented Nick. "This is a clever way to prevent handwriting experts from identifying the sender."

Poppy sighed and put the paper back down. "So it's another dead end."

"Not necessarily. The Forensic team might still be able to get something from it, although we *have* sort of buggered things up now by getting our fingerprints all over the note." Nick paused. "So... you were in here and you heard the person leaving the note?"

Poppy shook her head. "I wouldn't have heard them from inside the cottage. It was only because I happened to be outside already that I heard the sound of something being put in the letter box."

"What were you doing outside?"

"I was looking for Solly."

"Who?"

"You know, Solly—the slug that I promised to look after."

Nick laughed and smacked his head in mock dismay. "Oh God, yes, how could I have forgotten? The orphan gastropod... I still can't believe that you said yes, you know, especially after what she did to you."

Poppy shrugged, embarrassed. "Well, anyway, he's my responsibility now, and I really wanted to make sure that he was safe and comfortable for— well, however long slugs live. Except that he got loose! Oren knocked Solly's tank over and he escaped out of the greenhouse and into the garden. So I was out there trying to find him." She sighed. "But it was impossible in the dark. I don't think I'll ever find Solly again."

Nick looked at her incredulously. "Are you actually upset that you don't have to look after a slimy slug anymore?"

"Well... I feel bad. I mean, I did promise to look after him. And besides, I've... I've grown quite fond of Solly," said Poppy defiantly. "Don't laugh! He's actually a bit of a character, once you get to know him."

"Mm, I'm sure," said Nick, hiding a smile. "I'm sorry now I never made the effort to appreciate the finer points of slug personalities."

"Oh, shut up!"

"Well, I think you're just going to have to accept that Solly has gone for good and will now live out his days in blissful freedom in the garden—that is, until he ends up as a hedgehog's supper or something."

Nick chuckled. "But if it'll make you feel better, you can always imagine him going to the Great Lettuce in the Sky!"

CHAPTER SEVENTEEN

The next morning, Poppy hurried up the front steps of the South Oxfordshire Police Station and entered the foyer. She probably should have rung first to check that "Detective Inspector Whittaker" would be in that morning, but she had been hoping that the early hour meant that even if Suzanne had appointments elsewhere, she could catch her friend before she left.

"DI Whittaker?" The desk sergeant glanced curiously at Poppy. "Is she expecting you?"

"No, but—"

"Poppy!"

Poppy turned and was pleased to see Suzanne striding towards her. The detective inspector was wearing a coat, though, and had a bag over one shoulder and her car keys in the other hand.

"Have you come to see me? I'm afraid I'm just leaving," said Suzanne. "I've had an unexpected call from a colleague up in Durham—they've found some evidence which might tie in with a big case I've been working on and they need me to identify it urgently."

"How long will you be gone?"

"I'm not sure. Probably until tomorrow, although I might need to stay longer."

"Oh... I've got some things I wanted to tell you about Thales Georgiou's murder."

Suzanne glanced at the desk sergeant who was listening unabashedly to their conversation. "Come on, walk with me to the car. We can talk on the way."

Poppy fell into step beside Suzanne as the latter led the way out to the police station car park. "Have you got the autopsy report yet?" she asked.

"It was on my desk first thing this morning but I have to confess, I've only had a cursory look at it. It does confirm the forensic pathologist's initial guess of death by cyanide poisoning. Not by ingestion, though—they found no traces of cyanide in the stomach."

"You mean Thales didn't eat or drink anything that was poisoned?" said Poppy, thrown.

"That's what it looks like. His tox screen definitely shows evidence of cyanide in his system, though, so it's likely that it was absorbed through his skin or inhaled in the form of hydrogen cyanide gas."

"Oh, have they tested the aftershave in Thales's desk drawer?" asked Poppy eagerly. She told

Suzanne about Nick's theory and suspicions of Sidney Maynard. "It would be one way of poisoning him via skin absorption, wouldn't it?"

"Trust someone with Nick's imagination to think of a devious method like that," said Suzanne with a little smile. "I know Forensics have confiscated everything in Thales's desk, but I don't know if they'll have got around to checking the cologne bottle yet. I didn't see any mention in the autopsy report of lesions or contact dermatitis on the body, though, and you'd think that if Thales had applied aftershave with cyanide in it, it would have caused irritation to his skin at the points of contact."

"Oh," said Poppy, disappointed. "So you mean it couldn't have been the aftershave?"

"Well, it's worth checking—I wouldn't rule it out entirely—but it does seem unlikely. Of course, Maynard could still have administered the cyanide through other means. At this stage, I think the pathologist is leaning towards poisoning by inhalation, but we don't know exactly how." She paused, then added: "I did interview Sidney Maynard yesterday and it's obvious that there was no love lost between him and Thales. He certainly doesn't seem that upset about the death. But without any supporting evidence, I can't really say that he's a strong suspect."

Suzanne sighed. "Part of the problem is that, normally, we'd establish alibis for all the likely suspects, as a way to pinpoint or eliminate them. But in a murder case like this, the poison could have been administered well beforehand and the murderer could have been far away, in a totally separate place, by the time the victim was actually poisoned. So it makes alibis pretty irrelevant."

They'd reached Suzanne's sleek grey Audi by now and, as she opened the driver's door, she said, "If you think of something else—"

"Actually, there was another thing," said Poppy, hurriedly pulling a plastic ziplock bag out of her pocket. She held it up, showing Suzanne the crumpled note inside. "Someone left this in my letterbox last night. Nick told me I should bring it in to have it examined."

Suzanne's eyes widened slightly as she took in the words scrawled across the piece of paper. "Mmm, he's right. 'Malicious communication' is a criminal offence and should always be reported." She looked worriedly at Poppy. "The murderer is obviously feeling threatened by you. What have you been doing?"

"Nothing!" said Poppy. "I popped back to the Campana office yesterday to pick up my cardigan and I bumped into Sidney Maynard. We did talk about Thales's murder a bit, but it wasn't like I was interrogating him or anything. I also had a brief chat with Nina, Bill Campana's PA."

"This is the young woman you'd met with Thales? You thought there was something 'odd' between them?"

"Yes, although it wasn't some big thing. It turns out that Thales had asked Nina out several times and she'd turned him down. So maybe what I noticed was more like the awkwardness you get when you meet an old ex who dumped you—you know what I mean?"

"Did you see Nina as well when you were at the head office?"

"No, actually, I saw her at her home. She lives with her mother in the residential estate between Bunnington and the business park. I happened to be over at their neighbour's place. Einstein was with me and he ran off—well, it's a long story, but I ended up being invited to tea by Maggie, Nina's mother, and Nina came home from work while I was there."

"And you talked to her about Thales? Did she seem hostile? Defensive?"

Poppy thought for a moment. "No, not really. She admitted that she didn't like Thales but she laughed at the idea that she murdered him just because he couldn't take a rejection."

"Would she have known where you live?" asked Suzanne.

"Er... I suppose she could have found out. To be honest, though, anyone who knows I own Hollyhock Cottage Gardens and Nursery would know my address." Poppy didn't add that Maggie had also known where she lived, and *she* was someone who had *definitely* been hostile and defensive. But the woman's sudden animosity had been to do with her gardening ethos and her bias against Campana

AgroChemicals. Surely that had nothing to do with Thales's murder?

"Listen, can you do me a favour?" asked Suzanne. "I didn't have a chance to interview Nina yesterday but Sergeant Lee will hopefully be doing that today, so can you pop back into the station and show him the note? I want to make sure that he knows about it before he speaks to her. And if there's anything else bothering you, don't hesitate to contact Amos. He's in charge of the case while I'm gone."

"Really?" said Poppy in dismay. She had never liked Suzanne's sergeant, finding him both arrogant and pompous—and more concerned with wrapping up a case quickly than with investigating things properly. And she knew that Lee didn't like her either. Whenever she'd had dealings with him in the past, he'd always been disbelieving and contemptuous of anything she had to say. Her heart sank at the thought of having to deal with him.

Suzanne glanced at her watch, then gave Poppy an apologetic smile. "I really need to go. I'll speak to you when I get back." She started to get into the driver's seat, then paused and added: "And be careful, Poppy. You might think a poison case seems less violent, but that doesn't mean that the murderer is any less dangerous."

As Poppy watched Suzanne drive off, she realised, to her chagrin, that she'd forgotten to tell her friend about Maggie's report of seeing Thales with his ex-girlfriend at the garden centre café. She had meant to, but the unexpected news that Thales *hadn't* been poisoned by any food or drink after all had completely thrown her, and then she had been distracted by her eagerness to relay Nick's "aftershave theory". Now, she groaned inwardly as she realised that she would have to tell Sergeant Lee instead. Knowing the way he normally reacted, she was half tempted to say nothing, but if it wound up being vital information to the investigation, she knew she shouldn't let her own feelings prevent her from doing the right thing.

Dragging her feet, Poppy walked slowly back into the police station and asked to see the detective sergeant. A few minutes later, she was shown to Lee's desk and she eyed him with distaste as she approached. With his crooked tie, stained shirt, and protruding belly hanging over his trouser belt, Sergeant Amos Lee looked the complete opposite of Suzanne's cool elegance, and sadly, his approach to detective work mirrored his slapdash appearance as well. He was leaning back in his chair now, carelessly eating a chocolate digestive and dropping crumbs all over the report he was reading.

"Yes? What is it?" he asked importantly as he looked up. Then he scowled as he saw Poppy. "Oh, it's you."

He listened with barely concealed impatience as she told him about the note she'd received.

"It's probably just some prank," he said dismissively, ignoring the ziplock bag containing the note that Poppy held out to him. "We've had young lads in the village getting up to mischief before. No need for you to get hysterical about it."

"I'm *not* getting hysterical," said Poppy through gritted teeth. "I'm reporting a 'malicious communication', which, I understand, is a criminal offence."

Lee bristled at her tone. "I don't need *you* to tell me what constitutes a criminal offence. But I've got a murder investigation to run and I don't have time to follow every silly little joke that gets your knickers in a twist."

Poppy drew a sharp breath at his words and bit back the rude retort that sprang to her lips. Instead, she said in a falsely sweet voice: "Well, funnily enough, it was Suzanne—your boss, Detective Inspector Whittaker—who told me to come and report this to you. But I'm sure she'd be happy to know that you think she's just 'getting her knickers in a twist'..."

Lee snatched the ziplock bag out of her hands. "You didn't say the guv'nor sent you," he said gruffly. "Didn't know this could be evidence in the murder investigation. Very different situation."

Poppy had to really resist the urge to roll her eyes. "Suzanne especially wanted you to know about this note before you questioned the suspects today," she said. "It's likely that one of them sent—"

"Yes, I know how to do my job, Miss Lancaster," growled Lee. He made a show of shuffling some papers on the desk. "Now, if there's nothing else..."

"Actually, there *is* something else," said Poppy reluctantly. "I forgot to mention this to Suzanne but I think it could be important. I was chatting to a woman who often goes to the garden centre— actually, she's had run-ins with Thales a few times in the past. She's a real 'eco-warrior' type, you see, and she hated the fact that Thales was promoting chemical pesticides—"

"Don't tell me you think she murdered him because she didn't like him killing all the poor little bees?" said Lee, with a mocking laugh.

"No, I'm not saying that," said Poppy, annoyed. "What I wanted to say was that Maggie happened to pop into the garden centre café the day Thales was murdered and she saw him with a girl. I think it was his ex-girlfriend, Jules—Thales had told me that she came to the garden centre unexpectedly that day and he felt obliged to have lunch with her. Anyway, it seems that they were arguing. Maggie said the girl looked very upset. And Thales had mentioned that Jules had been trying to convince him to get back together with her, although he wasn't interested—"

"Forensics have already tested the chocolates in the car," said Lee, sounding bored. "There was nothing in them. And besides, the autopsy confirms that poisoning wasn't by ingestion. So the ex-girlfriend is off the list."

"But... surely you can't just discount her like that?" said Poppy indignantly. "I mean, she could have used another method to poison Thales!"

"Like what?"

"Like... like... I don't know..." Put on the spot, Poppy was frustrated to find that her mind went blank. "Maybe she gave him a cream to put on his skin or—oh! That reminds me: did they test the bottle of cologne in Thales's desk drawer?" Quickly, she told him about Nick's theory. "So you see, that could be a clever way for Sidney Maynard to poison Thales. Do you know if any cyanide was detected in the aftershave?"

Sergeant Lee glowered at her. "The forensic report is confidential police information and not to be shared with the public. Don't think, just because you're friendly with Inspector Whittaker, that you can come swanning in here, demanding access to case files."

"I'm not—"

"Now, I haven't got time to waste while you play at being Miss Marple. I've got a murder investigation to be getting on with. One of the constables will show you out."

Still protesting, Poppy found herself being escorted out of the police station, and she was left with no choice but to stalk, fuming, back to her car.

CHAPTER EIGHTEEN

What an absolute tosser! Poppy thought furiously as she started the engine and drove away from the police station. She spent most of the drive home seething and fantasising about ways to get even with Sergeant Lee, but as she was nearing Bunnington, she was distracted by the sight of a large billboard at the side of the motorway. It was advertising Mega Garden Town at the next exit. Suddenly, she recalled her decision to try the organic pesticide that Maggie had suggested.

Neem oil—isn't that what it's called? I bet I could find that at Mega Garden Town. They seem to stock everything there.

She took the upcoming exit and drove into the business park, swinging into a parking space in front of the huge garden centre a few minutes later.

Despite it being a weekday morning, the place was as busy as the last time she'd visited. Still, as she wandered through the crowded halls, Poppy found herself less overawed on this second tour. She arrived in the area devoted to pest control and felt a slight pang as she saw the deserted kiosk with the Campana banner. It seemed too unreal to think that Thales had been standing there just two days earlier and now he was dead.

There was a shelf for organic gardening products, and Poppy was pleased to find a bottle of neem oil concentrate. Clutching her purchase, she began making her way back to the front entrance. Somehow, the halls seemed to have become even more crowded since she had arrived, and Poppy found herself shuffling impatiently behind several large groups, who seemed intent on stopping to look at every display and promotion. Finally, she ducked into a side hall, determined to try and find an alternative route back to the front entrance.

As she rounded a corner, she was assailed by the smell of fresh baking, and she paused as she realised that she had come across the garden centre café. With cheerful green-and-yellow décor, and rustic wooden chairs and tables, it was an inviting sight. It had obviously only just opened for the day, and she could see the freshly baked breads and pastries being laid out in display baskets whilst, behind the counter, steam rose from an espresso machine, and the wonderful aroma of roast coffee combined with the smell of fresh baking in a heady mix.

Poppy's stomach growled and she remembered that she'd rushed out that morning without even having a cup of tea. Hesitating only a moment, she stepped into the café. A few minutes later, she was carrying a tray laden with a Danish pastry oozing with apricots and marmalade, a Cumberland sausage breakfast bun, a *pain au chocolat* thickly studded with chocolate chips, and two fluffy butter croissants over to the cashier.

"My goodness, are you really going to eat *all* that?" said the plump woman behind the counter with a chuckle. She eyed Poppy up and down with motherly interest. "Mind you, you look like you could do with some fattening up, dearie, so I don't suppose you need to worry about counting the calories."

"Everything looked so delicious, I just couldn't decide what to choose," said Poppy with a helpless laugh. "I actually wanted to take several other things too but I put them back."

"Well, you can always try them another time. We're open seven days a week, for breakfast, lunch, and afternoon tea."

On an impulse, Poppy asked: "Do you work here every day then?"

"Aye, it feels that way sometimes!" said the woman, chuckling. "I usually get alternate weekends off, and a day here an' there during the week."

"Were you here the day before yesterday?"

"Yes, why?"

"Oh… I just wondered… I don't know if you heard, but there was a young sales rep who was murdered—"

"Flippin' 'eck, yes! That young lad who worked for Campana AgroChemicals… Thales, his name was. Came in here all the time. Used to go for a vape outside during his morning break and he'd always stop by and pick up a coffee as well." She gave a sad smile. "Such a nice lad. Mind you, the serving girls were always giggling and mooning over him whenever he came in; had to have a sharp word with them or they'd never get any work done."

"It must have been a horrible shock for you when you heard," said Poppy in sympathetic tones. "I mean, if you saw him often… You just don't think that kind of thing could happen to someone you know, do you?"

"Too right!" said the woman with feeling. "It were the kind of thing you see on the telly. Don't expect it to happen in real life."

Poppy asked casually, "Did you see Thales the day he was murdered? That was the day before yesterday…"

The woman tilted her head to one side. "Hmm, now that I think about it… aye, he were here. With a girl. They were sitting right there." She nodded at a table nearby. "Didn't look very happy, I must say. Faces like thunder, the pair of 'em."

"Oh… were they fighting about something?" asked Poppy with innocent interest.

"Didn't really hear. I could tell that the girl had been crying though—her eyes were all red and her face blotchy." She frowned. "It were strange, actually. Thales's usually a real sweetie, especially with the ladies—you know, always buttering you up and the like—but he were awful stroppy with this girl. Even got up and stormed off at the end, leaving her alone at the table."

She sighed. "I felt really sorry for her, poor thing. I went over to clear their table after she'd rushed out after him, and I saw that Thales had left his vape behind. So I took it out, thinking that I might still catch him, but he'd already legged it. The girl were still standing there, though, in the middle of the hall, looking completely lost. I went up to her and asked if she were all right—I could see that she were right upset, you know, and I thought another cup of tea would do her good—but she weren't having any of it. Kept saying she were fine and she just needed to speak to Thales again." She shook her head. "Some people are gluttons for punishment, eh? I told her it would help her more if she didn't go running after him—you know, 'treat 'em mean, keep 'em keen'— isn't that what they say? But she wouldn't listen. Still, she saved me the hassle of having to find Thales later to give him the vape."

"What do you mean?"

"Well, she told me she were going off to find Thales at his kiosk-thing, so I gave her the vape to give to him."

Poppy stared at the woman as her thoughts whirled. Vaping involved inhaling a vapour from an e-cigarette device which vaporised the "vape juice", usually containing nicotine and maybe some herbal or fruity "flavours". *But a vape juice could also contain cyanide!* And the person using the vape would never know that they were essentially filling their lungs with poison—until it was too late. In fact, now that she thought about it, she could recall Suzanne telling her that the forensic pathologist thought inhalation was the most likely method of poisoning. A vape would have been the perfect delivery device! *And it would have been so easy for Jules to tamper with the vape before she gave it back to Thales*, thought Poppy. She would have known that he would use it later that day, but she could make sure she was a safe distance away by that time. The perfect way for a bitter ex-girlfriend to get revenge?

Where would Jules have got the cyanide from though? Poppy wondered as she carried her tray over to a free table and sat down to eat. As Nick had pointed out, unlike Sidney Maynard, the girl was unlikely to have a ready source of cyanide compounds. And another thing... there hadn't been a vape found with Thales's body, had there? Poppy frowned as she tried to remember the scene in the courtyard on the day of the murder. She couldn't remember seeing an e-cigarette device on the ground anywhere around Thales's slumped form, but it could have been trapped under him when he fell. If it had been there, the Forensics team would have found it when they processed the crime scene. She wished she could check to see if they'd found a vaping device, but she knew that it was no use ringing Sergeant Lee. He would never share the information in the reports with her and would only delight at the chance to snub her once again!

Poppy's thoughts were interrupted by the sound of her phone ringing. She was surprised to hear Nell's voice, and even more surprised to learn that her friend was calling from Hollyhock Cottage.

"But I thought you weren't coming back until tomorrow?" she said.

"I decided that two days was more than enough to spend with my sister," said Nell dryly. "Anyway, it's good to have a day to catch up with chores around the house before I start work again tomorrow. But my lordy Lord, Poppy, why is the fridge so empty? There isn't even any milk! And no eggs or butter either!"

"Sorry," said Poppy in an abashed voice. "I did mean to pick up some supplies, but I kept getting sidetracked with other stuff—"

Nell tutted. "Really, Poppy! I go off for two days and you let the pantry run out. How are you ever going to run a household when you become someone's wife? Anyway, where are you?"

"I'm in Mega Garden Town. I just came to pick up an organic pesticide I wanted to try." *And stuff my face with sixty-four pastries*, thought Poppy with a guilty grin. "Anyway, I'm leaving now and I'll be back soon."

"Good. You can stop off in the village shop and pick up some milk and eggs. And a packet of butter too. Oh, and see if they've got any nice potatoes. I might make a shepherd's pie tonight. And can you stop off at the butcher's as well to see if he's got any soup bones available? Mariam Hicks's niece has had her baby at last and I want to make a nourishing broth for the new mother—"

"...potatoes... soup bones..." muttered Poppy, hastily writing a list on her phone and trying to keep up as Nell continued talking.

"—have any to spare, I can put some in a thermos for Miss Finch as well. I gave her a ring earlier and she says her shoulder is a *lot* better. In fact, she was hoping to get out for some fresh air tomorrow and join her friends for morning tea. Of course, it's not really the fresh air she's interested in, you know—it's the gossip! Everyone's talking about the murder, all over the village. Some of the ladies in Bunnington had even met the murdered lad, you know. Apparently, he'd been in Bunnington a fair few times recently. They kept telling me they just couldn't believe it. I have to say, I could hardly believe it myself when you rang and told me what happened yesterday. Murdered by poison! That's the kind of thing that happens in books... oh, rhubarb—see if you can get some. It should be in season now. Nothing like a nice rhubarb crumble... and maybe some raspberries too. They should have had a new delivery. Actually, that reminds me: I must get that recipe for raspberry trifle cake off Mariam Hicks the next time I see her... which probably won't be until next week, more's the pity. She *was* planning to come into Bunnington earlier to pick up that bracelet she took in for cleaning, but now that the shop assistant's involved with the murder, things are a bit chaotic at the jeweller's and it might take—"

"What shop assistant?" Poppy cut in. "What do you mean, involved with the murder?"

"Oh, didn't I tell you, dear? Apparently, the girl who works in that antique jewellery shop on the village high street is the ex-girlfriend of the lad who was murdered! Talk about a small world, eh? That's why some of the ladies had met him, you see—they bumped into him when he came to see Julia Buckley. That's the girl who works at the jeweller's. She's been absolutely distraught, so she hasn't been in to work, and they haven't got anyone else—"

"Wait a minute, wait a minute..." Poppy said excitedly. "Are you telling me that Thales's ex-girlfriend Jules works in Bunnington?"

CHAPTER NINETEEN

"Yes, the poor thing," said Nell, clucking in sympathy. "Can you imagine what a shock it must have been for her, to learn that her ex-boyfriend had been murdered?"

Not if she's the one who murdered him, thought Poppy. She recalled what Thales had said when she'd told him she lived in Bunnington: *"Oh yeah, I know Bunnington. I've been popping in there a fair bit recently."* So the break-up must have been recent, and it seemed that Jules had been unable to let go of the hope that Thales might still get back together with her. Had that hope turned into bitter hatred when he refused to give them another chance?

"Is Jules back at work now? Do you know?" she asked Nell.

"I think so, although everything's dreadfully

backed up. Mariam thinks it might take weeks for them to get around to cleaning her bracelet and..."

Poppy tuned out Nell's voice as her thoughts began to follow a new direction. Sergeant Lee might have been convinced that the lack of poison in the chocolates meant that Jules was out of the frame, but he was wrong. The girl could still be guilty of the murder; she'd just chosen a different way to deliver the poison: Thales's vape, which had been conveniently given to her! And what was more, now that Poppy knew Jules worked at the jeweller's, the mystery of how she could have obtained cyanide was solved. Poppy thought back to the day she'd asked Bertie about cyanide. She could still hear the old inventor's voice saying:

"...you can obtain cyanide in the form of cyanide salts, such as sodium and potassium cyanide, which are widely used in laboratories... it is also used in industrial processes like steel manufacturing and electroplating and fumigation. Jewellers use it, too, to clean gold and silver..."

Yes, it all fit! A shop specialising in antique jewellery would probably need to clean gold and silver, and that meant that Jules would have been perfectly placed to access a ready source of cyanide.

Maybe I'll take Mum's locket into this place for a clean. If Jules is there, I might be able to get chatting to her, ask her about that vape that she was supposed to have given Thales...

Poppy came out of her musings to realise that Nell

was asking her something:

"I see the casserole I left you is all gone. Did you have it two nights running?"

"Oh... um, no, actually, Nick had dinner with me last night and we finished it off between us."

"Nick? Nick Forrest? What was *he* doing here?" asked Nell suspiciously.

"He just happened to be in the garden and he saw me when I went out to search for Solly." Poppy sighed. "That's a long story; I'll tell you about it later—anyway, so I invited him in for a bite to eat." She didn't mention the threatening note. It would only worry Nell and there wasn't much that could be done now anyway.

"I don't like the way he's always prowling around our garden at night," Nell grumbled. "It's just not normal to have a strange man wandering willy-nilly around your property any time he likes—"

"Oh, Nell—Nick is hardly a 'strange man'! Besides, you know that's the arrangement my grandmother had with him. She told Nick that he could come over whenever he needed it. And when I moved in to Hollyhock Cottage, I decided to honour her promise. It's not as if Nick disturbs us or anything—most of the time, we barely know he's there—and I think it helps him a lot with his writing, especially when he's stuck."

"He's got his own garden. Why doesn't he wander around in there?" said Nell.

"Because it's too neat and manicured," said Poppy

with a chuckle, visualising the garden next door, which was filled with carefully clipped hedges, low-maintenance shrubs, and evergreen perennials. It was a peaceful haven which complemented Nick's elegant Georgian-style house, but it certainly didn't offer the rambling nature and colourful exuberance—the *wild abandon*—of her cottage garden.

"Well, I don't like it," said Nell. "The thought of you here all alone, with Nick hanging around, and you know what they say about older men—"

"Nell!" Poppy gave an exasperated laugh. She could never understand Nell's wary attitude towards the crime author. With his brooding good looks and deep voice, she would have thought that Nick Forrest was the epitome of the type of romantic hero populating the romance novels her friend loved to read—and therefore, an instant favourite. Instead, Nell always acted like a protective mother hen, suspicious of his every move and intention.

"You talk as if we're in the Victorian era," said Poppy, chuckling, "First of all, Nick is thirty-nine. That's only, like, fourteen years older than me. And I'm not some innocent, helpless maiden needing a chaperone—I'm a modern woman, and I'm more than capable of taking care of myself! Besides, he doesn't view me remotely in a romantic way... and vice versa," she added quickly. "We're just friends."

"Hmm..." Nell didn't sound convinced. "He seems to be 'just friends' with too many women, if you ask me. Like that nice lady detective inspector—how come she's still so chummy with him? I thought they were sweethearts once."

"They were. But people can be friendly with their exes. They don't always have to be bitter and angry and want to murder each other," said Poppy wryly. "Anyway, Nick said your beef casserole was the best he'd ever tasted. He said he's even thinking of featuring it in one of his stories!"

"Did he now?" said Nell, sounding slightly mollified.

Okay, she was probably stretching the truth a bit and putting words in Nick's mouth. Not that the crime author hadn't been appreciative of the meal, but he hadn't gone quite as far as offering Nell's beef casserole a starring role in one of his future books. Still, Poppy thought a little white lie couldn't hurt once in a while, and it was worth it to hear Nell softening towards him. The way to a man's heart might be through his stomach, but the way to a woman's could easily be through her cooking!

Poppy duly made a stop in Bunnington's village centre on her way back to Hollyhock Cottage. Most of the shops in the village seemed to cater more to tourists, from art galleries and antique shops to boutiques selling knick-knacks and souvenirs of the local area. But thankfully, there was also a village post office shop, plus a small grocer's, to provide the local residents with more practical goods. There wasn't a huge amount of choice—this definitely didn't compare to a shopping mall or department store brimming with the latest trendy brands—but there was more than enough for fulfilling the everyday essentials.

Poppy stopped off at the butcher's first and bought the soup bones, before popping into the grocer's to see if she could tick the other items off Nell's list. She found a group of women gathered around the checkout counter when she stepped in, all busily talking. It looked like the local ladies of Bunnington were well into their morning gossip session! She gave them a quick wave and hurriedly ducked into the nearest aisle before they could engage her in conversation. Hopefully, she'd be able to make her purchases and get out without being accosted by the garrulous crowd. Poppy knew that they were mostly well meaning—in fact, many of them had known her grandmother, and now regarded her with the kind of affectionate interest reserved for a grand-niece or similar—but still, she preferred not to have to fend off their nosy questions if she could help it.

The shelves were well stocked and Poppy soon filled her basket with everything that Nell had asked for. As she arrived back at the checkout, she was surprised to see a familiar figure. It was Maggie Simmons. The other woman was leaning across the counter, glaring at the girl behind the cash register, as she pointed to the pyramid of egg cartons arranged on the counter next to her.

"...can't believe that in this day and age you don't stock free-range eggs! It's an absolute travesty!"

"S-sorry, miss," stammered the girl, who looked about sixteen and was probably rueing the day she'd decided to work in the grocer's part-time. "We do stock free-range eggs, but they've run out so we've only got the cage eggs left."

"Well, the fact that they've run out first just shows that everybody wants free-range, doesn't it? So why are you stocking the other kind? Any self-respecting shop should only stock free-range and nothing else these days, as a matter of principle!"

The girl squirmed, looking like she didn't know how to answer. Finally, she pointed at the spray bottle that Maggie was holding in her hands and said: "Um... so do you want me to put that through for you?"

"No! I'm certainly not buying this," said Maggie, regarding the bottle with disgust. Poppy saw that it was some kind of household cleaner with a label that boasted "instant sparkling results".

"Do you realise what damage this can do the environment if it goes into the waterways?" Maggie demanded. "You can achieve the same effect just with bicarbonate of soda and water and a bit of elbow grease! There's no need to use such harsh chemicals, and you shouldn't be stocking these and encouraging people to use them."

"Um... I'll pass that on to the manager," mumbled the girl. "But not everyone's, like, got the time, you know. Nowadays, people want what's convenient—"

"Convenient?" said Maggie, her voice rising with indignation. "Is that all you care about? Well, it won't be *convenient* when the Earth is destroyed and we've got no clean water or unpolluted air and the land is poisoned with—"

"Is there anything you actually *want* to buy? asked the girl desperately.

Maggie glowered at her. "I'll come back when you've got free-range eggs again." Turning, she shouldered her way past the crowd of women who had been watching, agog, and left the shop. The door swung shut behind her with a loud thud, and the girl at the counter sagged visibly in relief.

"It's all right, dear," said one of the women from the group. She reached over the counter and patted the girl's hand. "Don't take it personally. Maggie Simmons is like that with everyone."

"Yes, she jumped on me in the pub the other day and gave me a lecture for using a takeaway cup," said another woman, rolling her eyes. "Said I should be carrying my own reusable eco mug in my handbag."

"Well, she *is* right, really," said one of the younger women in the group, with a baby balanced on one hip. "I mean, we *are* supposed to be moving to more sustainable living habits, aren't we? I do try not to use disposable plastics if I can, and I've reduced the number of chemicals I use around the house."

"Yes, but Maggie is hardly going to convert anyone to her cause with a manner like that, is she?" said the first woman. "Most people see her coming and they run a mile!"

"I wouldn't be too hard on her, dear," a much older woman at the back of the group spoke up. "She's had a tough life, Maggie has. Especially after what happened to her mother…"

"What happened to her mother?" Poppy asked, going forwards to join them. She hadn't really wanted to catch the attention of the group, but she was intrigued in spite of herself.

The women looked at each other, then all began talking at once:

"I heard that it was a stroke—"

"No, no, not a stroke, it was an overdose."

"An overdose! Really?"

"That's nonsense. It was nothing to do with drugs—it was all in her head."

"You mean she imagined it?"

"No, I mean literally in her head. Something went wrong in her brain."

"Like a brain injury, eh?"

"I heard it was summin' to do with her brain cells and the connections—"

"She was poisoned," the older woman at the back of the group spoke up again.

"Poisoned?" said Poppy, startled.

The other villagers looked shocked too. "You're not saying that someone deliberately tried to harm her, Nora?" one of them said.

The older woman called Nora gave a shrug. "Well,

not deliberately but... what happened was: about twenty years ago, Valerie and Maggie were living closer to Oxford. I lived in the same village; that's how I knew 'em—"

"The daughter must have still been in primary school then," said the young mother, switching the baby to her other hip.

Nora nodded. "Yes. Maggie was a single mum and they were really struggling to make ends meet. And then Valerie saw an advertisement for volunteers to test a new product—some kind of pesticide, I think— and it was good money, so she signed up. It seemed really easy; all she had to do was spray it around her garden for a few weeks and then report what happened."

"Was the company who made the pesticide called Campana AgroChemicals?" asked Poppy quickly.

Nora frowned. "No, it was some small company... now, what were they called? Something 'Titanic'... 'Vanquish Titanic'—that's it. I remember thinking how silly it was that such a small business should have such a grand name."

"Oh," said Poppy, disappointed. She had thought for a moment that there might be a meaningful connection.

"So what happened?" one of the other women asked.

Nora pulled a face. "Well, it turned out that the volunteers started noticing side effects after a few months. Just small things at first—you know, forgetting odd things, people's names... getting a bit disorientated sometimes. And then it got worse. Pretty soon, Valerie was showing all the signs of early onset dementia."

"Oh..." Poppy thought back to the old lady sitting in the rocking chair with the vacant smile on her face. "That's awful."

"Was it that pesticide? The one she'd been testing?" asked the young mother, pulling her baby closer in a protective gesture.

Nora shrugged. "Who knows? Maggie was sure it was, though. She said the chemicals in this new pesticide must have had a toxic effect on Valerie's brain cells. Apparently there's loads of evidence that the pesticides we already use have bad effects on your nervous system and your brain. It's why more and more people are getting Alzheimer's and Parkinson's and MS and things like that—that's what Maggie told me."

There was an uneasy murmur as the other women looked at each other, no doubt thinking about the products they used in their own homes and gardens.

"So did Maggie do something about it?" asked Poppy.

"Yes, she contacted some of the other volunteers and found out that they'd been showing similar symptoms too," said Nora. "There was talk of a big lawsuit and media exposé and everything... but it all came to nothing in the end."

"But why?" cried Poppy. "Surely they had a case—

"

"Yes but they needed everyone on board for the case to have a chance. Just one case on its own could have been a coincidence. You know, people get early onset dementia sometimes, don't they? You can't prove that it was directly caused by the pesticide. If you had loads of cases, that would have been different. But it turned out that Vanquish Titanic had got in touch with the other volunteers and offered them a settlement out of court. So the whole thing was hushed up. I think the company withdrew the product and that was the end of it."

"And Maggie?" asked Poppy. "Did she get a good payout then?"

Nora shook her head sadly. "No. She wouldn't take the money. Said it would have been selling out—
"

"What a ninny!" cried one of the other women, shaking her head. "I would have taken the money and run. What good are morals when you need to put bread on the table? Whatever happened to Valerie can't be undone now. She might as well have got the compensation."

A few other women nodded and made noises of agreement.

"You can see why she's gone a bit doolally on pesticides and chemicals, though," said the young mother sympathetically. "I would, too, if something like that had happened to anyone in my family."

"She's gone a bit far over to the other side, though,

if you ask me," said the woman beside her. "Maggie thinks any kind of chemical or drug is bad for you. Won't even take normal medicines half the time now."

"Yes, I met her in the pharmacy the other day and got chatting about my sister, who's having chemo for cancer. Maggie started going on about how my sister should be taking homeopathic alternatives instead, like apricot kernel extract—"

"Oh no, that's terrible stuff," cried another woman. "Haven't you read the stories? There was this man in Australia who took that for prostate cancer and he ended up getting terrible side effects and poisoning himself!"

"Well, you try telling that to Maggie," said the first woman, shaking her head. "She thinks that anything that comes off a plant is safe and anything that comes from a lab is evil. She's always brewing up homemade cordials and tinctures in that shed of hers and insisting that they're superior to anything you could buy in a pharmacy." She rolled her eyes. "You just can't reason with that woman."

"Well, I still think I might stop using chemical pesticides and switch to organic products," said the young mother, stroking her baby's head tenderly. "Don't want to take any chances with the little one."

Maybe Maggie can get a bit of cold comfort from that, thought Poppy as she turned to the girl behind the checkout and handed over her basket of goods. At least her personal tragedy might have helped convince some others to opt for more eco-friendly choices!

CHAPTER TWENTY

Poppy crossed the village high street with her shopping in tow and was just about to head over to where her car was parked when she spotted the sign above a shop further down the street: *SANDERS' FINE JEWELLERY*.

She paused. *Isn't that the place Nell mentioned when she was talking about Mariam Hicks's bracelet? So that must be where Thales's ex-girlfriend Jules works,* she thought excitedly. She hesitated a moment as she glanced at the shopping in her hands, then turned and hurried across to the jewellery boutique. The bell attached to the door tinkled as Poppy stepped in. It was a quaint little shop, filled with dark wood cabinets and display cases, and there were vintage pendant necklaces, antique gold rings, art deco brooches, and Victorian chokers gleaming from behind the glass panels.

A young woman stood behind the counter at the far end of the shop and Poppy eyed her speculatively. Could this be Jules? She seemed to be about the right age and she had a bruised look around her eyes, as if she hadn't slept well or had been crying. She was busily polishing a piece of sterling silver jewellery with a cloth, and she looked up with a polite smile as Poppy entered the shop.

"Hello, can I help you?"

"Um... yes," said Poppy, going over to join her at the counter. She indicated the silver that the girl was polishing. "Do you clean gold jewellery too, by any chance?"

"Oh yes, we're experts in all forms of jewellery cleaning, both by traditional means and with the newer ultrasonic equipment. As specialists in antique jewellery, we're used to dealing with very old pieces which may have been sitting in a jewellery box for years and have become grimy and tarnished." The girl looked at Poppy enquiringly. "Do you have a particular piece of antique jewellery that needs cleaning?"

"Oh... well, not an antique, really," said Poppy with an embarrassed laugh as she put down her shopping and reached under her shirt to pull out the gold locket she normally wore around her neck. She unclasped it and handed it to the girl. "It's just an old locket that belonged to my mother. I don't suppose it's very valuable but—"

"Oh, it's lovely," said the girl, taking the locket and holding it up for a closer look. The front sprang open under her fingers to reveal a tiny photograph of a beautiful girl with honey-blonde hair smiling mischievously over her shoulder. "Wow—who's that? She's gorgeous."

"That's my mother," said Poppy with some pride.

The girl turned the locket over with knowledgeable fingers, saying excitedly: "I think it actually *is* a vintage piece, you know! You see this engraving on the back? It's a hallmark—it tells you that it was assayed in Birmingham in 1900... '9.375 for 9ct Gold'... there, see? And that's the maker's mark—'PP Ld'—which stands for Payton Pepper & Sons Ltd. They were well-known jewellers in Birmingham. It's even rumoured that when the Crown Jewels were returned to the Tower of London after the Second World War, it was Payton Pepper who reset the stones."

Poppy looked at her with new respect. "Wow... you really know your stuff."

The girl laughed self-consciously. "I've always been mad about vintage jewellery. When I got this position, it was like landing my dream job." She gave Poppy a friendly smile. "I'm Jules, by the way."

Poppy returned the smile, trying not to look too elated. "I'm Poppy." She looked back down at the locket. "I never realised this was an antique."

"And worth quite a few quid too, I'll bet," said Jules. "I can have it valued, if you like, at the same time as cleaning it."

"Do you think you could find out where it might have been purchased?" asked Poppy on an impulse. "I've... er... always wondered who might have given it to my mother. If it was an expensive piece, I don't think she could have bought it herself."

"Sure, I can try." She looked at Poppy curiously. "Couldn't you just ask her, though?"

"She passed away last year."

"Oh, I'm sorry!"

"No, it's all right," Poppy reassured her. "In any case, I don't know if Mum would have told me. I'm hoping... I mean, I think it's possible that my father might have given this locket to her. Mum would never talk about him, but I recently discovered that there's another photo in the locket—in the back—there..." She showed the girl the hidden mechanism which opened a second compartment with another photograph, this time showing a handsome young man with brooding good looks and soulful dark eyes. "I know it's a long shot, but I thought... maybe if I can find out where this was bought, it might give me a clue... you know, something to help me track him down..."

Poppy trailed off, suddenly embarrassed. Why on earth had she started blurting all this out to Jules? She had come in here to ask about Thales's murder, not go down rabbit holes about the mystery of her own long-lost father!

"Omigod, this is so romantic!" cried Jules, staring

at the second photograph. "So your dad was, like, your mother's secret sweetheart? And this could be him? I'd love to help. Yeah, leave it with me and I'll see if I can dig up any information for you." She reached under the counter and pulled out a docket pad. "If I can just get your name and phone number..."

As Poppy watched the other girl fill out the pad, she reflected that now that she'd met Jules, it was a bit hard to reconcile her preconceived image of a bitter, revenge-obsessed, jilted ex with the friendly, chatty girl in front of her. And it was especially hard to think of a way to broach the topic of Thales's murder and ask Jules about the vape as a potential murder weapon!

She glanced around the shop, then asked casually: "Will you be doing the cleaning here? I'm a bit nervous about losing my locket if you have to send it somewhere else—"

"Oh no, we do all the cleaning on the premises. There's a workshop out the back and, in fact, I do a lot of the cleaning myself," said Jules proudly. "It's a really simple process, actually. We soak the pieces in a special chemical solution of hydrogen peroxide combined with potassium cyanide, and they come out gorgeous and clean and sparkling, without having to use any kind of hard, abrasive polishing. It's brilliant."

"You use cyanide?" said Poppy with exaggerated horror. "Isn't that, like, really poisonous?"

"It's not too bad if you know how to handle it and take the proper precautions."

"So it's not kept under lock and key?" said Poppy jokingly. "Can you get access to it any time?"

"Well, it *is* kept in a special sealed container, in a locked cupboard, but Mr Sanders trusts me. He knows that I'm really careful and I wouldn't ever give the key to anyone el—" Jules broke off suddenly and narrowed her eyes. "Wait a minute... are you some kind of undercover cop?" she demanded.

"W-what?" said Poppy, taken aback by the girl's abrupt change. Gone was the warm, friendly manner; instead, Jules was eyeing her with open hostility.

"All these questions about whether I have free access to cyanide... I'm not stupid. This is about Thales's murder, isn't it?" she spat. "I know I'm one of the suspects. I've already had that bloody sergeant in here this morning, and I told him I don't know anything about it! But I suppose they thought they'd send a woman to try again? You think trying to get chummy with me using that fake sob story about your mother's secret lover would—"

"No, no! That wasn't a fake story—I really don't know who my father is," cried Poppy. "And I'm not an undercover policewoman or anything like that. Although I *am* involved with the case," she admitted. "I was actually the person who found Thales's body. I... er... Thales sold me some pesticide," she said tactfully, thinking that it would probably be best if

Jules never knew that Thales had had a romantic interest in her!

"I've been questioned by the police too," she added, hoping to generate some solidarity with the girl. "That... er... Sergeant Lee has given me a really tough time as well." *Which is certainly not a lie*, she thought sourly.

"Oh," said Jules, calming down. "Sorry to jump on you like that. It's just that it's been horrible enough without having the police practically accusing me of murder. I loved Thales!" she burst out, her eyes welling up. "I would have done anything for him. How could they think that I would have hurt him?"

"Well... I suppose people always go for the clichés first, don't they? I mean, people are always suspecting the spouse or partner or something. Maybe the police found a... um... a gift or something you gave Thales which showed your special relationship?" asked Poppy ingenuously.

"Well, I did give Thales a box of chocolates that day, and that had a card with it. I suppose they must have seen that," the girl admitted, sniffing and wiping her eyes with the back of one hand. "But like I told the sergeant this morning: if I was going to poison him, I wouldn't be daft enough to put the cyanide in a box of chocolates with my name on it, would I?"

No, but you might have cleverly added it to the e-juice in his vape, thought Poppy. Even if Jules seemed friendly and sympathetic, that didn't mean that she couldn't still be the murderer. True, she seemed genuinely distressed, but she could also simply be a very good actress...

"So... um... you don't have any idea how Thales could have been poisoned?" Poppy asked.

Jules shook her head. "He seemed totally fine when I saw him. We had lunch together at the garden centre café."

"And that was the last time you saw him?"

Jules hesitated, looking down and fiddling with the silver polishing cloth. "Well, not exactly. We... we sort of had a row at lunch and Thales stormed off. I was going to follow him because I hadn't finished what I wanted to say—and also, he'd left his vape behind. One of the café ladies found it and I said I'd take it to him. But then... well, when I went to find Thales's kiosk, he was with a customer, and he looked so annoyed when he saw me. I thought maybe it would be better if I let him cool down first. I was planning to go back the next day..." She looked back up at Poppy, her eyes filling with tears again. "And then I heard the news. I... I couldn't believe it! They say you should never part in anger, you know? I can't bear the thought that the very last time Thales and I were together, we were rowing. I wish I had stayed that day and tried to talk to him again!"

Poppy waited until the girl had pulled herself together, then asked delicately: "So that vape—you didn't manage to return it to Thales?"

"No, I've still got it here." Jules reached into her jeans pocket and pulled out a small rectangular device. "That sergeant was such a plonker—he really annoyed me! So I didn't tell him about the vape and trying to see Thales again. I just told him I had lunch with Thales at the café and that's it."

Poppy stared at the vape device. It was obviously expensive, with a sleek metal body and beautiful enamelled panels on each side. She could just see the initials *"T. G."* engraved on the end. Disappointment washed over her. *There goes my theory about the vape as a murder weapon*, she thought. If Jules still had Thales's e-cigarette, then it couldn't have been used to deliver cyanide to him.

"I'm probably supposed to hand this in to the police, aren't I? I'd really like to keep it though." Jules lifted the vape and sniffed it, then gave a wistful smile. "Thales always used this e-juice that had a cinnamon flavour. It was like his signature scent. Just smelling this reminds me of him. Do you think I have to tell the police about this?"

"Yeah, I think it would be considered evidence in a murder investigation," said Poppy, thinking that, in any case, keeping your dead ex-boyfriend's vape just so you could sniff it occasionally was slightly odd and creepy!

Jules sighed. "Okay. I suppose I'd better let them know. I just hope that sergeant doesn't give me any grief for not handing it in earlier." She shoved the vape back into her pocket, then tore the top page off the docket pad and handed it to Poppy. "Here you are... this is for your locket. I'll let you know when it's ready and also if I find any information about it."

"Thanks. I'd really appreciate that," said Poppy, glad in a way that Jules seemed to be off the list of suspects.

"Do you live near here, by the way? I don't think I've seen you before," said Jules.

"Yes, actually, I live on the other side of the village, but I haven't been out and about much," said Poppy with a rueful smile. "I inherited a garden nursery, you see, and I didn't know anything about plants, so it's been a bit crazy the past few months just getting to grips with everything—"

"Oh, I know the place!" said Jules, her eyes lighting up. "Hollyhock Cottage, isn't it? I've been meaning to pop in to check it out. I just moved into my own place. It's only got a balcony, but I wanted to get a couple of plants to put in pots."

"Oh, well, you're welcome any time. And actually, I'm holding an Open Day in a couple of weeks. There'll be lots of promotions and discounts, so that would be a good chance to pick up some bargains."

"Ooh! Sounds great. I'll definitely try to pop in if I'm free," Jules said with a smile.

Poppy bid the girl goodbye and left the shop, thinking to herself: *Now I really hope she doesn't turn out to be the murderer!*

CHAPTER TWENTY-ONE

Back at Hollyhock Cottage, Poppy walked in with the shopping to find Nell in the kitchen, busily scrubbing the oven tray over the sink. The entire house looked like it had been freshly dusted and vacuumed, and all the taps in both the kitchen and bathroom were gleaming.

"Didn't you clean that before you went away?" she asked, watching Nell scrub vigorously at a barely visible stain in one corner of the tray.

"Well, I was giving all the saucepans a wash and I thought I might as well give this a once-over as well," said Nell, pushing a flyaway tendril of hair off her face and leaving a smear of soap suds on her cheek. "I can't believe it, but I seem to have missed a couple of spots last time!"

"Really?" said Poppy, leaning over the sink to look

at the tray. "That looks clean to me."

"It might *look* clean, but there's still residue there—I can feel it," said Nell, running her gloved fingers experimentally over the surface of the tray. "And if you keep baking it with those food residues, it'll cook the carbon black, and then it'll be a nightmare to remove. Might even have to use soda blasting," she said with relish.

Poppy hid a smile. All the practical reasons didn't hide the truth, which was that Nell loved cleaning with a passion. Her friend was probably the only cleaning lady in the world whose day job really was her favourite hobby!

Poppy busied herself putting away the shopping, then made herself a cup of tea and sat down at the table with a sigh. "My God, what a morning—and it's barely lunchtime! Thank goodness the nursery is closed today, otherwise I'd really be in a tizzy."

Nell paused her scrubbing to look up enquiringly. "What do you mean? I thought you just went over to the garden centre to buy some kind of organic pesticide."

"I did, but before that I popped into the police station to speak to Suzanne about the murder. Oh, it's terrible, Nell! Suzanne has to go away, and that pompous git Sergeant Lee is taking over the case," moaned Poppy. "He's so obnoxious, he gets everyone's back up and puts them off wanting to help the police. Like Jules, Thales's ex-girlfriend—she didn't even tell him that she had Thales's vape!

Although I suppose that was lucky in a way, since I would never have known about it if it *had* been handed over to the police..."

She saw that Nell was looking at her blankly and had to explain her theory about the vape as the poison delivery device.

"...it all fits perfectly! If Thales was poisoned by inhalation—which is what the autopsy seems to suggest—then the vape would have been the easiest way to get him to inhale a large dose of cyanide. But since Jules never gave it back to Thales, it can't have been the vape, after all," she finished, crestfallen.

"Couldn't the girlfriend have put the cyanide in some other thing for Thales to inhale?" asked Nell.

"Like what?" asked Poppy. "There aren't many things you'd sniff really deeply. And besides, Bertie told me that if it's inhaled, cyanide acts very quickly—so it couldn't have been something that Thales inhaled earlier in the day. He would have already started showing symptoms by the time I met him. And I know he was fine for an hour before his death because I was with him the whole time and he was perfectly normal! So he had to have inhaled the poison just before he collapsed. I thought it could have been the vape because, although I didn't see him use it, he could have taken it out for a quick 'smoke' when I went to the loo. But since Jules never gave his vape back to him, that's out."

"Well, maybe there was something else in his house that he inhaled? Did you see any candles or essential oil burners? What about air fresheners?"

Poppy shook her head impatiently. "Nell—Thales was a typical 'bloke'! He wasn't going to be putting scented candles or aromatherapy diffusers around his house! It was a real 'bachelor pad' kind of place— you know, full of headphones and sound systems and game consoles and stuff like that." She paused and thought for a moment. "And besides, he was out in the garden when he collapsed, so it had to have been something he inhaled while outside..."

"A flower with a poisoned perfume?" suggested Nell.

Poppy laughed. "Now we're getting into the realm of fantasy! Besides, if it was already growing in Thales's garden, wouldn't he have sniffed it and been poisoned before? It doesn't make any sense!"

"Well, maybe you should leave it to the police to sort out," said Nell. "I'm sure when Suzanne gets back, she'll know the best way to proceed with the investigation. And in the meantime, don't you have a bunch of diseased roses to treat, dear?"

"Oh God, yes," cried Poppy, springing up guiltily. In all the excitement that morning, she had completely forgotten about her gardening troubles! "I'd better be getting on with that, especially as the nursery is closed today. It's a good chance to spray everything."

"It's nearly lunchtime," said Nell, glancing at the clock on the wall. "Why don't you have something to eat first and then do the spraying afterwards?"

Poppy patted her stomach ruefully. "I stuffed my face at the Mega Garden Town café—I'm not really that hungry. But actually, waiting might be a good idea. I remember Maggie saying that you shouldn't spray when bees are actively foraging during the day, so I suppose it would be better to wait until this evening, when they've gone back to the hive."

Accordingly, late that afternoon, Poppy retrieved the bottle of neem oil concentrate she'd bought and took it into the greenhouse to mix up a spray solution. She was just pouring the mixture into a garden sprayer when she heard a familiar, demanding voice:

"*N-ow? N-oww?*"

She turned and smiled involuntarily as she saw a big orange tomcat slink through the gap in the greenhouse door and stroll over to join her by the potting bench.

"Hello, Oren." Then, recalling that she was supposed to be annoyed with the ginger tom, Poppy changed her smile to a mock scowl. "Actually, I shouldn't even be talking to you after your little stunt with Solly's tank!"

She glanced over at the corner of the greenhouse, where the empty glass tank stood. She had pushed it back upright and swept up the mess after Nick had left the night before, but she hadn't had a chance to search for the missing slug again. In any case, she knew in her heart that it was a lost cause: how could she possibly hope to find one small slug in the dense tangle of greenery spread through the whole garden? Besides, even if she *did* come across a brown slug, how would she know that it was the right one? She had no way to distinguish Solly from any other random garden slug going about its slimy business!

"*N-ow?*" said Oren, leaping up onto the potting bench and rubbing his chin against the side of the sprayer.

"Oi! Stop that! You're going to tip it over," Poppy admonished, lifting the sprayer out of his reach.

She twisted the top securely closed and then pumped the handle several times before lifting the large bottle and taking it outside. There, she spent the next twenty minutes carefully spraying all the rose bushes by the path, drenching them in the neem oil solution until it ran dripping off their leaves. Remembering Maggie's instructions, she took particular care to get into the nooks and crannies, spraying under every leaf and thoroughly coating each stem. Finally, satisfied with her handiwork, she went back to the greenhouse.

Oren had made himself comfortable on a kneeling pad she'd left on the wooden bench. He opened one eye as she came back in and yawned widely, showing his impressive canines. Then he rose and arched his back in a perfect cat stretch before trotting over to the door that led from the greenhouse into the cottage kitchen.

"*N-ow?*" he said, looking back at her hopefully. "*N-oww?*"

"No, Oren, it's not time for dinner yet. And anyway, you know I can't feed you," said Poppy reproachfully. "I'll get in trouble with Nick again. You've got your own perfectly good dinner at home. Yummy cat food... wouldn't you like that?"

"*Nooo-ow!*" said Oren sulkily.

Poppy sighed. "Well, don't complain to me. Go and talk to Nick about it."

Oren stalked back to where she was and watched sulkily as she examined a row of young penstemons. These were some of her favourites: *Penstemon 'Sour Grapes'*, a wonderful perennial with elegant spires of rich purple, bell-shaped flowers, perfect for growing in sunny borders or in pots on the patio. They were vigorous seedlings, growing well, and, in fact, looked ready to be potted up into a bigger home. Poppy decided that now would be a good time to tackle the job, and she turned to an enormous collection of plastic pots arranged in stacks along the greenhouse wall.

When she'd first moved into the cottage, she had tutted at her grandmother for hoarding so many discarded plastic plant pots and had nearly thrown them all out. But once she had started growing plants herself, she began to appreciate Mary Lancaster's thriftiness. She realised that her grandmother's years of careful stockpiling meant that she now had a ready-made supply of different-sized containers when she needed to move plants up to the next stage. After deliberating a moment, she selected one of the stacks and carried it back to the bench. She picked up one of the young penstemons, squeezed it gently out of its pot, and carefully positioned the root ball in one of the new pots from the stack. It slid in with an inch to spare on all sides. Poppy smiled. *Perfect.*

As she began to work, transferring each young penstemon into its new, bigger home, she remembered the early days when she'd thought she could save herself work by skipping the gradual "potting up" process and just putting baby plants straight into the big final pots. It had seemed a good idea, but what she hadn't realised was that a little plug plant in a huge pot was a recipe for disaster: the seedlings were left stranded in the middle of a vast sea of soil, with their tiny roots unable to reach the bottom of the pot where the water had all settled. Meanwhile, with no roots to absorb the excess moisture, most of the soil in the pot remained wet for far too long and quickly turned sour, leading to fungal diseases and root rot. Yes, she had certainly learned her lesson the hard way! Now she diligently repotted her batches of young plants every few weeks into slightly bigger containers until they were ready for their final pots.

But this should be the last move for this batch, she thought, looking down at the group of young plants with satisfaction. She was also pleased with how efficiently she was getting through the batch. Gone were those early days of fumbling with the plants, squashing roots, tearing off leaves by mistake, and spilling soil everywhere. Now her movements were deft and quick, honed from hours of practice, and the plants remained fresh and intact as she transplanted them into their new homes.

Poppy began to hum a tune, with Oren interjecting a bossy "*N-oww!*" every so often as he watched her work. She was just getting to the last plant in the batch when her bag of potting compost ran out.

"Bugger..." muttered Poppy, annoyed at having to open a whole new bag of compost just for one plant. Still, there was no way around it.

She went over to the far side of the greenhouse, where several sacks of peat-free potting compost were leaning against the wall, and heaved one up in her arms. The action made her think of Thales—the way he had been trying to show off while lifting that heavy bag of mulch out of his car—and she felt a twinge of sadness. He might have been a womaniser and, okay, maybe even a petty thief, but there had been something about Thales, a certain charisma, that made you like him in spite of everything. He was like the handsome, naughty little boy at school who was always pushing boundaries and doing things he shouldn't, and yet you couldn't help softening when he looked at you with his cheeky grin.

She carried the bag of potting compost over to the work bench and dropped it with a thud on the top. Grabbing a pair of gardening scissors, she sliced across the top of the bag and pulled it open, then reeled back, coughing violently as a cloud of fine mist billowed from the mouth of the bag.

"*Noooo-ow!*" cried Oren, jumping away.

"Ugghh!" Poppy cried, waving her hand in front of her face to try and clear the air.

But that only seemed to fan the cloud of dust around even more, making her cough even harder. Her eyes began to water and she lost her grip on the bag, which slumped sideways.

"Argh! No!"

She lunged to grab the bag and keep it upright, but it was too late. Potting compost fell out, spilling everywhere. Thankfully, the dust from the bag was slowly settling, although the strong, musty smell still lingered in the air. Poppy sighed as she looked at the mess of potting compost all over the workbench and in piles on the floor. Now she had an extra cleaning job to do!

"Wonderful," she muttered, annoyed at herself and feeling a stab of guilt as she recalled Nell's nagging the other day. She hadn't followed any of the advice for safe gardening: she hadn't donned a mask, she wasn't wearing gloves, she hadn't opened the bag of potting compost at arm's length, nor done it outside in a well-ventilated place.

"*...poor man died in intensive care after he was infected by fungal spores while gardening... all these cases in Scotland where people ended up in hospital with legionnaires' disease, all because they got* *infected through soil or water in their gardens..."*

Poppy winced as Nell's voice echoed in her head and she grimaced even more she glanced down and caught sight of a little icon on the side of the bag, next to a label with the words:

WARNING: This product contains micro-organisms that may be harmful to your health. Avoid breathing dust or mists from the bag and always wear gloves when handling. Wash hands immediately after use.

Poppy peered warily into the mouth of the bag. *I hope I haven't inhaled any fungal spores or bacterial particles*, she thought, eyeing the dark piles of compost. *The last thing I need is to catch legionnaires' pneumonia or—*

She froze. As she stared down at the bag in front of her, slumped on its side with compost spilling out, she suddenly saw, in her mind's eye, a similar bag slumped sideways, with its contents also spilling out... the bag of mulch that had been lying next to Thales's body when she found him.

"Oh my God," she whispered. "It was in the mulch!"

CHAPTER TWENTY-TWO

Yes, it's the only thing which makes sense! thought Poppy excitedly. Thales had opened the bag of mulch after she'd gone to the toilet, and the poisonous fumes must have billowed from the bag and enveloped him. He would have choked and coughed, and staggered sideways, knocking the bag over and spilling the mulch everywhere as he slumped to the ground.

And in fact... if she had rejoined him earlier, she would probably have breathed in some of the poisonous cyanide gas, too, Poppy realised with a shudder. As luck would have had it, her little mistake with the toilet door had actually saved her. Bertie had mentioned that hydrogen cyanide gas was less dense than air and dispersed quickly in open spaces. So by the time she had finally managed to open the jammed door and get out of the toilet, the cyanide gas must have dissipated and been blown away.

Yes, it all fit! She had to ring the police. It was crucial to let them know that the bag of mulch was the potential murder weapon. But even as Poppy reached for her phone, the memory of her unpleasant interview with Sergeant Lee flashed through her mind. She paused. She could just imagine Lee's sneering face as he listened to her theory. No, she couldn't go to him with just a hunch—she needed evidence to back up her idea.

If only I knew whether Forensics has tested that bag of mulch yet and whether they found any traces of cyanide, she thought in frustration. But she doubted if Sergeant Lee would share that information with her, no matter how much she pleaded. Without knowing if the mulch had contained cyanide, it was almost impossible to check if her idea was correct.

Then, as she glanced again at the potting compost spilled all over her workbench, an idea came to her: there might still be some of the mulch left in the garden at Thales's property! She knew from experience that it was almost impossible to completely sweep up soil, compost, and other things spilled in the garden. There were always remnants left on the ground. And the Forensics team wouldn't have been concerned about tidying the place, only with removing a large enough sample for their own purposes. So it was more than likely that they would have left a lot of the spilled mulch on the ground.

But even if I can sneak over and remove some, how am I going to test it? wondered Poppy despairingly. After all, she didn't have access to the police Forensics department.

Then a slow smile spread across her face. She didn't need a Forensics department! She had an entire lab right next to her house and a "mad scientist" who'd be more than happy to help test anything for her.

***

Poppy had been worried that Bertie might not be home but, to her relief, the old inventor opened the door on her first knock.

"Poppy, my dear—how lovely to see you!" he said, beaming at her.

Poppy looked at him uncertainly. Bertie was dressed in a bright yellow penguin-patterned bathrobe, and his usual shock of wild grey hair was obscured by a foamy mountain of soap suds. "Er... Bertie, is this a bad time? I didn't mean to disturb you—"

"No, no, not at all," said Bertie. "I am just in the middle of testing my waterless shampoo formula. It foams without any application of water, you see, and then the soap suds just evaporate as they dry."

"Oh—how cool!" said Poppy. "That would be really useful. So you can shampoo your hair without water and don't need to rinse it off?"

"That is the goal, although I have not quite perfected the evaporation part of the formula. Unfortunately, once generated, the soap suds seem to solidify instead."

Poppy looked closer and realised that the mountain of foam was actually a solid mass of rigid bubbles. "Oh. So how do you get it off your hair?"

"I haven't figured that out yet," said Bertie cheerfully. "But never fear, the answer will come to me in time."

And in the meantime, you're just going to walk around with a mountain of bubbles permanently on your head, thought Poppy, smothering a laugh. It was no wonder that most of the villagers gave Bertie a wide berth!

"I was just about to have some home-made salt-and-vinegar ice cream," said Bertie as he led her into the house. "Would you like a scoop?"

"*Salt-and-vinegar?*" Poppy struggled not to make a face. "Um... do you have another flavour?"

"There is vindaloo curry, if you fancy something spicy, or stewed prune... I have created a machine that can make ice cream out of everyday foods, you see, and I am testing the limits of what it can churn. So I have been trying various things in my fridge. Ah, I have also made some 'frozen oyster' flavour—would you like to try that? It doesn't seem to have set very well though. The oyster chunks have congealed at the top."

"Er... actually, I don't think I will have any ice

cream, after all," said Poppy, feeling slightly queasy. "Listen, Bertie, are you free at the moment? I was hoping you might be able to help me with something."

"Certainly, my dear. I would be delighted to help if I can."

"You know the man who was murdered recently with cyanide? Well, so far the police haven't been able to figure out how he was poisoned, but I think I might have an idea." Quickly, she repeated her theory of what had happened with Thales and the bag of mulch. "So is there some way someone could have hidden some cyanide gas inside the bag?" she asked as she finished. "Like, could they have injected it into the bag or something?"

"Oh no, my dear. Any gas injected into the bag would have leaked out again through the opening made by the needle. The only way your young man could have been fatally poisoned was if there had been a build-up of hydrogen cyanide gas trapped inside the bag, which was then released in a sudden, large dose when he opened it."

"Oh," said Poppy, deflated. "So you mean my theory doesn't work?"

"On the contrary. If two compounds, which react to generate hydrogen cyanide, had been placed in the bag, you could get the gas build-up required. For example, an acid would combine with the cyanide salt of an alkali metal to generate gaseous HCN— that's hydrogen cyanide—and in fact, that reaction has often been the basis of accidental poisonings in laboratories. But you know, my dear, one might not necessarily even need to place special compounds in the bag," Bertie said thoughtfully. "The cyanide gas could have been generated by the mulch itself."

Poppy looked at him in surprise. "What do you mean?"

"Well, you may remember that I told you cyanide is present in many fruits and vegetables?"

"Oh, yes, that's right," said Poppy, recalling the conversation in her car on the day she had dropped Bertie off at the train station. "You said it's in lots of things that people eat every day?"

Bertie nodded. "Spinach and almonds and chickpeas and butter beans... and, in particular, there are significant amounts of cyanide in the seeds of apples and pears, and the members of the *Prunus* family."

"The *Prunus* family?"

"Peaches, nectarines, plums, apricots, and cherries, among other things," Bertie elaborated. "In fact, apricot kernels can contain enough cyanide in their stones to be lethal if ingested. Of course, you are perfectly safe to eat peaches and apricots as long as you only consume the flesh and leave the pit alone, but there have been some instances of people attempting to crack open the pits and eat the kernel within."

"Why on earth would they do that?" said Poppy with an incredulous laugh.

"Ah, it is due to the mistaken belief that amygdalin, a compound found inside apricot kernels, can kill cancer cells."

Poppy stared at him, her mind whirling. Suddenly, she remembered the scene at the grocer's that morning and the gossiping women of the village talking about Maggie's obsession with alternative natural remedies. One of them had mentioned Maggie touting apricot kernels as a cure for cancer. Was it all just a coincidence? Or could Maggie have something to do with Thales's murder?

"Are you saying if you fed someone apricot kernels, you could poison them with cyanide?" she asked Bertie excitedly.

"Oh, depending on the amounts consumed, most certainly. Amygdalin is a cyanogenic glycoside that can release cyanide anions upon enzymatic action. Now, it is true that the cyanide anion is toxic to cancer cells, but the problem is, it doesn't just selectively target *cancer* cells—it also kills *all* the other cells in your body too."

"So, you mean people are poisoning themselves faster than they can cure their cancer?"

"I suppose you could put it like that," said Bertie. He shook his head. "Sadly, there is just no scientific evidence that taking amygdalin supplements can help to treat cancer, but because of the misinformation, many cancer patients have inadvertently poisoned themselves when they attempted to self-medicate with amygdalin."

"Oh God, yes, I remember the ladies in the village talking about a man in Australia who poisoned himself taking apricot kernels for cancer. I just can't believe people can be so stupid!"

"Ahh, but you must not forget, anecdotes can be very persuasive to the average layperson. It always sounds impressive when you hear the story of someone's sister who was dying and then was miraculously saved. People do desperately want to believe in 'miracle cures', my dear, and they're especially vulnerable when it is touted as a natural ingredient."

That would be Maggie all over, thought Poppy. Still, it was one thing for the woman to be a "natural-therapies eco-warrior maniac" and quite another for her to be a potential murderer. If nothing else, why would Maggie want to kill Thales? She had no real motive. Poppy thought back to Sergeant Lee's sneering question: *"Don't tell me, you think she murdered him because she didn't like him killing all the poor little bees?"* The memory of his mocking voice made her fume, but she had to admit that the detective sergeant had a point. Even *she* couldn't quite believe that Maggie would kill Thales just because he was selling chemical pesticides.

Poppy turned back to the old inventor. "Bertie, I don't understand—it sounds like you have to eat apricot kernels to be poisoned by the amygdalin. So how does that relate to the bag of mulch?"

"Aha! Well, I posit that the mulch mixture could

have contained pieces of crushed apricot kernels," said the old inventor eagerly. "You see, the cyanide is only released if the kernels are pulverised. In your body, the apricot kernels are broken down by the digestive acids in your stomach, and thus the poison is released. But in the case of your bag of mulch, if the apricot kernels are crushed and then placed in the bag, the inherent enzymatic reaction together with the moisture in the bag could still convert the amygdalin into hydrogen cyanide. It would be a much slower process, of course, but if the bag were sealed and left alone for some time so that the cyanide gas could accumulate, I believe that it would be the perfect delivery mechanism for a large dose of toxic gas!"

"So if we can get hold of a sample of the mulch and test it, will that give us proof that it was used to poison Thales?" asked Poppy. "But how will we know that there are apricot kernel fragments in the mulch? If they've been pulverised, they would be really small and probably just look like the rest of the mixture—"

"Fear not, my dear—that is where my portable laser polarimeter prototype will come in!" said Bertie. "My meeting in Oxford was most successful, and several of the chemists and biophysicists at the University believe that it will be a brilliant diagnostic tool for the dispersion composition of organic soil components. However, with a few small adjustments, I believe I should be able to adapt it to test the composition of a solid organic mixture too." He rubbed his hands with glee. "In fact, this will be the perfect opportunity for me to test its functional parameters! If my modelling is correct, then one should be able to extrapolate the light scattering matrix data and map it onto a greater spectrum using the T-matrix code—"

"Er... that's great, Bertie," said Poppy, cutting him off hastily. "Why don't you explain it to me in the car on the way there?"

CHAPTER TWENTY-THREE

The residential estate seemed quiet when they arrived, with residents obviously indoors for the evening. As she drove slowly through the grid of streets, Poppy felt reassured by the lack of people out and about. Hopefully that meant they'd be able to slip in and out of Thales's place without anyone seeing them. She pulled up outside the house. It was the last in a row of terraced houses and she noted with relief that the adjoining house was dark, with no lights showing. It looked like Thales's immediate neighbours weren't at home. Still, she cast nervous looks over her shoulder as she hustled Bertie up the front path.

There was a wide strip of crime-scene tape across the front door, and she didn't have the key, in any case, but Poppy hoped that they wouldn't have to break into the house. She remembered the side alley that connected the front and back of Maggie's house and Miss Finch's, as well. Thales's house was smaller and narrower, but there was a good chance that the estate developers had opted for a similar design...

They had. Poppy smiled as she crept around the side of the house and found a narrow alley running towards the rear of the property.

"Bertie! This way!" she called in a hushed voice. She glanced over her shoulder. "Do you need help?"

"No, no, I am fine, my dear," said Bertie, coming up to join her with the box containing his laser polarimeter in his arms.

Poppy threw one last look around them to make sure that they weren't being watched, then she ducked into the side alley with Bertie ambling after her. They emerged in the rear courtyard garden, with its neat zigzag borders and paved path running down the centre. Poppy paused for a moment, seeing in her mind's eye again the sight of Thales's body slumped on the ground, then she pushed the memory away and approached the spot warily. Crime-scene tape had been looped around some of the trees and bushes, so that the area was sectioned off where his body had been, and Poppy's heart sank for a moment as she saw that the path was bare: the bag of mulch was gone. Of course, the Forensics team would have taken that.

Then her spirits lifted as she caught sight of several small piles of bark chips and organic debris around the edges of the path. *Yes!* She had been right—Forensics hadn't cleared all the mulch away. Hopefully there would be enough here for a test sample. Carefully, she ducked under the crime-scene tape and crawled over to one of the piles. Scooping up a handful, she looked back at Bertie, who was busily unpacking his case.

"How much do you need, Bertie?"

"Oh, just a small handful should suffice, my dear."

A few minutes later, Poppy watched anxiously as the old inventor placed the sample of mulch mixture into a chamber within his apparatus, then pressed a few buttons on the operations pad. A soft humming noise began to issue from the machine. Poppy glanced nervously around. They were well concealed here in the back garden, with the dense foliage of the surrounding trees and hedges hiding them from sight. And the humming was hopefully too soft to be heard from the street at the front of the house. Still, she didn't like to push their luck.

"How long is this going to take?" she asked Bertie in a whisper.

"Well, it will need to calibrate the sample, and then it will require several minutes to perform the scan. Good analysis cannot be rushed, my dear."

Poppy fidgeted nervously. "It's just that, the longer we stay here, the more we risk—"

She broke off as she realised that the hum from the device seemed to be getting louder and louder. She had thought that it was simply the noise of the machinery working, but now she realised that the hum was actually beginning to have a musical quality. The next moment, it morphed into a cheerful tune backed by a lively fiddle and tin whistle.

Poppy stared at the machine in disbelief. "Is... is that music coming out of the laser polarimeter, Bertie?"

"Oh yes, that was one of my special modifications," said Bertie, beaming and beginning to tap his toe in time to the tune. "You know, it can get awfully boring for scientists with all the waiting around while tests are being completed. So I thought: why not liven things up with a bit of music? I integrated an audio player into the design of this prototype, which enables it to play songs while simultaneously performing the analysis."

Before Poppy could respond, a warbling voice joined the tune coming out of the machine:

"...when Irish eyes are smiling, sure, it's like a morn in spring—

In the lilt of Irish laughter, you can hear the angels sing..."

Bertie hummed and swayed along to the music. "Hmm-mm-mm... *when Irish hearts are happy—*"

"Bertie!" Poppy hissed. "What are you *doing*?"

The old inventor blinked at her in surprise. "Do you not like it, my dear? It is one of my favourite songs."

"I... it's great... but we can't have music now! We need to be *quiet*," Poppy whispered urgently. "People in other houses are going to hear this and wonder what's going on, and then they'll come over and discover us!" She gestured frantically at the machine. "Turn it off! *Turn it off!*"

"But if I do that, the analysis will stop," protested Bertie. "The two functionalities are linked."

Poppy groaned. "Well, can't you put it on mute or something? Or at least lower the volume?"

"Well, I hadn't thought to include a volume control, but I suppose I could try adjusting the variable resistor," said Bertie, bending over the machine.

Poppy hovered around him, almost frenzied with impatience, as Bertie opened the side of the machine and began tweaking the wiring inside. The music was agonisingly loud and she felt like everyone across the whole county of Oxfordshire could hear it. Finally, Bertie twisted something with a flourish and the tune cut off abruptly.

"Oh thank God!" said Poppy. "Let's just hope—" She stiffened as she caught sight of a light moving in the corner of her eye. Whirling, she saw that it was coming from the other end of the side alley: the waving beam of a torch. Someone was at the front of the house. The next moment, she heard voices, faint but unmistakable:

"...sure I heard singing, Barry!"

"I don't hear anything. You're probably imagining

things."

"No, I'm telling you, there was someone here singing. A woman, I think. Sounded like one of those Irish ballads—"

"Irish ballads? Give me a break! Who would be out here singing Irish ballads at this time of the night? I think you've had one too many gin and tonics, Irene."

"I have not! I heard it! Just go and have a look, would you?"

Poppy froze in horror. These were probably some of Thales's neighbours in one of the nearby houses. Would they come through to the back? She grabbed Bertie's arm and looked wildly around for a hiding place. There were precious few possibilities in Thales's neat courtyard garden, but she dragged the old inventor across to a large *Fatsia japonica* at the far side of the path and pushed him down behind it. Then she crouched next to him and waited, hoping that the big palmate leaves of the glossy green shrub would give them enough cover.

She strained her ears for the sound of footsteps approaching but, to her relief, she didn't hear any. Instead, she heard the man's voice again, sounding weary and irritable:

"...not going in there, Irene. That's where that bloke was murdered recently, wasn't it? Look, I can see crime-scene tape... we'd get into trouble! Anyway, we've been here for five minutes now and I can't hear any singing at all, can you?"

"No... but I'm sure I didn't imagine it—"

"This is daft! I'm going home."

The roving beam of light disappeared and their voices faded away. Poppy let out the breath she had been holding and slowly climbed out from behind the *Fatsia*. "Bloody hell, that was close," she said to Bertie. "How much longer does the scan need? I don't think my nerves can take—"

There was a loud beeping from the laser polarimeter and, for a moment, Poppy thought the device was going to break into a rendition of a 70's disco tune. But to her relief, Bertie exclaimed: "Ah, the analysis is complete!" and hurried over to his machine.

She followed and watched as he examined the output screen. It all looked like a lot of gibberish to her, but Bertie nodded excitedly as he scrolled through the numbers.

"Yes... yes... mmm... yes... It appears that you are right, my dear. There are discrete fragments of *Prunus armeniaca*, with high trace concentrations of hydrogen cyanide associated."

"So there are definitely apricot kernels in the mixture? That's wonderful, Bertie!" cried Poppy. "It's the first step I need to convince Sergeant Lee that Maggie Simmons might be the murderer. Although..." She frowned as her earlier doubts returned. "I have to say, I don't really understand *why* Maggie would want to kill Thales. It doesn't make any sense. She might hate what he sells, but it's not as if he owns Campana AgroChemicals and is personally—"

"Did you say Campana, my dear?" said Bertie, looking up from the output screen.

"Yes, it's the name of the company that Thales worked for. I'm assuming it's named after the CEO, Bill Campana—"

"Ah, Bill!" cried Bertie, his face lighting up. "Yes, I thought it might be him. It is not a common name, Campana, and the mathematical probability of encountering another man with the same moniker is close to the null value."

Poppy looked at him in confusion. "Bertie—are you saying you know Bill Campana?"

"Yes, indeed. We used to be laboratory partners in my Oxford days," said Bertie with a reminiscent smile. "Bill is a brilliant chemist, you know. Always thinking outside the box, always pushing the boundaries of what is possible. He once attempted to generate spontaneous lightning in the laboratory, as a method to create ozone." Bertie chuckled. "That did not go down well with the university authorities, I can tell you! He was known around the department as the 'Mad Chemist'."

That's rich, coming from you, thought Poppy with a smile. "I met Mr Campana the other day, actually, but you might not recognise him now, Bertie," she said, thinking of the distinguished older man she'd met with Thales. Somehow, she couldn't imagine the CEO as a risk-taking, crazy scientist. "He seems to have mellowed a lot and now looks more like a corporate executive."

"Ah, well, Bill did always say that he wanted to be the head of a big chemical company one day. How nice to know that he achieved his ambitions. Mind you, he had a few false starts. His first company, Vanquish Titanic, had to be liquidated after a scandal erupted concerning one of the first products he developed—"

"What?" Poppy cried. Hadn't the gossiping village women mentioned Vanquish Titanic when they were telling her the tragic backstory of Maggie's mother's condition? "Bertie, what was the product?" she asked urgently. "What was the scandal?"

Bertie frowned. "It was a pesticide, I believe. Bill was always obsessed with the neonicotinoids. He was determined to come up with a formula that could still be effective, while addressing all the usual environmental and health concerns—"

"Oh my God," Poppy gasped as a dozen thoughts began churning in her head, like the spin cycle of a washing machine gone crazy. "Bertie, I think... I think I've just realised where we might have all gone wrong! It didn't seem to make sense for Maggie to be the murderer—even with the proof of the apricot kernels in the mulch—because I just couldn't think of why she would want to kill Thales. But what if the intended victim *wasn't* Thales? What if the person Maggie really wanted to poison was your old friend, Bill Campana, the CEO of Campana AgroChemicals?"

Bertie looked at her in astonishment. "But why should she want to kill Bill?"

"Because he was the manufacturer of the pesticide that destroyed her mother's life! It was his first company, Vanquish Titanic, that recruited volunteers for the trial of the pesticide, and I'm sure Maggie blames him for her mother's condition. She must have been nursing a bitter grudge all these years..."

"You mean she wants to kill him in revenge?"

"Yes, and this also explains why Maggie hates Campana AgroChemicals so much! I thought her bias against the company was a bit extreme, even if she was against chemical pesticides; it was more like... like a personal hatred, you know? You should have seen her the other day, Bertie—she was so friendly to me until she realised I had a connection with the company. Suddenly, she turned completely against me!"

Poppy thought back to the day she had been at Maggie's house and recalled the tense conversation between mother and daughter. It was clear now why Maggie was so angry with her daughter for working as Bill Campana's PA—she must have seen it as a personal betrayal. Maybe it had even triggered her to act after all these years.

"Yes, Maggie has finally decided to get revenge," said Poppy grimly. "Since Bill Campana 'poisoned' her mother, she's decided to do the same in return: kill him by poisoning."

CHAPTER TWENTY-FOUR

Bertie was silent as he considered Poppy's words, then he said: "Your hypothesis has merit, my dear, but there is one significant contradiction in your assumption. If the lady's intention was to poison Bill, why would she have placed the apricot kernels in a bag of mulch for your young man?"

"Because that bag was never meant to go to Thales!" cried Poppy. "I think it was originally supposed to go to the CEO's house, as part of a batch of factory rejects..."

She flashed back to the day she had returned to the Campana head office to retrieve her cardigan and happened to meet the warehouse manager. She could hear the man's voice once again: "*Ainlie saw him yesterday—came tae pick up 'at mulch fo' the gaffer—an' we had a blether about th' footy...*" He'd had a thick Scottish accent and used some slang, which had made it a bit difficult to understand him, but he'd clearly said: *came tae pick up 'at mulch fo' the gaffer*—"came to pick up that mulch for the boss". Thales had obviously been asked to pick up the bags of "reject" mulch from the warehouse and drop them off at Bill Campana's home.

"Yes, it's all coming back to me now!" said Poppy excitedly. "When I met Bill Campana during that tour of the head office, he thanked Thales for 'dropping things off' at his place. What must have happened was that Thales dropped off most of the bags but decided to keep one for himself. Sidney Maynard mentioned that Thales had a habit of 'stealing' office stationery and other supplies for personal use, and, in fact, Thales even admitted as much to me when he told me that he'd got that bag of mulch 'for free'." She shook her head. "He really paid for his petty theft this time. It was his bad luck that the bag of mulch he nicked happened to contain the poison... which was originally intended for Bill Campana."

"It was unfortunate for the murderer that Fate intervened, but it was still a remarkably clever plan, executed with significant strategy and preparation," observed Bertie.

Poppy thought back to the cluttered bookshelves in Maggie's house: there had been a well-handled volume of Sun Tzu's *The Art of War* resting on one of the shelves, and she remembered the woman quoting from it as well. As one of the most famous books ever written about strategy and tactics, studied in military academies around the globe, *The Art of War* would have provided more than ample guidance for Maggie's lethal campaign.

The question was—what was she going to do now? Her first attempt had failed, but Poppy was sure that the woman would have a back-up plan.

"I've got to tell the police so they can warn Bill Campana," she said suddenly. "Maggie wouldn't let one failed attempt stop her; she'll try again and God knows what she'll do the second time. In fact, given the distraction and confusion around Thales's murder, now is probably the best time to strike again. Isn't that exactly what a military strategist would advise? We've got to warn Campana so that he can be on his guard!"

She dug out her phone to call the police. It was late, though, and so she was disappointed but not unduly surprised when the duty sergeant told her that Sergeant Lee was no longer at the police station.

"Can't you put me through to his mobile?" she asked. "It's really urgent that I speak to him! It's about the Thales Georgiou investigation. I've got information that could be key."

"I can take a message and pass it on tomorrow morning."

"No, tomorrow morning might be too late! Please, can't you just give me his mobile number—"

"We don't give out officers' numbers to members of the public without permission."

"Okay, but you can patch me through to him, surely?"

The duty sergeant sighed. "DS Lee left instructions that he wasn't to be disturbed tonight unless it's an emergency—"

"This *is* an emergency!" insisted Poppy. "Someone's life could be in danger."

"If it's an emergency, you should really be ringing 999."

"No, no, not that kind of emergency. This is different. It's about the murder case. Please, I wouldn't be asking if it wasn't important."

The duty sergeant hesitated. "All right, I'll see what I can do."

Poppy waited tensely. Finally, after what seemed like an interminable period, Sergeant Lee's voice came on the line. "Yes, what is it?"

"Sergeant Lee, this is Poppy Lancaster. Look, I'm sorry to bother you but it's really important. I've worked out who the murderer is in the Thales Georgiou case! We were all wrong, you see: Thales wasn't the intended victim. It was Bill Campana, the Campana AgroChemicals CEO, that the murderer was really after—"

"What? What are you going on about?" said Lee irritably.

Poppy took a deep breath and began to explain the whole thing whilst Lee listened with ill-concealed impatience. He barely let her get to the end before he cut her off, saying:

"If I were you, Miss Lancaster, I would give your imagination a rest—"

"It's not my imagination! This is real and serious. It's information that's absolutely crucial to the investigation—"

"Fine. Come in to the police station in the morning and a detective constable will take your statement—"

"This can't wait till the morning!" said Poppy, her voice shrill with frustration. "We've got to warn Bill Campana *now*. Maggie could try again tonight and—"

"I'm not going to disturb the CEO of Campana AgroChemicals on the basis of some cock-and-bull story from a hysterical female about mistaken identity and poisonous mulch and revenge conspiracies... blah-blah-blah." Sergeant Lee gave a contemptuous laugh. "It's ludicrous when you think about it!"

"It's not—it all makes sense! In fact, it's the only way that the facts of the case fit together, and if you were doing your job properly, you'd take the time to consider it instead of just dismissing it out of hand!" Poppy retorted.

Sergeant Lee made an angry noise. "All right, Miss Smarty-Pants, if you're so clever, then explain something to me: how did Maggie Simmons get the apricot kernels into the bag of mulch?"

"I... what do you mean?" said Poppy, taken by surprise. "Those bags were warehouse rejects: you know, the ones that had damaged packaging and couldn't be put on display for sale. In fact, I remember now that Thales's bag had duct tape across parts of it, obviously to seal up rips and tears. It would have been easy for Maggie to open one of the damaged bags, add the crushed apricot kernels, and then seal it back up again."

"Yes, but how would she have done that? She would have had to sneak into the Campana Agrochemicals warehouse to tamper with the bag, and that, I can tell you, is practically impossible. The doors are all monitored and locked after hours, and what's more, there are security cameras all around the site. My DCs have gone through the footage and there are no signs of any break-ins in the past week. So how was Maggie Simmons supposed to have been able to enact this brilliant master plan that you're suggesting?" he asked mockingly.

"I... I don't know," Poppy admitted. "But that doesn't mean that she didn't do it! We just haven't figured out that part yet. It doesn't change anything. She's still a risk to Bill Campana and—"

"Well, I suggest you go away and dream up that part of your little story, then come back to me."

"Wait, I—" Poppy stopped.

He had hung up.

"AAARRGHH! THE BLOODY TOSSER!"

She lowered her phone, seething. What should she do now? She could wait until the morning and go back to the police station, try to find another detective inspector who might listen to her... but she couldn't shake off the sense of urgency. What if Maggie tried something tonight? She'd never be able to live with herself if Bill Campana died as a result of a poisoning that she might have prevented.

"I've got to warn him myself," said Poppy.

"Eh?" Bertie looked up from where he was still fiddling with his laser polarimeter.

"Quick, Bertie, we've got to pack up here. I've got to go to the Campana AgroChemicals head office," said Poppy, glancing at her watch. "Bill Campana was there pretty late the day I was touring the place with Thales and he might still be there tonight as well. I've got to take the chance!"

CHAPTER TWENTY-FIVE

Several minutes later, Poppy hustled a slightly bemused Bertie back into her car, dumped the laser polarimeter case on the back seat, then threw herself into the driver's seat and started the engine. As they zoomed out of the residential estate, she tried to rehearse what she was going to say to the Campana AgroChemicals CEO. She needed a succinct, plausible version of her story—she didn't want to get the same sceptical reaction she'd just received from Sergeant Lee!

The Campana head office seemed quiet and empty when they arrived, but Poppy hoped that the fact that the front entrance was still open meant that not all the employees had left the premises yet. Even if she couldn't find Bill Campana, maybe she could find a member of staff who would at least know how to contact him. Leaving Bertie happily fiddling with his laser polarimeter in the car, she took a deep breath and went into the building. The reception desk in the foyer was empty and she hurried past it to dive down the familiar corridor she'd taken before. She didn't know where Campana's private office was, but she hoped there might be signs on the doors, or perhaps she might bump into someone who could direct her...

As it turned out, it was easier than she expected to find the CEO's office. Perhaps it was luck, but as she was wandering down the maze of corridors, she came across a door with the sign reading:

BILL CAMPANA
CEO, Campana AgroChemicals Ltd.

Poppy hesitated a moment, then knocked on the door. A male voice called "Come in!" and she stepped inside. She found herself in a large, plush office, with a sleek leather sofa suite arranged around a glass coffee table at one end and an enormous executive desk at the other end, flanked by floor-to-ceiling bookshelves and cabinets. A large window looked out onto the landscaped gardens of the business park, dark now in the gathering dusk, and a series of vintage maps and aerial photographs of the Oxfordshire area decorated the walls.

Bill Campana looked up in surprise from his laptop. "Yes? Can I help you... er, Miss...?"

Poppy felt a rush of relief at the sight of him,

seemingly healthy and unharmed. She hurried forwards. "Mr Campana, I don't know if you remember me. I met you the other day with Thales—"

"Ah yes... I remember now. Miss Lancaster, isn't it? Mary Lancaster's granddaughter."

"Yes, that's right." Poppy gave him a nervous smile. "I... I'm sorry to disturb you, but I needed to come and warn you: I think your life might be in danger. I think someone is trying to kill you!"

Campana gaped at her. "I beg your pardon?"

"I know it sounds crazy, but I'm not making it up! The person who murdered Thales—her real, intended victim was you. The poison was in the bag of mulch, you see, and it was only because Thales nicked that bag out of the batch he was supposed to deliver for you—that's why he ended up dead... he was poisoned by mistake. But the original plan was for *you* to open the bag and inhale the cyanide gas inside. It was from the apricot kernels—the gas, I mean—the amygdalin—you know, crushing it..."

Poppy realised that she was babbling and stopped, trying to regain her composure. She probably sounded exactly like the kind of hysterical female that Sergeant Lee had described. If she hoped to convince Campana of anything, she had to sound more coherent and authoritative. Taking a steadying breath, she tried to calm herself and speak again.

"The person who murdered Thales is a woman called Maggie Simmons. She put crushed apricot kernels into a bag of mulch intended for you. The kernels would release hydrogen cyanide, and she hoped that you'd inhale the lethal gas when you opened the bag. But Thales took the bag by mistake and ended up the inadvertent victim."

"That's... that's an extraordinary suggestion!" said Campana, looking at her doubtfully. "I don't understand... why would this Maggie Simmons want to... er... murder me?"

"Because your first company, Vanquish Titanic, made a pesticide that caused dangerous side effects in humans, isn't that right?"

Bill Campana stiffened and his expression became chilly. "There is no legal basis for that claim," he said. "The product was withdrawn after early trials showed that it was unsuitable for the conditions it was initially designed for, that was all."

"Nothing might have been proven in court, but it doesn't change the fact that Maggie's mother, Valerie Simmons, who was one of the volunteer testers, developed early onset dementia after exposure to the pesticide," said Poppy. "And Maggie blames *you* for that. She's very bitter about the whole thing and she's decided now to get revenge for what you did to her family. She—"

There was a soft knock on the door to Campana's office and then it swung open to reveal Nina standing in the doorway.

"Sir, I've got your wife on Line One. She wants to speak to you urgent—" Nina broke off as she saw

Poppy. "Oh. I'm sorry. I didn't realise you were in a meeting."

"No, it's all right," said Bill Campana quickly. "I'm not in a meeting. Miss Lancaster just... er... had something to tell me."

Nina looked at Poppy curiously but she didn't comment.

Bill Campana turned back to Poppy. "I'm afraid I need to take this call, Miss Lancaster. Perhaps... er... we could arrange another time—"

"No, no, I'll wait," said Poppy, not wanting to lose the chance to finish what she had to say. Then, realising that the man probably wanted privacy for his conversation with his wife, she gestured awkwardly towards the door of his office. "I can wait in the corridor outside."

Campana looked as if he would argue, and Poppy was beginning to worry that he might insist on her coming back the next day, when Nina said:

"Why don't I take Miss Lancaster to Meeting Room A? She can wait for you there until you finish your call and then you can join her, sir."

"Yes, that's a good idea," said Campana, looking relieved.

Poppy hoped he would keep his word and join her after his call. It would be terrible if he slipped out while she sat there waiting! Still, she had no choice but to follow Nina as the girl led her out of the CEO's office and a short way down the corridor to a meeting room furnished with a large conference table and several chairs.

"If you wait here, I'll bring Mr Campana as soon as he's done," said Nina. She hesitated, then asked: "Would you like a drink? Tea? Coffee?"

"Actually, tea would be great," said Poppy gratefully. A hot cup of tea might help to calm her nerves and enable her to speak more coherently when she faced Bill Campana again.

As the PA turned to leave, Poppy called out: "Nina?"

The other girl turned around. "Yes?"

"Um… do you happen to know where your mother is right now?"

Nina looked surprised but she answered readily enough: "I think she's at home, although…"

"Although what?"

Nina looked slightly uneasy. "Well, I rang her a short while ago, just to tell her that I'd be running late tonight, and there was no answer. It's a bit odd as I thought she'd be home with Gran. I tried her mobile but she didn't answer that either." She frowned at Poppy. "Why are you asking about my mother?"

Poppy wondered what to say. Things might have been tense between Nina and her mother, but that didn't mean that the girl would appreciate someone telling her that they thought her mother was a murderer!

"Um… never mind," she said at last. "Forget I asked."

Nina gave her an odd look but, to Poppy's relief, she didn't press further. Instead, she left the meeting room, closing the door softly behind her. Poppy sank into one of the chairs around the conference table and leaned back with a sigh. The tension of the furtive expedition to get the mulch sample, combined with the excitement of solving the mystery of Thales's murder—not to mention the headlong dash to the Campana head office and the strain of the interview with Bill Campana—were all beginning to tell on her. She felt absolutely drained and exhausted. All she wanted to do now was to go home and change into her comfiest old pyjamas and curl up with a hot cup of tea. Instead, she had to psych herself up for another difficult interview with the Campana AgroChemicals CEO. Her heart sank just in anticipation of it.

Still, at least I've got the 'hot cup of tea', she thought, sitting up with a smile as Nina returned bearing a steaming teacup.

The PA placed this in front of Poppy and said: "Mr Campana shouldn't be much longer now," then quietly left the room again.

As Poppy picked up the cup and began sipping the soothing brew, she reflected that, even if Nina was cold and aloof, the girl made a brilliant PA: she was smooth and efficient, her manner quiet, her demeanour professional. She radiated competence. In fact, just knowing that she was liaising seemed to already make you feel more relaxed.

Poppy put the teacup down and sat back with a weary sigh. The chair was deeply upholstered, very plush and comfortable, and she could feel the warmth from the tea seeping through her body, making her feel almost as if she was melting into the cushions. Her eyelids began to droop. She was so tired... so tired...

CHAPTER TWENTY-SIX

Poppy groaned as she slowly came to. Her mouth felt dry and horrible, and there was a nauseous sensation at the back of her throat. When she tried to lift her head from where it was resting on a large, smooth table, the room spun crazily around her and she hastily laid it down again.

What happened? Where am I?

Carefully, she tried to raise her head again, and this time she managed to push herself upright. She found that she was sitting in a chair, slumped against a large oval table. She looked slowly around. From the whiteboard on the wall and the number of chairs arranged around the oval conference table, she guessed that she was in some kind of meeting room, but she had no idea how she had got there. In fact, she found that she couldn't seem to remember anything that had happened recently at all. The last clear memory she had was of driving with Bertie to the Campana head office.

Is that where I am? she wondered, looking around the room again. She tried to get up from the chair but found, to her horror, that she couldn't quite seem to control her body. Her limbs wouldn't move where she wanted, and she had trouble even orientating herself. Her legs trembled as she attempted to stand up, and she barely managed to struggle into a semi-upright position before she had to pause, leaning heavily against the conference table. A wave of dizziness overwhelmed her and she fell back into her chair again.

Just as she was mustering the will to try once more, the door swung open and a young woman walked in. Sleek dark hair pulled back in a low ponytail, simple trouser suit, discreet make-up... Poppy knew that she knew this girl, but it took her a long moment to dredge the name up from memory: *Nina.* Yes, that was it. The girl was called Nina and she was the PA of the CEO of Campana AgroChemicals, but she was also something else, something important... Poppy furrowed her brow, straining to remember. *Maggie Simmons... the 'eco-warrior' woman from the garden centre... yes, Nina was her daughter...*

"Oh, so you're awake."

Poppy blinked and tried to focus on the girl, but she found that Nina's face swam in front of her eyes.

The other girl laughed. "Feeling a bit ropy, aren't we? Well, GHB will do that to you. I wasn't sure how long you'd be out for—I didn't have much time to calculate the dosage when I was making up your tea—but at least it knocked you out pretty fast, which is all I wanted." She looked at Poppy thoughtfully. "Actually, it's good that you're awake. Makes it easier for me to get you to the lab."

"Mmwwha—?" Poppy tried to speak but her tongue felt swollen and unresponsive, her jaw weirdly slack. She made a supreme effort and only managed to slur a few sounds: "Whachoo... doooh... mmme?"

"Are you wondering what I did to you?" said Nina, looking amused. "You mean Little Miss Marple hasn't figured it out yet? I've doped you with GHB— otherwise known as gamma-hydroxybutyrate. Or you might know it better by its street names. 'Gina'? 'Easy Lay'? 'Liquid Ecstasy'? Any of those ring a bell? No? Well, you don't look like the type that goes clubbing much. No, you like to spend your time sticking your nose in where it doesn't belong, don't you?"

"Mmmbbfff," mumbled Poppy. "Youuu... mmbbbluumbbb..."

"Sorry, you seem a bit incoherent," said Nina with a snigger. "But don't worry, I can guess what you're trying to say. You want to know why I'm doing this. Haven't you guessed? You were nearly there, you know. You almost had all the pieces: Vanquish

Titanic and its vile pesticide, Gran volunteering and getting ill, the company trying to cover things up... I heard you when you were talking to Campana. I was standing outside his door and I heard everything you said. You were even right about Bill Campana being the original intended victim." She thrust her face close to Poppy's. "You just got one important thing wrong: the mastermind behind the whole plan wasn't my mother—it was *me*."

Poppy stared at the girl in front of her. That impassive face was now alive with hatred, the bland eyes burning with a feverish intensity. She couldn't believe how the cool, aloof PA had morphed into this seething madwoman.

Nina drew back and said in a calmer voice, "Not that I can't give my mother credit. She used to read me Sun Tzu's *The Art of War* before bed every night, did you know that? So I learnt his lessons *very* well." She looked into the distance and quoted softly: *"All warfare is based on deception. Hence, when we are able to attack, we must seem unable; when using our forces, we must appear inactive; when we are near, we must make the enemy believe we are far away; when far away, we must make him believe we are near."*

She turned back to Poppy and smiled. "That's one of my favourite quotes from the book. It was what inspired me when I decided to kill Bill Campana: to use deception to get close to him, to bide your time and not attack, even when you are able..." She sighed. "Mum never understood though; she was so angry when I applied for the job as Campana's PA. She couldn't see that I was just pretending to admire the man, to like him, to support him, so that I could allay suspicion."

"H-howrron?" Poppy asked. Licking her lips, she tried again, slurring the words badly: "How long... had you been... planning this?"

Nina shrugged. "About a year, I suppose. It took me a while to get that job as Campana's PA. Mum almost ruined it by trying to block me from working for the company. She kept accusing me of 'selling out'... Sell out? *She* should talk!" said Nina indignantly. "*She* was the one who sold out! Mum always liked to talk big, you know. All I heard growing up was how she had stood up for her principles, how she hadn't accepted the payout from Campana like the other volunteers. But then last year, when I was sorting through some old papers for her, I unearthed documentation on the ownership of our house.

"And do you know what I found out?" Nina looked angrily at Poppy. "She never bought the house—it was *given* to her. Yes! By Campana AgroChemicals! There was Bill Campana's own signature on the deed documents. We've been living on Campana's generosity for the last ten years!" A mixture of horror, disgust, and disbelief filled the girl's face. "I couldn't believe it. All these years, I thought we were being strong and true, full of integrity, standing up for

Gran... but actually, we were just like all the other pathetic volunteers, letting Campana buy our silence." She met Poppy's eyes, her face grim. "That's when I decided: Bill Campana couldn't get away with it. He had to pay."

"*You're* the one who put the crushed apricot kernels in the bag of mulch," said Poppy, realising now that it was the only explanation that made sense. Unlike her mother, Nina wouldn't have had to worry about breaking into the warehouse or dodging security cameras on the premises. She had free access to all parts of the head office site and knew the routines of the place, so she could have easily picked a time to slip into the warehouse unnoticed. As Campana's PA, she would have known about the CEO's habit of taking the "reject" products home, and also his preference for doing his gardening himself, his love of "getting his hands dirty". The very nature of the bags—with their damaged and ripped packaging—made it easy for her to add the crushed apricot kernels. All she had to do was seal up the bags again using duct tape, something which no one would remark on since it was common to see that on the warehouse rejects. And it would have been natural for her to personally oversee the collection of the mulch for her boss, so that she could ensure that the tampered bag went to Campana's house.

Poppy suddenly recalled the day she was at Maggie's place, when Nina had escorted her to the door and they'd talked of Maggie's hostility towards her daughter's employer. The girl had defended her job as Bill Campana's PA, saying: "It's a great position working directly for the CEO, which could lead to all sorts of opportunities... It's a means to an end."

Nina had practically confessed *what she was up to*, Poppy thought with chagrin. *Why didn't I see it?* It had all been meticulously planned, just as you'd expect from a disciple of *The Art of War*—the only thing Nina hadn't reckoned with was Fate in the form of Thales's interference.

As if reading her thoughts, Nina scowled suddenly and said: "Bloody Thales—he had to muck things up for me. I knew that he was a womanising wanker, but I hadn't realised that he was a scumbag thief as well! If he hadn't stuck his sticky fingers in the pie, Campana would already be dead by now!" Then she smirked. "Still, he paid for it, didn't he? And anyway, it doesn't matter in the grand scheme of things. I've still got Plan B."

"What's Plan B?" said Poppy, almost afraid to ask.

Nina smiled. "Gamma-hydroxybutyrate, of course. You've been a good test run, actually, and I can see now exactly why it's one of the most popular date rape drugs. It's brilliant! Colourless, odourless, tasteless, dissolves easily in liquids, and works in minutes. What more could you ask for in a poison?" She laughed. "I probably should have just used a GHB overdose to start with, I suppose, instead of cyanide—it would have made things a lot simpler.

But it would have been too easy for Campana, just going off to sleep like a baby. I wanted him to *suffer!*" she said savagely. "I wanted him to know what it was like to have a chemical invade your body through your lungs and kill the cells in your brain while you fight uselessly against it. I wanted him to feel everything that Gran went through."

Poppy was surprised to see the sudden shimmer of tears in Nina's eyes.

"You don't know what a wonderful woman Gran was," Nina said, her voice wobbling slightly. "When I was a little girl, she used to take me everywhere and do all sorts of things with me. We went hiking and camping and swimming in the nude; we did baking and painting and sang karaoke and took part in protest marches. She was so full of life, up for anything, interested in everything and everyone— and now she's just an empty shell... and it's all Campana's fault!"

In spite of the situation, Poppy felt a flicker of sympathy for the girl. She had never known her own grandmother, and there was a part of her that yearned for the kind of childhood that Nina had described. She could understand the anguish, the bitterness when all that was snatched away, and the fierce need to make those responsible pay. *Still, is that an excuse for murder?*

"There are other ways to punish Campana," Poppy said weakly. "You don't have to resort to killing him."

"What—you mean like a lawsuit?" said Nina

scornfully. "It was hard enough to get him through the formal justice system back when he owned a small company—do you think there's any chance now that he's the rich CEO of a big corporation? Besides, what would happen? He'd just lose a bit of money—so what? He can well afford that. He wouldn't suffer personally; he wouldn't know what it feels like to have your life destroyed and your family unable to do anything but watch."

"Murder is still wrong," said Poppy desperately. "I'm sure your grandmother wouldn't have wanted you—"

"Shut up!" snapped Nina. "Don't you talk about Gran! You don't know anything about her!" She leaned down suddenly and grabbed Poppy's arm, hauling her roughly to her feet. "Come on, we've wasted enough time talking. Let's go."

CHAPTER TWENTY-SEVEN

"Where... where are we going?" gasped Poppy, stumbling as Nina hustled her out of the meeting room. Her legs felt as if someone had taken them off and reattached them to her body backwards.

"To the lab," said Nina, hurrying down the corridor and dragging Poppy with her.

It was an agonising journey to the R & D laboratory. Poppy tripped and stumbled, struggling to control her legs as they buckled beneath her, but Nina kept her cruel grip on her arm, forcefully dragging Poppy even when she fell to the floor. When they finally arrived at the lab, Nina marched to the far end of the room where she gave Poppy a hard shove, sending her reeling towards the wall.

Poppy fell against a side counter and clutched at it for support. Next to her, there seemed to be a collection of strange glass shapes, and she stared at them, desperately trying to focus, as another wave of dizziness caught her. When it finally receded and her head cleared, she realised that she was staring at an arrangement of volumetric flasks, test tubes, and glass pipettes. Then the sound of glass clinking made her turn around. She saw Nina on the other side of the laboratory. The girl was hovering over a similar set of glassware and equipment, set up on the end of the workbench near the door.

"Chemistry used to be my favourite subject at school, you know," said Nina in a conversational tone. "I even thought I might do it at uni. But then we couldn't afford for me to spend more years being a student when I could have been working and helping to earn some money. Still, I remember everything I learned. I used to devour the textbooks, and my Chemistry teacher even let me read some of the advanced stuff. Came in pretty handy recently— and, of course, it's nice having a well-stocked laboratory to hand. A bit of flirting and eyelash-fluttering at one of the research assistants, and suddenly I had access to all the chemicals I needed," she said with a sly smile.

"What are you doing?" asked Poppy, nervously watching the other girl gently swirl some clear liquid in a glass beaker with one hand.

Nina laughed at her expression. "Oh, don't worry, this is just cyclohexane. A bit temperamental, you could even say *flammable*—" She winked. "—but overall, fairly harmless stuff, really. As long as you don't set it on fire by mistake." She turned and reached out with her other hand to pick up a different beaker filled with a pale liquid. "Of course, if I mix it with a strong oxidising agent, such as this ammonium nitrate solution... now *that's* a different story." She looked back at Poppy, grinning, and said in a mock whisper: "*Boom.*"

Poppy lurched to her feet and started stumbling towards the door of the lab. But her legs folded like soft rubber beneath her, and she would have fallen to the floor if she hadn't clutched at the side of the counter and saved herself. Leaning against it, she began to shout in a hoarse voice: "Help! *Help!*"

Nina laughed again. "Shout all you like. No one's going to hear you. The building's empty—I checked."

"But... Bill Campana... he was going to come—"

"Campana? Oh, he's long gone. I went back to his office where he was still trying to figure out why his wife wasn't on Line One—yes, I made that all up," said Nina, chuckling. "It was a bit lame, I suppose, but I couldn't think of anything else on the spur of the moment. Anyway, he was delighted to hear that you'd changed your mind and left. I might even have hinted that you were a bit... er... under the effects of alcohol, shall we say?" Nina sniggered. "So don't think you'll be getting any help from good ol' Bill."

"You still won't get away with it," said Poppy. "There'll be an investigation, and when the police question him—"

"I'm sure Campana isn't going to voluntarily

mention the crazy girl who came here after hours, spouting conspiracy theories about murder plots and mistaken identities—*especially* if it involves him dredging up all the scandal surrounding Vanquish Titanic again. And anyway, he's not going to live for much longer himself so he'll hardly be able to contradict my story when he's dead, will he?" said Nina with a complacent smile.

"It doesn't matter. The police will still suspect you!" cried Poppy. "How could you possibly explain why I was here in the lab—"

"Oh, that's easy. I'll simply say that when I returned to the meeting room, it was empty and you were gone, and I thought you'd left and gone home. But in actual fact, you'd sneaked off by yourself." Nina smirked. "I remember that day, the first time we met, you were hovering furtively around the R & D lab with Thales. And I've heard Sidney Maynard complaining about finding you wandering around the place. So everyone will just think that you were snooping around where you shouldn't have been, sneaked into the lab without permission, and accidentally knocked something over." She shook her head in mock regret, tutting loudly. "Laboratory fires are so common, you know, especially when there are so many flammable chemicals lying around…"

"You… you…!" Poppy was so angry, she could barely speak. She couldn't believe that she had actually felt sorry for the girl, had felt some sense of empathy with her. Nina was a cold-blooded psychopath who didn't care who she hurt or what she destroyed, as long as she achieved her single-minded goal of revenge.

Nina shrugged. "Don't get upset with me. You only have yourself to blame. In fact, you're the one who made it easy for me by snooping around in the first place. And I did try to be nice and warn you from getting involved, but you ignored my note, didn't you?" She turned back to the equipment next to her. "Now, I think it's time for a little chemistry experiment..."

Poppy realised that she had been so intent on what Nina was saying that she hadn't noticed what the girl was doing with her hands. Nina was no longer holding the two glass beakers. Instead, she had placed them to one side, and she was now spooning a dark purple, almost-black powder into a glass petri dish. Onto this, she swiftly emptied a large test tube of clear, viscous liquid. Poppy held her breath, bracing herself for an explosion or billowing fumes or *something*, but nothing happened.

Relief made her feel more confident and her fear turned to defiance. "Looks like your little experiment didn't work," she said tauntingly.

Nina didn't reply. Instead, she strolled over to the door of the lab before looking back with a cool smile and saying, "I still remember the first time my chemistry teacher showed me this. It was like magic. Enjoy the show." The next moment, she was gone and the door swung shut behind her.

CHAPTER TWENTY-EIGHT

Poppy swung her gaze fearfully back to the pile of dark powder in the petri dish but it still sat, now slightly damp, inert and innocuous. The tension in her shoulders eased slightly. *Maybe Nina was just bluffing.*

But even as she had the thought, the first wisps of smoke began appearing from the dark mound. These rapidly became large streams of grey rising from the powder, and then Poppy jerked back in alarm as the petri dish suddenly burst into flames. It was a vivid, intense fire, but only a small one, which remained contained in the petri dish.

Poppy gave a nervous laugh of relief as she tried to calm her racing heart. So—Nina had just been trying to scare her. Or maybe the PA had overestimated her own chemistry abilities and failed to set up the reaction properly. At any rate, that small fire wasn't going to harm her. Still, the sooner she got out of here, the better.

With agonising slowness, Poppy began to make her way across the laboratory towards the door. Her legs were still weak and uncoordinated, and she was frustrated with how she couldn't control her own body, couldn't do the simplest things that she'd always taken for granted. The horrible dizziness kept coming and going, too, so that she had to pause often as the room spun around her. She was exhausted by the time she made it halfway down the lab, but she didn't dare stop.

Still... she relaxed slightly as she shot a wary glance at the small fire in the petri dish and saw that it seemed to be burning down now. She would have to skirt around the end of the workbench where it was placed to reach the door, but she could probably do it safely. The only thing was... shouldn't she try to put the fire out? What if it spread somehow and then something else caught fire? She'd feel horribly responsible if she could have prevented a disaster but did nothing. This was a chemical laboratory, and all sorts of dangerous compounds in here might explode and blow up the whole building. *Which is why you should get out as soon as possible*, a voice in her head said. She could see a fire extinguisher on the wall beyond the lab door. It would mean making a detour instead of heading straight for the door. She hovered uncertainly, torn over what to do.

Then all thoughts went out of her head as the end of the workbench erupted suddenly in yellow flames.

Poppy gasped and reeled back. For a moment, she thought that the workbench itself had caught fire, then she realised that the flames were oddly coming from one of the two beakers that Nina had been playing with earlier. It must have been the one containing the flammable cyclohexane. Nina had left both beakers right next to the petri dish and the heat from the spontaneous fire had warmed the liquids, causing the vapours to catch fire.

That had been Nina's devious plan all along, Poppy realised suddenly. The girl had needed time to make her own getaway so she had engineered a reaction that would only ignite after a short delay, knowing full well that the small fire would then be magnified by the chemicals in the beakers.

And not just magnified, thought Poppy with a chill of fear as she remembered Nina talking about the ammonium nitrate solution in the second beaker. She looked fearfully back at the end of the workbench. Thick black smoke was now mingling with the flames rising out of the cyclohexane, which licked in every direction. Some of the flames were engulfing the second beaker and Poppy wondered suddenly how heatproof both beakers were. If they shattered and the contents mixed... Nina's smirking face flashed in her mind and she heard once more the girl say in a mock whisper: *"Boom."*

Oh God, I've got to get out of here, thought Poppy,

lunging towards the lab door.

But she hadn't gone two steps when she began to choke and cough violently. Fumes and thick black smoke were rising out of the fire and filling the air. Poppy staggered back, clutching her throat, her eyes watering. She threw an arm over her face, covering her mouth with the crook of her elbow, and tried to stop the violent coughing, but it only got worse as more fumes billowed towards her. She was forced to retreat back down the lab.

How am I going to get out now? she wondered desperately. The lab had only one door and there were no windows either. It was completely sealed.

"Help!" she began to shout feebly. "HELP!"

But she knew that no one could hear her, deep in the centre of the building; and besides, her voice was weak and hoarse, her throat raw from the coughing.

My phone! she thought suddenly. *I can call for help!* Why hadn't she thought of it before? But when she dug her hand into her pocket, it came out empty. Her phone was gone. Of course, it had been a vain hope. She should have realised that someone as devious and methodical as Nina would never have left a loose end like that. The girl must have removed the phone from her pocket when she was unconscious.

Poppy bit down hard on her lip, fighting the urge to cry, as fear and despair washed over her. The room was filling with smoke, and already she could feel her throat catching and the coughing take over again as fumes reached her end of the lab. The fire had spread and the entire end of the workbench was now ablaze. She could hear glass shattering and see embers and soot whirling through the air.

Poppy ducked down and huddled against the side counter, bracing herself for an explosion. It was hard to think clearly, though, as the fumes and smoke engulfed her once more, reaching like a hot branding iron down her throat and searing her lungs. She coughed and retched, her vision becoming fuzzy as spots danced in front of her eyes. She could feel the darkness reaching out for her, and although she tried to fight it, it was like someone shoving a suffocating blanket against her face whilst she struggled uselessly.

She slumped to the floor, gasping for breath, her ears filled with the roar of the fire.

And then... she heard something else.

Music.

Poppy raised her head, her eyes widening in disbelief. Yes, it was there... faint but distinct... the warbling tones of a woman's voice singing...

"...when Irish eyes are smiling, sure, it's like a morn in spring..."

The fire seethed and roared, and more glass shattered, but through the rush of sound, the music drifted, sweet and lilting.

I must be hallucinating, thought Poppy wildly. *The toxic fumes must be affecting my brain.* She'd read that, under times of great stress, people's minds could begin to play tricks on them. Maybe hers was trying to protect her, to lull her into a sense of peace as she knew that the end was near...

"...in the lilt of Irish laughter, you can hear the angels sing..."

And then suddenly she heard it. Not angels singing, but something even better: shrill and unmistakable—the wail of a siren.

The fire brigade. Emergency services. Help is here.

Poppy felt relief overwhelm her, leaving her weak and trembling. She slumped down against the floor again, feeling the concrete cool and hard against her cheek. The darkness reached for her once more, but this time she fought it with grim determination, dredging up the strength to hang on, whilst in the distance, the lilting melody played on:

"...and when Irish eyes are smiling... Sure, they steal your heart away!"

CHAPTER TWENTY-NINE

Sunlight gleamed on the freshly painted front gate, which stood open invitingly, showing the path into the garden. A large wooden sign had been erected next to the gate and the words "HOLLYHOCK COTTAGE GARDENS AND NURSERY – OPEN DAY" had been painted in a rainbow of colours to match the cluster of balloons tied to the base of the sign. More balloons decorated various points along the path, and long loops of bunting had been strung up among the tree branches and against the side of the cottage in the centre of the gardens.

Poppy stood beside the cottage and looked around with a happy sigh. She couldn't quite believe that the Open Day was finally here. It was a glorious English summer day, with a cornflower-blue sky and a balmy breeze stirring the leaves in the trees. Music drifted across the gardens, mingling with the sounds of talking and laughter, and everywhere she looked, she could see people admiring the borders and flowerbeds. Taking centre stage was the bed of roses alongside the path, and Poppy felt a wave of pride (and relief!) as she gazed at the display. There were still some signs of damage and disease—shrivelled leaves and scarred stems didn't magically heal themselves overnight—but the neem oil had worked wonders. She felt a wave of gratitude to Maggie for teaching her about the organic treatment. It had taken effect faster than she'd expected and had even somehow enabled the deformed rosebuds to open up into beautiful blooms. True, several of the outer petals were a bit blemished or distorted, and not all the blooms were a perfect cup shape, but it didn't detract from the overall beauty of the roses. It certainly didn't fail to impress the visitors, if their constant oohing and ahhing was anything to go by!

And it wasn't all just empty admiration either. Poppy smiled with delight as she watched a steady stream of people come up to the trestle tables displaying plants for sale and help themselves to several pots. Nell, who was manning the till and happily gossiping with each customer, could barely keep up with the queue of people lining up to pay. *At this rate, I'm not going to have enough stock to last the whole day*, thought Poppy. *It's a good problem to have!*

Beyond the trestle tables, several stalls had been

set up next to the path, each offering visitors even more entertainment. There was face-painting for children, a lady selling little cupcakes designed to look like miniature flower pots, a gentleman proudly showing off his hand-carved wooden plant labels, a stall filled with herb-scented candles, and a pair of sisters presiding over a motley collection of pottery, all made by local artists. When Poppy had put out a tentative invitation for volunteers at her Open Day, she'd been surprised and overwhelmed by the enthusiastic response from the villagers, with many offering to come and help, even if they weren't selling anything themselves. Chief among these had been Mrs Peabody, one of the bossiest busybodies in Bunnington. Now she presided happily over the "Refreshments" stall, directing other volunteers as to how to serve the tea and coffee and cakes and scones.

"Congratulations—your Open Day looks like a great success."

Poppy whirled to see an elegant woman with a sleek, dark bob coming up the path towards her. "Suzanne! How nice of you to drop by," she said, smiling in delight.

"Well, I haven't really seen you properly since getting back from Durham, other than that rushed visit in hospital. I know you've been dealing with Sergeant Lee to wrap up the case, but I did want to personally check that you're recovering okay. I had some time off today, so I thought I'd come by and say hello," said Suzanne, returning her smile.

"Aww, thanks! I'm fine, really. I had some of the GHB withdrawal symptoms for a while—the tremors and insomnia, especially—and my memory of that night is still pretty hazy, but overall, I suppose I was pretty lucky."

"Mmm… I hope the next time you decide to go haring off to confront a murderer and blow up a lab, you might consider informing the police first."

Poppy acknowledged Suzanne's gentle reprimand with a shamefaced look. "I did call the police station first that night," she protested. "But Sergeant Lee—" She hesitated, not wanting to sound too rude about Suzanne's junior officer. "—he… um… he didn't quite share my opinion of the urgency of the situation."

Suzanne compressed her lips. "I've had a word with Amos already, and I will talk to him again about giving more credence to your suspicions. But I must say, Poppy, even if you can't get police support immediately, that doesn't mean that you should go rushing off into danger yourself."

"I didn't realise that it would be dangerous! I thought it was just a case of warning Bill Campana to be on his guard against any attempted poisonings. How was I to know that it was his PA who was the murderer?" Poppy said ruefully. "Anyway, it wasn't as if I was completely alone. I had Bertie with me."

"I'm not sure Professor Noble can be counted on as a reliable source of back-up," said Suzanne dryly; then she conceded, "Although he did raise the alarm in this case. I'm still not sure how he knew you were in danger, though?"

"He didn't, actually," admitted Poppy. "It was really just sort of luck. I'd left Bertie in the car, fiddling with his laser polarimeter. It plays music while performing the analysis, you see, although Bertie had forgotten to add a mute option, so he was trying to fix that while waiting for me and—well, he got the wiring wrong or something. It went a bit nuts, blasting out music at hundreds of decibels, which, of course, alerted security guards patrolling the business park. So they came and found Bertie, and when they asked him what he was doing there—" Poppy smiled to herself as she imagined the scene of the bewildered security guards confronting the strange old man in a penguin bathrobe, with a mountain of soap suds on his head. "—he told them about me going into the Campana building. So they went in to investigate and found the fire and called the emergency services," she finished with a rush.

"I... see," said Suzanne, sounding slightly bemused. "Well, you were very lucky. A few more minutes and it might have been very different, Poppy."

"Yes, I know," said Poppy, sobering. "And I *will* be more careful in the future. I promise." She hesitated, then asked, "What's going to happen to Nina?"

"Well, she'll be facing multiple charges, including murder, attempted murder, and assault, among others."

"Do you think they might be a bit lenient with her,

given the circumstances?" asked Poppy.

Suzanne looked at her in surprise. "You sound almost like you're asking for compassion for Nina. I would have thought you'd want her to have the maximum punishment, given what she did to you."

"Well, a part of me does," Poppy admitted. "But a part of me..." She thought back to the day she was in Maggie's house, standing in the front hallway, looking at all the framed photos—the many wonderful moments Nina had shared with her grandmother, the childhood filled with love and wisdom, and then the later ones showing the fierce tenderness and protectiveness towards Valerie.

"She really, really loves her grandmother, you know," she said to Suzanne. "I never knew the kind of bond Nina had with Valerie... I wish I could have had that in my own childhood. I can't imagine what it must have been like to have a figure like that in your life and then to see her become such a shadow of herself. You can sort of understand how Nina might have felt, how you could become so angry, so tormented—"

"There's never any justification for murder," said Suzanne firmly.

"No, I know, I'm not condoning how Nina behaved. I just... I feel like I can understand why she did it. I mean, you always think you'd never commit murder, but how do you know what you'd really do when you're pushed? When someone you love is threatened?"

Suzanne gave her an amused look. "You're beginning to sound like Nick. He's always going on about the shades of grey and how justice isn't always a straight line. Well, if it makes you feel any better, I know the crown prosecutor who will be taking the case and he's a very compassionate man."

"And... Maggie?" asked Poppy. "Do you know how she is? I thought about calling on her, but I wasn't sure if she'd want to see me—"

"She's coping all right. Probably as well as you can expect, in the circumstances. Actually, one good thing that's come of all this is that, following the media coverage, Maggie has gained quite a following in the press and on social media. She's been invited onto TV shows to tell her side of the story, and I even heard that there's the possibility of a book deal. Plus, one of the big national charities for environmental concerns has got in touch with her. They've appointed her as their new spokesperson, and she'll be spearheading a campaign which will aim to educate the public on the potential dangers of chemical pesticides and similar household products."

"Oh!" said Poppy, delighted for Maggie. It might not have mitigated the stress and shock of her daughter's arrest, but it was a relief to hear of something good coming out of all this for the woman. If nothing else, it might comfort Maggie to know that she would now reach a far bigger audience and achieve far more than she could ever have done as a one-woman rabble-rouser, protesting outside a garden centre.

"What about Campana AgroChemicals?" asked Poppy. "Will they be subject to some kind of injunction or punishment for the damage their products have caused?"

"Well, that's not really the remit of the CID," said Suzanne. "But from what I understand, there isn't a legal case—"

"What d'you mean? What about the cover-up with the pesticide that Valerie was testing?"

"'Cover-up' is a strong word, Poppy. It suggests malicious intent—but it's hard to prove that. The original case was settled out of court and, aside from Maggie, none of the other volunteers are admitting any kind of complaint."

"But they were paid compensation! Doesn't that imply that the company was at fault?"

"Not necessarily in a legal sense. They could have been compensated for 'emotional distress' or something similar, without the product itself ever being proven as 'toxic'. At the end of the day, it's all about proving a causal link and that can be very difficult. Remember, correlation and causation are two different things," said Suzanne gently. "Just because two things are linked doesn't prove that one caused the other. In this case, the defence lawyers could argue that Valerie might have developed early onset dementia even if she hadn't been using the pesticide—"

"But surely it's too much of a coincidence that she should develop the symptoms so quickly after using it? The most likely explanation is that the pesticide caused it."

"Yes, but even if you know it's very likely, you still have to provide evidence to prove it. An isolated case just doesn't provide enough proof. It would be different if there were large numbers of cases over a long period of time—that kind of data is hard to refute. But even then, it can still be difficult to prove a definitive causal link. If something is acceptable in small doses, companies will get around things by keeping the concentrations low and thus be able to state that their products are 'safe'."

Poppy was suddenly reminded of Bertie telling her about cyanide and how it was manageable in small doses, such as the amount found in everyday fruit and vegetables, but highly toxic in large amounts. "Yes, but if you're constantly exposed to a 'small dose' over a long period of time, that still builds up to a big dose, which may *not* be safe at all," she argued.

"Oh, I agree," said Suzanne. "But like I said, it can be difficult to prove. And to make things even more complicated, the research to test the safety of these chemicals is often funded by the pesticide companies themselves so..." She gave a cynical shrug. "In many ways, Campana is no worse or better than many other companies out there currently manufacturing pesticides. And unless people start demanding alternatives and voting with their wallets, companies will keep making these products because it's profitable for them."

"Maggie was right all along," said Poppy, feeling slightly guilty as she remembered her own impatience with the woman's impassioned lectures. "She kept saying that people themselves were partly to blame because they wanted an easy 'quick fix'."

"Sadly, she's probably right. There are lots of things being used which are suspected to have carcinogenic or other harmful effects, but... you know, they're quick, cheap, and convenient, so we all tend to turn a blind eye to the negative stuff." Suzanne made a rueful grimace. "I know I'm guilty of it myself—like microwaving things in plastic containers! Even the so-called 'microwave safe' materials probably release tiny amounts of nasty chemicals, and if you're using them all the time..." She glanced up as a couple approached, holding one of the plants for sale and obviously wanting to ask Poppy a question. "Anyway, I'll leave you now—I'm going for a wander around your gorgeous gardens," she said, backing away. "By the way, is Nick around? Yes... over on the other side? No, no, don't worry... I'll find him myself. I'll catch you later!"

With a cheerful wave, she was gone. Poppy turned to the couple and, for the next hour, found herself busily seeing to customers. She was just handing over a tray full of vigorous snapdragon seedlings when she looked up and saw a familiar, distinguished-looking older man stepping through the front gate. It was Bill Campana and he was escorting a middle-aged woman dressed all in black. From her Mediterranean colouring, striking good looks, and sombre but stylish attire, Poppy had a good guess who the woman was, and she was proven right a few minutes later when Campana introduced her as Thales Georgiou's mother.

"Mrs Georgiou particularly wanted to speak to you, Miss Lancaster," he said with a smile. "And I'd seen your Open Day advertised locally, so I've been keen to make a trip as well to see your nursery."

Poppy turned to Thales's mother. "I'm so sorry for your loss," she said, feeling that the words were terribly inadequate but not knowing what else to say.

"Thank you," said Mrs Georgiou quietly. She had a stoic dignity that was somehow more heartbreaking than tears. "Actually, that was why I wanted to come and see you—I wanted to say thank you in person. For catching Thales's killer."

"Oh, I... it wasn't just me," Poppy stammered. "I mean, the police..."

"I've spoken to Detective Inspector Whittaker. I know how much you did to help bring the real murderer to justice." Mrs Georgiou paused, then looked at Poppy curiously. "Did you... know my son well?"

"We actually only met a couple of weeks ago at the garden centre," Poppy confessed. "I needed some pesticide and Thales was there promoting his company's new range of products. But we hit it off immediately and... er... Thales invited me out to dinner," she added, blushing slightly.

The flicker of a smile lit Mrs Georgiou's face. She obviously knew about her son's penchant for pretty girls. "I'm sure he was very persuasive." She turned to look out across the garden, her gaze sweeping over the rose bushes along the path. "I love roses—yours are absolutely gorgeous."

"Thank you. Actually, those bushes were the reason I went to the garden centre. I was having some pest trouble and all the flowers were being destroyed." Poppy gave a slight smile. "You could say those blooms were the reason I met Thales."

Mrs Georgiou turned back to her, her eyes bright. "Really? Did you know that Thales's name means 'to bloom'? Yes, it comes from '*thallo*', which is ancient Greek for 'to blossom'. It's strange, don't you think? Almost as if it was meant to be."

"I'm... I'm really glad to have known your son, Mrs Georgiou, even if it was for far too short a time," said Poppy impulsively. "Thales was... well, he was one of those people who made you want to love life and enjoy it to the full."

As she said it, Poppy realised that she really meant it. She wasn't just saying platitudes to soothe a grieving mother—she really *was* glad that her path had crossed with Thales's. Yes, he had been no angel, and there were aspects of his character that were potentially deplorable—but there had been a wonderful charisma, too, and an enviable ability to grab life and make the most of every moment... something that Poppy felt she could well learn from.

Mrs Georgiou smiled and touched Poppy's hand. "Thank you. That's a lovely thing to say. Now, I hope you'll excuse me for a moment, but I must go over to have a closer look at your beautiful roses..."

As she wandered off, Bill Campana stepped up and said: "I actually wanted to say thank you as well."

Poppy looked at him in surprise. "For what?"

"For saving my life, Miss Lancaster. If it weren't for your efforts, I might not be standing here today." Campana gave her an apologetic smile. "In fact, I must apologise for not treating your words that night with more... er... consideration."

"Oh, that's okay," said Poppy with a laugh. "I think you probably reacted as well as anyone could have if they'd been faced with a strange girl running into their office, raving about poison murder plots and mistaken identities!"

Bill Campana inclined his head. "Well, I am very grateful. And as a small way of showing my appreciation, I was thinking I could offer you a special VIP arrangement as a stockist of Campana products where you would not need to make any upfront payments to be supplied with stock. You would only have to pay Campana a small percentage of any profits you made. That way, you wouldn't have to worry about any financial outlay in terms of stocking products that might take time to sell. And I would enable you to have access to all our marketing and promotional support for free."

He nodded at the crowds of people milling in the gardens. "I'm sure your customers would appreciate being able to buy horticultural products and supplies, in addition to plants, from your nursery. It would put you in a much better position to compete with the big garden centres as well, since you'd be able to offer things like fertilisers and pesticides. What do you say?"

CHAPTER THIRTY

Poppy looked out across her gardens, remembering that first day she had wandered through Mega Garden Town, and how she had wished she could offer a similarly wide range of products. Now, here was a chance to start making that dream a reality—and at practically no cost or risk to herself! But partnering with Campana would also mean adopting their ethos of chemical solutions for everything. Even their new mulch was to be coated with chemicals!

She hesitated for a long moment, thinking of what Suzanne had said about companies continuing to manufacture and promote potentially harmful products unless people demanded alternatives and voted with their wallets.

Finally, she looked back at Bill Campana and

said: "Thank you for that incredible offer. I'm really overwhelmed by your generosity, but... I'm afraid I have to decline. I... I would prefer to garden organically, and I think that is the ethos I would like my nursery to promote as well."

"Organic gardening is a *lot* more work."

"Yes, I know." Poppy raised her chin. "I'm not afraid of work."

Campana gave her a grudging look of respect and a reluctant smile. "You know, Miss Lancaster, you're more like your grandmother than you realise. I could never persuade Mary to stock my products either, despite trying many times. Well, you might be interested to know that Campana AgroChemicals is actually investing in a new organic range. Yes, I have set up a new R & D division specifically to develop products which meet certified organic and sustainability standards... so perhaps we could talk again in a couple of years' time?"

Poppy returned his smile. "Oh, that's great to hear! Yes, I'd certainly be up for that."

He nodded, then looked around. "I heard that my old friend Bertram Noble might be here. It would be wonderful to see him. Do you know where he is?"

"I think he's in the back garden, by the greenhouse, doing some fun science demonstrations for the children," said Poppy, thinking: *At least, I hope that's what he's doing and not blowing up the children!*

"Great. I'll go and see if I can find him." With a

nod, Campana went down the path and disappeared around the side of the cottage.

Poppy watched him go, hoping that she'd made the right choice. It heartened her to know at least that her grandmother had made the same decision. Surely she could do no worse than to walk in Mary Lancaster's footsteps?

Her thoughts were interrupted by a gentle tap on her shoulder, and she turned to see Miss Finch in a hat and pretty floral dress, with one arm in a shoulder brace.

"Hello, my dear—I simply had to come over and tell you what a lovely event this is!" the old lady gushed. Then she indicated the very tall man standing diffidently beside her. "Oh, and I also wanted to introduce you to my nephew. This is Dennis, who was—" For a horrified moment, Poppy thought the old lady was going to say: "—*born with a wonky willy*". But Miss Finch finished with: "—going to take me out to lunch, and I persuaded him to bring me here first."

Poppy breathed a silent sigh of relief, although— as she looked up into Dennis's laughing eyes—she had a sneaking suspicion that he had read her mind.

Embarrassment made her more formal than usual. "Er... how do you do?" she said stiffly. Unable to meet his eyes, she dropped her gaze, then realised with horror that she was staring at his groin. Hastily, she jerked her eyes back up and was relieved to see that Dennis looked more amused than insulted.

He said, in a gallant attempt to change the subject: "I heard that you had some trouble with pests on your roses. I grow roses myself and I'd love to hear any tips you might have."

Grateful for his help in steering the conversation back to normal, Poppy hastily launched into an account of her trials with the rose bushes. She had just finished telling them about the neem oil spray when they were interrupted by a bloodcurdling yowl.

The next moment, an enormous ginger tomcat vaulted over the open front gate and came bounding up the path. He was followed a moment later, not by a bad-tempered crime author this time, but by a scruffy black terrier, barking at the top of his voice.

"Oren! Einstein!" gasped Poppy as the two animals rushed past her in a blur of motion.

They paid no attention to her shouting as they chased each other around the gardens, in and out of the flowerbeds and up and down the main path, to the delight of the customers, and especially the children, who squealed with excitement. Everyone cheered when Oren finally outwitted the terrier by making for his favourite drainpipe and swarming up the side of the cottage to sit on the roof. There, he looked smugly down at the dog, then gave a pointed yawn and began to wash his face, whilst poor Einstein remained jumping up and down in frustration, still yapping furiously.

"Here, mate... a bit of a consolation prize," said a deep baritone voice.

Poppy turned to see Nick Forrest coming up the path. He bent to pat Einstein and handed him a biscuit, which quickly mollified the dog. A minute later, a group of children had gathered around the terrier, eager to pat him, and he went off with them, his tail wagging, the cat forgotten.

"I would apologise for my cat's behaviour, except that I think he'd revel in that," said Nick, shooting Oren a dirty look as he came up to join Poppy.

She smiled, not fooled by his manner. She knew that Nick really doted on the ginger tom, even if they did often behave like two grouchy old men living in the same house and constantly getting on each other's nerves!

"I must say, you've put on a great event," said Nick, looking around with approval. "I've been chatting to a lot of the villagers and visitors, and they absolutely love it. In fact, I think many are hoping this could become an annual event in Bunnington."

"Oh, I'd love to do that," said Poppy with a dreamy sigh. "I could invite even more local artists and maybe have a corner set aside for a petting farm— the children would love to see some baby animals! And we could also offer stalls for the local ladies to sell home-made jams and chutneys—"

"Yes, that's all great, but the one thing you *must* do is change the music next year," said Nick, pulling a face as the warbling tones of a woman singing *"...when Irish eyes are smiling..."* drifted across the air towards them.

"What do you mean? Don't you like it?" asked Poppy innocently, trying not to laugh. "Your father helped choose the music for today."

"I might have guessed," said Nick with a groan. "But I'm surprised you went along with it. Since when do you like cheesy Irish ballads?"

Since one saved my life, thought Poppy with an inward smile. Aloud, she said: "I think it's rather catchy," and hummed along to the tune.

"Oh God, please don't," said Nick, making a face. "I'm going to have that stuck in my head for days as it is." Then, to Poppy's surprise, he lifted a hand suddenly and held something out to her, saying gruffly, "Here... this is for you."

"For me?" Poppy stared down at the beautifully wrapped package.

Carefully, she unwrapped it, then gasped in delight as she held up the ceramic sculpture of a slug draped daintily over a leaf, its tentacles alert and curious. It was the one she had seen in the art gallery at Mega Garden Town, and she held it up now, admiring it even more in the dazzling sunshine.

"Ohhhh... it's that gorgeous piece I saw at the garden centre, but I never thought I could afford—" She broke off, feeling too overwhelmed for words.

"It won't replace the real thing, but at least it'll take any further abuse from my cat much better," said Nick.

"I love it. It looks so much like Solly!" said Poppy, thinking to herself that it was just like Nick to seem totally unsympathetic when she had been so upset at losing the slug, and then to surprise her with such a thoughtful, valuable gift. She looked up at him with shining eyes. "Thank you." Then, on a crazy impulse, she reached up and kissed him on the cheek.

Nick blinked, looking slightly startled. There was an awkward silence, then he cleared his throat and said, "Well, I'd better go and see what my father's up to. Last time I walked past the greenhouse, he was asking for volunteers to test his explosive bubblegum. I bloody hope no child put their hand up!"

As Poppy watched him walk off, she thought about how far Nick and Bertie had come in the past year. When she'd first moved into Hollyhock Cottage, the father and son were barely on speaking terms, despite being such close neighbours. While she knew that Bertie could be exasperating, even infuriating sometimes, Nick's hostility towards his father had seemed excessive. She still didn't know what had caused their estrangement—somehow, despite her closeness to Bertie and her familiarity with Nick, she had never felt comfortable asking—but she was delighted to see that they seemed to be slowly rebuilding their relationship. Whatever it was that had caused the rift between them, Nick seemed to be finally finding it in himself to forgive his father and even appreciate Bertie's quirks and idiosyncrasies.

Poppy turned towards the front door of her cottage. However robust Nick might have thought it was, she wasn't taking any chances with her precious new gift, and she wanted to put the ceramic slug somewhere safe indoors. She went inside and made her way to the large bay windows in the sitting room. Several ornaments had been placed on the windowsill and she moved some of these carefully aside to make room for the slug.

The sound of laughter made her look up, and she gazed out through the windows—at the gaily bobbing balloons and bunting fluttering in the breeze, the billowing flowerbeds and verdant borders, the proud stallholders busily showing their wares, and the crowds of people wandering through the garden, enjoying the festive atmosphere. Poppy felt a wonderful sense of accomplishment, and she liked to think that, if her grandmother had been there, she would have been proud of Poppy for once again making Hollyhock Cottage part of the local community.

Not that she would have told me, Poppy thought with a wry laugh as she recalled what Nick and the villagers had said about the prickly woman who had lived there before. Mary Lancaster had been a stern perfectionist, especially when it came to gardening, and had had a brusque, no-nonsense manner that was unlikely to include compliments or praise.

Still, she's my *grandmother*, thought Poppy, smiling as she looked back down at the windowsill where a trifold frame stood amongst the ornaments. A few months earlier, she had been delighted to find a rare picture of Mary Lancaster in a clipping from an old horticultural magazine. She had carefully cut this out and placed it in the frame, alongside a photo of herself and one of her mother. Now, she picked up the triple-picture frame and held it up, looking at the three generations of Lancaster women side by side.

She might never have a warm, smiling photo of herself standing with her arms around mother and grandmother, nor have known the kind of doting childhood that Nina had experienced, but...

Bill Campana's voice echoed suddenly in her mind: *"You know, Miss Lancaster, you're more like your grandmother than you realise."* And as she looked back out through the windows, Poppy felt, for the first time, a real connection with her family and the woman who had left her Hollyhock Cottage Gardens and Nursery.

THE END

ABOUT THE AUTHOR

USA Today bestselling author H.Y. Hanna writes fun cozy mysteries filled with clever twists, lots of humor, quirky characters - and cats with big personalities! She is known for bringing wonderful settings to life, whether it's the historic city of Oxford, the beautiful English Cotswolds or the sunny beaches of coastal Florida.

After graduating from Oxford University, Hsin-Yi tried her hand at a variety of jobs, including advertising, modelling, teaching English, dog training and marketing... before returning to her first love: writing. She worked as a freelance writer for several years and has won awards for her poetry, short stories and journalism.

A globe-trotter all her life, Hsin-Yi has lived in a variety of cultures, from Dubai to Auckland, London to New Jersey, but is now happily settled in Perth, Western Australia, with her husband and a rescue kitty named Muesli. You can learn more about her and her books at: www.hyhanna.com.

Join her Readers' Club Newsletter to get updates on new releases, exclusive giveaways and other book news!

https://www.hyhanna.com/newsletter

Made in the USA
Thornton, CO
07/14/22 23:00:58

ce6e9df0-a679-433d-ab99-c7995734f209R01